Mistletoe and Holly

....

S.N. Moor

Copyright © 2023 by S.N. Moor

All rights reserved.

No part of this publication may be reproduced, distributed, or transmitted in any form or by any means, including photocopying, recording, or other electronic or mechanical methods, without the prior written permission of the publisher, except as permitted by U.S. copyright law. For permission requests, contact authorsnmoor@gmail.com

The story, all names, characters, and incidents portrayed in this production are fictitious. No identification with actual persons (living or deceased), places, buildings, and products is intended or should be inferred.

Contents

Hey Dad	VI
Dedication	VII
Introduction	VIII
1. EVERLEE - CHESTNUTS ROASTING IN A SAUNA	1
2. EVERLEE - CHRISTMAS TREE HAIR DON'T CARE	14
3. CALLUM - COMING DOWN HER CHIMNEY	19
4. EVERLEE - ROCKIN' AROUND THE DANCE FLOOR	27
5. EVERLEE - DRESS SHOPPING	30
6. EVERLEE - MERRY BUNCH OF ASSHOLES	40
7. JAX - MAKE ME PEG FOR IT	51
8. EVERLEE - RIDE THE PONY	62
9. CALLUM - RAINBOW AFTER THE STORM	67

10.	EVERLEE - SIGHTSEEING IN FRANCE	70
11.	EVERLEE - PRIVATE EVENT	76
12.	EVERLEE - SURPRISES	82
13.	CALLUM - SEVENTEEN MINUTES	90
14.	EVERLEE - LOVE IS LOVE	96
15.	KNOX - CALL ME BLITZEN	110
16.	EMMETT - I BURN FOR HER...	118
17.	JAX - JIGGLER THE ASS TICKLER	123
18.	CALLUM - LOVE THE UNEXPECTED	129
19.	EVERLEE - EIFFEL TOWER IN FRONT OF THE EIFFEL TOWER	133
20.	CALLUM - GLITZED UP WALK OF SHAME	139
21.	EVERLEE - MISTLETOE	143
22.	EVERLEE - WINE TASTINGS	148
23.	KNOX - KINKY FUCKERS	156
24.	EVERLEE - IUD OR TREE ORNAMENT?	163
25.	KNOX - HOME SWEET HOME	170
26.	EVERLEE - MAKING UP	176
27.	KNOX - CANOEING	183
28.	EVERLEE - NEW YEAR'S EVE	189
29.	EVERLEE - NO PHONE IN THE SEX CLUB RULE IS THERE FOR A REASON	197
30.	KNOX - MORNING SURPRISES AND NEW BEST FRIENDS	207

31.	JAX - THANKS A LOT PHIL	217
32.	EVERLEE - LUNA AND WYATT	223
33.	EVERLEE - OVARY EXPLOSION	234
What's Coming Next?		244
About the Author		245

Hey Dad

Well, ho ho ho. Alas, Christmas miracles don't exist. Well, not in this specific case anyway. This is yet another book that will not be wrapped up for you under the Christmas tree, because... well, you can't read it. What?? Shut the front door! I know, you're probably like "Shut the elf up! This is ridiculous!" But don't get your tinsel in a tangle! There will be a book... one day. Naughty or nice, my smutty book lovers will get what they want. But until then, here is recap of this story. It's Christmas and Everlee and her.... friends travel to Paris to visit Sophie and well... there's a surprise... and then another surprise... and then they have dinner at the Eiffel Tower. Yum! You can walk around asking friends, "Can you believe what happened at the Eiffel Tower?" Throw your hands in the air for a bit of dramatic flair, and you'll be good to go. They also visit a vineyard while they're in France, then come home and exchange Christmas gifts. All above board and boring. Think socks, shirts, cologne. The standard. They have a New Year's party and there's a balloon drop. Woo! Very exciting stuff. Maybe next year will be your year, maybe...but regardless, thank you for your continued support!

To all you good girls and boys who say 1 day of coal or 364 days of smutty fun... I'll take my chances.

Introduction

Mistletoe and Holly is the 7th book of the series. It's Christmas and let's just say there will be a lot of Christmas cheer and a grinch. Our fave fivesome travels to France to spend Christmas. There will be some big surprises, sightseeing, and vineyards!

It's recommended you read Cupid's Contract, Bunnies and Bowties, Rainbows and Unicorns, Stars and Stripes , and Gobble 'til you Wobble first. If you haven't read those yet, stop here, because there are spoilers below (the title links will take you to the books).

In **Cupid's Contract**, Everlee meets her four delicious men who give her the time of her life and the confidence she lost after dickface, Rich, destroys her. The only problem is the men make her agree to only sleep with them two times before they part ways. By the end of the arrangement, Everlee gets attached but doesn't know how the men feel, so she honors the agreement against her own desires and leaves. She's scared of getting hurt again.

Bunnies and Bowties, picks up two months later. She's been absolutely miserable, and unbeknownst to her, so have the men. Lizzy, being the amazing BFF she is, gets her back out on the scene, but she runs into her men and things are as hot as ever. She wants to talk with them about a future, but she's already committed to visiting her family for Easter. We get to meet her eccentric brother, Beckett, and her mother and father. Her mother is hellbent on a marriage and grandkids for Everlee and uses every opportunity to remind her, going as far as setting her up on a date with a lawyer. Everlee does her part but is missing her men desperately. The church her family attends is hosting a birthday party for one of their members and during the celebration Everlee comes face to face with her men (while on her date). They were all in foster care together a few towns over from Everlee growing up. Small world. As you can imagine, fireworks ensue, and Beckett picks up on all the sexual tension between them all and calls out she's in a poly relationship. Our favorite fivesome is formed and it is HOT! HOT! HOT!

Rainbows and Unicorns picks up soon after Bunnies ends. This one centers around Memorial Day and Pride Month. Sammie, a woman from the men's past enters the picture with a proposition for them that is hard to refuse. Because of personal reasons, Sammie has to go back to Texas, but offers to sell Allure back to the guys. Allure was their first successful business, a sex club, that gave them the funds to open Vixen and Bo's. Scared of how Everlee will react, they are hesitant to tell her, but when they do, she shocks them when she's excited about it. Sammie sets up a night where our fave five can visit Allure and experience Eden and Infernus (hello fave wood scene), two other areas of the club she added. While at Allure, Knox and Everlee participate in a Shibari demonstration that is... ahem... hot AF and we learn that Knox's nickname in the SEALs was Knots. In the end, they all decide to buy the business, Everlee included, so she's now an official owner of a sex club with the boys. Things continue to progress with the relationship and by the end of the book everyone says they love one another with hints of something more developing between Emmett and Jax. Lizzy is still in wedding planning mode so who knows what she'll decide about her wedding, and we also finally get to meet Betty's husband.

Stars and Stripes gives us our summertime vacation feels! Our fave five head away for a week of fun in the sun, with Beckett, Will, Lizzy and Tony, but when Beckett stupidly invites his and Everlee's mom, things get tense. She never travels alone, so why would she now? Several days later, the knock on the door shocks them all. Dearest Donna took a page out of Ev's book and travelled on her own... to the beach house... the forbidden love nest with Ev and her men. Things are awkward and their bedroom activities are put on hold, but when Everlee's life is in danger and all the men jump in to save her, the cat is out of the bag. Everlee and her mom talk, and Ev admits she's in a poly relationship. With the weight of the world off Everlee's shoulders, she can finish out the week relaxing and Donna can really meet the men. Also, in Stars and Stripes, we see Emmett and Jax's relationship start to heat up as Jax begins to explore the feelings he's been pushing down. Everlee's love and unconditional support give him the courage to explore. What does this mean for the future?

Deal with a Djinn is the fifth book in the series, however, it can be read as a standalone. Like some of our favorite shows do, Deal with a Djinn breaks from the series and our favorite characters are transported to another realm- a paranormal world, where they meet again for the first time. It's a paranormal retake on Cupid's Contract. If you've read the series, then you will likely see Easter eggs that have been planted throughout in this book. Hope you enjoy!

Gobble 'til you Wobble is the sixth book of the series. Our men decided they were ready to take their relationship to the next level and propose, but when Everlee is involved in a serious accident their plans take a detour... but not for long. Of course, hilarity ensues anytime Lizzy is around and even though she has a heart of gold, and was managing Allure for Knox and Ev, she accidentally sent a bouquet of vibrator roses to Everlee in the hospital. Because of the accident, Thanksgiving plans changed and our fivesome is no longer flying down to meet her parents. This really bums Ev out, because the guys were finally going to meet her dad in person (as her boyfriends), and because she's never missed a Thanksgiving dinner with her family. The guys decided to surprise her and bring her family to town, but made the mistake of not telling her. It's been weeks since the accident, and the guys have been scared of hurting her, so their sexy time has been put on hold, but Everlee said NO MORE! She decorated the table and undressed herself to surprise the guys when they got home from their errand (of picking up her family from the airport). Surprise is on her when her mother and brother turn the corner and find her on the table in nothing but whipped cream and pumpkin pies. The guys get some time alone with Dave and ask for Ev's hand in marriage and he gives an amazing speech and his blessing. The guys plan to ask Ev after dinner, but then Beckett surprises everyone with a proposal of his own. Our guys decide to wait until after her family leaves so it doesn't overshadow Beckett and Will. They plan a super romantic game for her around the house, taking her back through the memories and their journey from the beginning. She says yes and bow-chicka-bow-wow.

EVERLEE – CHESTNUTS ROASTING IN A SAUNA

EVEN WITH THE SUN shining bright in the sky, the cold still nips at my fingers and toes as we trudge through the foot high snow up the hill to find the perfect Christmas tree. I wore several layers of pants and the down jacket that Callum bought me at Valentine's, and covered my head and ears, but it's doing nothing. The guys are all dressed in jeans and some combination of sweater and vest. I don't know how they aren't cold. We've already had several in-depth discussions about fifteen trees, but they weren't *it*.

They didn't speak to Knox- so we continue.

He really wanted us to cut our own tree, insisting we make it a yearly tradition. He meticulously selected this tree farm after reading countless positive reviews online, and was convinced the three-hour drive would be worth it. It doesn't matter that we got a load of snow dumped on us this past week.

Nope!

We had to find a Christmas tree today. Which makes sense looking at our schedule coming up... but this farm was three hours away! Luckily, the great thing about it being a Monday is that no one else is really here, and it's fairly quiet.

When I called Sophie to share the news about the engagement after Thanksgiving, she insisted we come to visit her in France for the holidays, *because there was no better place than the French countryside*. I was hesitant at first until I found out my parents won a holiday cruise, Will and Beckett had to work since they got Thanksgiving off, and Lizzy and Tony were going to visit Tony's family since they didn't see them at Thanksgiving. After all that, it made the decision a lot easier to travel. Our Vixen holiday party is next weekend and we leave the Monday after, for almost a week and a half. We get back a few days before the New Year, because Vixen has to have a New Year's party.

"Fucking Christmas tree farm," Jax mumbles, batting a snow-covered branch out of his way. "Can we please pick a tree? We've been out here for an hour looking at row after row of trees."

"I'm ready to go back and sit by the fire and drink some hot chocolate," Emmett agrees and tosses a playful wink at me, causing a surge of warmth to flow through me.

Knox made up for his three-hour drive by finding a beautiful chalet. It's very triangular looking, but the entire back of the house is floor to ceiling windows overlooking the mountains. The view is stunning. The living room has an oversized fireplace with large comfy couches. Deep down, I wish for a snowstorm so intense that the roads become inaccessible, trapping us in a cocoon of snowy tranquility.

Trying to get rid of the cool burn on my face, I cup my mouth and nose with my hands and blow a warm breath into them. It does little to take away the chill.

"You should have bundled up jellybean," Knox says, bouncing by me.

"I did!" I yell after him just before he tucks between two more trees.

"This one's great," Jax calls out, stopping in front of a tree. Callum and Emmett walk back to stand beside him just as Knox comes hopping around a tree.

"How the fuck do you have so much energy?" Jax chimes.

"I love this time of year. It makes me so happy, and this is the last piece for the house."

It was the last piece.

The Monday after Thanksgiving, he had all the decoration boxes strewn across the floor by the time we all rolled out of bed with garland and lights already wrapped around the stair banister. He'd gone to the café on the corner and bought us an assortment of muffins, noting the special candy cane ones they released for the holidays. He was wearing a pair of red sequin elf shoes with bells on the top of the curved piece and a santa hat and santa apron. Again, nothing else with the apron, so his ass was on full display.

So needless to say, we spent the rest of Monday and Tuesday putting up decorations and then, randomly, throughout the rest of the week, we would all come home to find more. It was like Santa's workshop had taken over the house.

Callum said he's like this every year, but he was a little extra this year.

He's glowing, and it's hard to take that light away from him, so I don't. I just wrap myself up in his joy and let it feed me.

"No. Not this one. There's an enormous gaping hole in the back. Come on Jax. Let's look around the tree," he says, moving his hand and arm in a large circle.

"Fuck off." He pushes Knox's head, but instead of Knox retaliating, he takes off between another set of trees. "We could just leave him out here?"

"Stop." I shove his shoulder, smiling. "But I would love to find a tree so we can go back to the house. I think the sauna, some hot chocolate, and a fire are calling my name."

"Sauna," Callum and Emmett say in unison, pumping their eyebrows at me.

The heat from their stares races through me from my toes to my head and suddenly, the chill I was feeling is gone.

Jax barks at Knox, "Five minutes, Knox. I'm putting your jolly ass on a timer. Find a tree or walk home."

Knox yells something back, but none of us can make out what he's saying, but we all confirm that it sounds nothing like 'I found the one'.

Ten minutes later, we're standing around a large tree. It has to be every bit of five feet wide and over ten feet tall.

"This is it," Knox says, looking up at it, like it's shining.

"It's huge, Knox," Jax says, his voice dripping with exasperation.

"Why thank you." He pumps his brows and his hips at the same time.

"Mature," Jax snides.

"Also thank you."

Jax doesn't take the bait and just shakes his head, keeping his lips sealed.

"Where are we going to put a tree this big? How are we going to even get it in the house?"

"It will go into the living room. It's tall enough, and through a door. Obviously."

"Obviously," Callum repeats with less enthusiasm.

Knox is bouncing up and down with his hands clasped together under his chin.

Callum looks at everyone who shrugs. Likely some combination of not caring, wanting to get inside somewhere warm, and not being the one to burst his bubble... because that face. It's almost enough to melt the snow on the ground. "Fine. Let's go."

"Thank you, daddy," he says, slinging the saw from around his shoulder.

"Nope. Not your daddy."

I slip my arm around Callum's waist and press my cheek to his warm chest. He wraps his arms around me, pulling me in tight before brushing his lips across the crown of my head.

Knox drops to his knees and begins sawing quickly while Emmett and Jax eventually walk over and help by grabbing the tree and tilting it back some.

"This tree is enormous," Jax sighs, looking over his shoulder at us.

I toss him a quick wink, not wanting to leave the warmth of Callum's arms, while I watch my men hard at work.

An hour later, we're back at the chalet, stripping out of our cold, wet clothes and climbing into the sauna. The hot steam prickles my skin like needles when I first walk in. Knox decided to take a shower, wanting to wash the dirt, snow, and pieces of tree out of his hair before he joined us. There's a relaxing lavender scent infused with the steam that makes it smell wonderful.

I take the top bench in the corner, leaning my back against the wall and closing my eyes, letting the heat warm me from the inside out. I don't see where the others sit, but can feel someone just to the left and right of my legs on the lower bench.

When we got to the chalet late last night- rather, early this morning- we fell into bed, so we haven't been able to enjoy the amenities, and Knox had us up at the ass crack of dawn to go look at trees. He keeps saying when we have kids, they won't be sleeping in, so we should get used to being up early.

I haven't told them I have an appointment this week with my lady bits doctor to remove my IUD. Callum saw the message come through by accident. We were expecting news from Knox about something at Allure when the reminder popped up on my phone. He suggested that maybe I just get it taken out and not replaced, but not to tell the guys yet. I was going to put it in a box under the tree, but thought that was weird as fuck, so I took a picture of it in the trash can and put that under the tree instead.

My hand absentmindedly rubs across the lower part of my stomach for a second while I imagine where we'll be this time next year.

When a hand runs up my leg, my thoughts transition from the future to the present, where I'm currently sitting in a sauna with three- now four, because Knox just walked in wearing only a Santa hat that has been permanently affixed to his head- extremely hot, naked men, who are all mine and they're looking up at me with that want and need in their eyes. With the businesses doing so well, we have been so busy, but we have started discussing more long-term plans of getting the right people in place to free up our time. Low has been doing phenomenal, so she'll be ready to take over Vixen soon and manage without Callum and Jax there, but Allure is still too new. While we have a good team in place, there's still that need to baby it and build a good foundation.

"Everlee," Jax says my name like a warning. "What are you thinking of?"

My head falls forward and I look at him. His eyes are fiery, pupils blown, and cock hard. A dream. That's what he is. "The future."

"The future?" He slowly rolls to his knees and perches himself between my legs, forearms gently laying across my thighs. "What exactly about the future?"

"Nothing in..." my words drop as he plants a kiss on my stomach, specifically my scar. He lifts his head and kisses the other side near my hip bone.

"Nothing in?" He asks before feathering more kisses on me.

"Particular. Nothing in particular."

He lets out a low hum and slides back, kissing further down my hips to the apex of my thighs. My stomach tightens as I watch him travel further and further down. The expectation and thought of his mouth on my pussy sets me on fire.

"I think..." He kisses right above my clit. "That you are..." He kisses on my clit and my legs try to clench together, but he holds them apart. "Thinking about something." His tongue softly swipes up the center.

My head falls back into the wall and my hands press firmly on the bench as tingles shoot through my body.

"May I?" Emmett asks, scooting beside Jax, pushing my legs even further apart.

My pussy is on full display right now and I can't help but think the old me would have been cringing at the thought of it just being... there. For anyone to see. But these men. God. The confidence they have given me.

Emmett dips his head between my legs and presses his tongue in as he swipes up to my clit, running it back and forth a few times before he pulls back. "Let me taste her on your lips," he says to Jax and they both look at me as they lean in for a kiss.

Between my legs.

Fuck me.

Emmett pulls away a minute later, looks at me, then smiles.

I'm so fucking wet right now I can nearly feel my pussy pulsing come out of me, clearing the way for theirs, like a boat who's taken on too much water with a storm brewing in the distance.

Knox climbs up the bench and lays down, gently cupping my left breast in his hand before leaning down and whispering something before he kisses it. "I call booby duty."

"So mature," Jax snipes.

"Fuck off. These are mine. Holy shit!" Knox shouts like he just realized something. "Guys! Guys! What is this?" He crouches on the top and thrusts his hips in my direction so his cock is near my face, but his hand is motioning to something lower.

"What are you doing?" Emmett asks, laughing.

"Come on, guys. This is perfect!" Knox says, waving his hand back and forth quickly between my breasts and his balls.

When no one says anything, Knox lets out a dramatic sigh. "Chest and nuts... chestnuts... Christmas... oh my god! Classic!" he says, laying back on the bench so happy with himself.

"Fucking idiot," Jax mumbles before turning his attention back to me.

"Whatever. It was brilliant. Scrooge," he huffs before whispering to my breast again, running his hands across them before taking them into his mouth.

Out of the four of them, he has a special fondness for my breasts, which makes me feel an overwhelming desire to shower him with affection. My hands run along his back and around his neck as I give him a quick squeeze. He looks up at me, his chin resting on the side of my boob. "It was funny," he whispers.

"It was," I wink, lifting his chin to give him a quick kiss.

Callum is over a second later on my right side. When Knox and I finish kissing, Callum wraps his hand around my neck and uses this thumb to turn my head to look at him.

"Have you been a good girl this year?" he asks, eyes dark and sultry, voice low in his chest.

"I have."

All the men let out a laugh at the same time, like it catches them off guard.

"I've been a very good girl...most of the time." Callum's eyes lock on mine. "Some of the time." His brows raise to his forehead. "Fuck off. I'm a good girl."

Callum chuckles before swooping in and pressing his lips to mine in a needy kiss. My skin erupts as his tongue presses its way in, pulsing, matching pace with... fuck me.

Emmett and Jax are fucking... goddamn.

A moan escapes.

They're eating my pussy together, tongues intertwining, licking, pulsing. It's like they're making out with my pussy.

My ass clenches, pressing my needy little cunt closer to their mouth as my body prepares. My left arm loops around Knox, holding him to my breast while he sucks, and my other arm grips around Callum's neck, holding him in place. I'm trying to focus on kissing him, but with Emmett and Jax between my legs... fuck... shit...mother ass.

A moan shoots out of my mouth as my orgasm slams into me, sending me spiraling into a sweet oblivion as sweat drips down my body and scents of lavender fill the air. My body is tingling, and my head is spinning. I latch onto Callum's cock and pump, like moving my hand faster on him will help expel the energy yearning to burst out of me.

A second later, my ass is being lifted off the bench and rotated slightly in the corner. Emmett is bent over, lapping up all my come while his ass is in the air. Judging by the lube tube on the bench, Jax is preparing him and my stomach tightens even further. Emmett's eyes watch me while he eats me out, and I watch Jax. It's the sexiest thing in the world.

Emmett pulls my legs up higher, placing them over his shoulders, so I'm nearly laying on the top bench. He stands, pressing his cock at my entrance and without waiting longer than a wink, wraps his arms around my legs and slams into me, his piercings doing things to my body only he can. My body pulses in waves around the pressure as he fills me completely, lifting my ass into the air to get those extra inches. A tightness aches in my belly, telling me he hit my cervix, and a mangled noise shoots out of my mouth as everyone pauses to look at me.

"All good. Nothing to see here! Please continue." I wave my hand, dismissing their nonsense, and smile when a smirk creeps along Emmett's face.

"Bend," Jax commands, pressing Emmett over without waiting, sending my legs further back, causing my hamstrings to scream.

Should have stretched.

It only lasts for a second because his arms fall from my legs as he shoots his hands to the bench to balance himself.

Knox keeps his hand firmly planted on my breast, but looks towards Jax and speaks in a deep growly voice, "Me, Jax. Me, Abominable Snow monster. Me want to fuck."

Emmett and I chuckle, while Jax just glares at Knox.

Knox continues with his deep growl. "Grr. Shut the fuck up, even though you speak the truth, wise one."

"I draw the line there. You were right with the first part of the sentence and that's about it," Jax says, stepping up to Emmett.

My eyes flicker between Jax's and Emmett's, with Emmett's cock frozen inside of me.

Jax tosses me a quick wink that tells me he's about to press in, so I watch Emmett. Second best thing to having that first thrust in me, is watching Emmett when Jax presses into him.

It's like the world stops spinning or at the very least moves in slow motion. Emmett takes in a slow breath and his eyes get wide as his stare becomes more intense. His lips part as a puff of a breath escapes and his eyes slowly close, savoring the feeling before his head nods up like he's saying yes. Yes, take me.

It takes a few thrusts and some more lube, but I can tell when Jax is fully inside of Emmett, because I can feel Emmett's cock jerk inside of me.

And then it's like the world resumes its normal speed and Emmett lets out a puff of air and drags his length out before pressing it back in.

"You feel so good," Jax hums, fingers gripping into Emmett's hips as he unleashes his speed.

He's been getting more vocal with Emmett when we're all together. When it's just the three of us, he's fine, but when it's all five of us, for a while he would be quiet, like he was wrong for letting the others know how much he enjoyed Emmett.

"Yes," I scream out. Using my other hand to wrap around Knox's hard shaft. I think I startle him because his hips buck and he clamps on my nipple a little too hard, causing me to scream out.

I roll onto my side and guide Callum's cock to my mouth, eager to have him fill it.

"Ev," he pants out, placing his hand on my head.

I hum around him like the vibrations humming through my body. Damn, I've missed these men and their glorious cocks. It's not been that long, but this is the first time since the accident they haven't hesitated once, or asked to make sure I'm ok, or not in pain, or if they're being too rough. They just... fuck me.

Having a fivesome in the sauna probably wasn't the best idea, since it's close to a bazillion degrees in here and only getting hotter.

"Yes. Ev. Yes. Take my cock. Suck it like the queen you are. Fuck. It feels so good in your mouth. Fuck, you *are* such a good girl." His hand swipes back my hair and it stays because of the sweat and moisture in the air. "You suck cock so good. I'm going to come down your throat and you're going to swallow all of it like a good girl."

"Mmhmm," I hum and he jerks as his hands tighten in my hair. Knowing he's close, I suck him all the way in until he hits the back of my throat and hold him there for a second until he pulls out.

His gaze sets on me like he knows what I'm doing. Since the one time in the bathroom, where he made me watch as he fucked me, we haven't tried breath play. However, he found a teacher and is planning on bringing them to Allure in January, which will be very exciting. They are going to give us a private session beforehand to show us what they'll be teaching.

"Are you being naughty?" He moves his hips faster and faster until he shoots into the back of my throat a minute later. His ass muscles clench as he jerks, thrusting in quick pulses while his fingers grip at the root of my hair. When he's done, he drags his cock out, then leans down and brushes his lips across my forehead.

Knox slides out of my hand and looks up at me. "I'm going to come on your chest after I fuck your breasts." He glances at Jax and Emmett. "Hurry boys, my cock has places to be and titties to see."

Jax levels a menacing glare at him while Emmett completely ignores him, wrapped up in the sensations of Jax fucking him while he fucks me.

"Ohh," Jax groans out a second later. His fingers tighten onto Emmett's hip, causing his skin to blanch under the pressure.

A few more thrusts and Jax is unloading inside of Emmett, and my orgasm rips into me again, watching him. Pulses and waves of electricity erupt across my skin, setting it on fire, while the muscles in my legs tighten to the moment just before they cramp.

"Fuck me," Emmett cries out, no doubt feeling me clamp around his cock like a vise. Another two thrusts and Emmett is coming inside of me. He presses his cock in as far as it will go and holds it there. I can't help but wonder if this has anything to do with his newfound breeding kink.

He pulls out and then drops to his knees in front of me and presses his finger inside. His eyes roll into the back of his head as he plays with our come mixing together, pressing it back in.

"She's not getting pregnant yet," Jax says.

"Fuck. It still gets me off just thinking about me – us – inside of her." He runs his tongue along my opening and over my highly sensitive clit.

Jax, Callum, and Emmett all leave, noting they're going to stand outside to cool down. Fortunately, there is no one around for at least a mile and the back deck faces the mountains.

"My turn," Knox says, swinging my feet and lifting me so I'm sitting on the top bench. He hops down and runs his hands across my breasts, slick with sweat and hints of my body lotion as the heat has pulled it out of my skin. "Fucking perfect." Before stepping forward, he grabs them and feels their weight in his hands. "I've missed fucking your breasts and right now they are so slick."

It's like someone rubbed baby oil all over my entire body with the heat.

I lean forward as he takes another step in and runs his length up the valley between my breasts. Knowing this is between him and my breasts, I lean back enough to plant my hands on the bench. His hands press on the outside of each, squeezing them around his cock until he lets out a low hum and pulls his shaft down.

"So fucking perfect."

He drives his cock back up, his balls dragging across parts of my stomach, so I tilt my head down and stick my tongue out, licking the tip of his head.

"No, baby girl. You just sit back. I'm going to watch my come explode across your chest, not in your mouth."

He moves faster and faster and his breaths become shorter and shorter until the muscles in his legs tighten and a second later, he releases my breasts, grabs around the base of his cock and aims it at my chest. He puffs out, eyes on fire, then collapses on the bottom bench, head on the top turned toward me.

"If I wasn't so fucking hot right now, I'd be using my fingers to press that so deep inside of you."

I climb down and crawl onto his lap, pressing my chest against his, then run my fingers through his hair as I lean in and whisper, "I can't wait until my IUD is out and you can get me pregnant."

His fingers run firmly up my back. "Say things like that and we will die in this sauna because I will fuck you repeatedly."

"Promises, promises."

EVERLEE - CHRISTMAS TREE HAIR DON'T CARE

My hand rubs across the scar on my stomach while I stare at the thin white line in the mirror. It's been just over a month and a half since the accident that left my car totaled and me in a coma with this scar. I've still not driven much since then. I thought I could take my parents to the airport after Thanksgiving, but I freaked out.

Taking a deep breath, I pull up the dark green velvety fabric and loop my arms through the sleeveless top. The skirt poofs out to the sides with tulle layered underneath and has a bright red fur trim around the outside. The guys complain I'm always showing my stomach, so allowing them this one Christmas miracle, I bought a dress for tonight. Rubbing my hands down the soft fabric, I toss myself a wink in the mirror. It may be a dress, but it falls right at my ass line. Obviously, I'm wearing panties- red and white striped since it goes with my sexy elf outfit and matches my knee-high socks.

Turning to look at the ribbon in the back, I grab both ends that are dangling and pull them tight, cinching the crisscross pattern up my back. Before I can tie it into a knot, the doorbell rings downstairs. Must be Lizzy. We're riding to Vixen together tonight for their last themed holiday party of the season - Mistletoe and Holly.

We technically have just over a week until Christmas, but the guys have given everyone the week before it off. It really worked out well at Thanksgiving and we had a great response from the employees. We'll come back just before the New Year, and while we're having a party to ring it in, it's not themed.

By the time I get downstairs, the sound of packages shuffling along the hardwoods and sighs fills the air. Lizzy must have let herself in and decided to start rifling through the gifts under the Christmas tree.

"Hey Lizzy," I say, walking up on her.

She jumps, then yells, "What the hell?" But doesn't turn around, head under the tree and ass still in the air.

"What?" I laugh, watching her move packages around, reading the names on each.

"I only have one gift?" she asks, turning around seeing me for the first time. "HELLO!" She stands from her crouched position and walks over to me. "Did I speak too soon? Yes, yes, I did. This is all the gift I need," she says, holding me at arm's length, looking me up and down. "You're like a naughty, sexy elf!"

A heat races through my body, flushing my cheeks.

"The guys are going to lose their shit tonight!" She claps jovially. "Your eyeliner..." she tilts her head to the side. "Love it!"

With the red and white stockings and underwear, I matched my eyeliner, doing a white and red candy cane stripe into a wing. For good measure, I added some sparkles on my cheekbones to really make them pop.

"And your hair." She covers her eyes. "I really love how you have fun up top and sexy on the bottom." She walks around me. "How did you get your hair to look like a Christmas tree?"

"I flipped my hair over, got a twenty-ounce soda bottle, put it on my head, tied a hair bow around the lid and flipped it back over. I just made sure to have it tight."

"And the decorations?"

"Dollar store." I found a short, thin silver garland and twisted it at the top, then wrapped it around my hair, then added some mini ornaments.

"I absolutely love it!"

"Thanks!" Walking over to the tree, I sigh, nudging a small box back under with my foot. It's a new one I hadn't seen before and I can't help but think the guys were trying to hide it from me.

After our engagement, we had a long discussion and agreement about gifts for the holiday, however it appears they are not honoring the deal we made. An enormous flat gift is wrapped and wedge behind the tree against the wall. Even though there's not a tag on it, we all know it's for Jax from Knox. Jax threatened to throw it away without even opening it, but Knox insisted it wasn't for Jax. I don't care if they buy gifts for one another. I just don't want them going overboard on me. They just bought me this stunning engagement ring, which looks like it cost more than my car. It's absolutely spectacular and I still can't believe it's mine and we're getting married.

"When do you leave?" Lizzy asks. It's the third time she's asked in two days.

"Do I need to tattoo it on your hand?"

"No. I won't ask anymore, I promise." She holds three fingers in the air, clamped together, for scout's honor. She feels like she can use it whenever she wants to, even though she was only in the Girl Scouts for three months, because she wanted to go camping with them.

"We leave on Monday."

"Two days. Cool, cool, cool."

"Why are you acting so weird?" I cast a side eye at her.

"No reason. I'm just a little bummed I won't see you this year. We've only spent like two Christmases apart since we've known each other."

"You could always come with?"

"Yea. Jax would love for me to come along." She tosses her head back, laughing, and then stops. "Maybe I should?"

My cheeks are starting to hurt from smiling so much.

A car door closes outside, catching both of our attention. "Brady must be here."

Lizzy hands me a lemon drop martini and says, "We aren't going anywhere before our pre-club drink. It's a tradition and you know how I am about traditions. Though it looks like we'll need to create new traditions since we're both getting hitched!" She nudges me with her elbow.

"Yes, we are." It was only when they got down on one knee that I understood how much I wanted to marry them. I had successfully convinced myself I didn't need to marry to be happy, because it wasn't a possibility, but when it became one... I haven't told anyone, not even Lizzy, that it's all I've been thinking about the last couple of weeks. I've been making boards on my socials of inspiration for our wedding, rather union. My thoughts are scattered, and I can't seem to settle on a location, color scheme, or even a date.

Jax made it very clear he wouldn't wait until the end of next year, but they've given no other date. Because it's a union, we just need to find a date that we like. It's going to be small only because a lot of people don't know. I'd like to do a destination wedding, somewhere tropical and beachy, I think, or cozy and woodsy, or maybe somewhere in between.

We finish our drinks and wash the glasses, then hang them back in their spot before we meet Brady outside. He takes one look at me and his eyes quickly dart down and his lips pinch into a hard line.

"Brady."

"Everlee." He's gotten better with using my name since our talk after Thanksgiving. Occasionally, he'll still call me Ms. Everlee, but that's only when the guys are around.

"Do you like?" I point towards my hair.

"Very creative," he smiles just a bit.

"Woah, B man! Don't break your face!"

"Ms. Lizzy, always a pleasure."

"Right back at you!"

We climb into the second row of the Audi and wait for Brady to get in. I have to slouch a little in the seat so I can fit my hair. I didn't fully think through the Christmas tree on top of my head being too tall for the car.

"Hey!" Lizzy whisper shouts.

"Yes?"

"Do you have time tomorrow to run by La Belles? I'd love for you to look at the bridesmaid's dresses I've picked out. I'm down to two styles and need to get them finalized this week, since I'm less than six months out."

"Sure. Can we do it in the morning? I want to spend the afternoon washing clothes and packing since we leave Monday."

"Yea, that works. I think they open at ten, so we'll go then."

"Sounds good."

"I'll swing by and pick you up around nine fifteen and we can grab breakfast and coffee at the corner café."

I cut my eyes at her.

"Stop. You're leaving in two days for France for, like, what, a week, week and a half?"

"Yes."

"Fine. So I'm going to get my time with you, boo boo."

"Ok, fine, that works."

She squeezes my hand before she claps excitedly.

CALLUM - COMING DOWN HER CHIMNEY

THE FOUR IMAGES OF the club rotate every five seconds on the screen in the office. I was trying to get a jump on our paperwork for the month, so I didn't have as much to do when we get back from France, but the text message I got a few minutes ago from Brady has completely distracted me. He'd just left the house and was on his way here with Ev and Lizzy.

I knew they were coming tonight, because it's a holiday party. Ev only missed the Halloween one, and she was so bummed. Allure isn't doing a holiday party this year, but she and Knox talked about doing it next year. The Halloween one was such a success, they need more time to plan. They did, however, do some holiday themed decorations. They converted the white room we stayed in for Halloween into a Winter Wonderland, complete with a snow machine and ice shaped dildos. It's been their most popular room since the change.

The image on the screen has a car pulling up to the side entrance.

She's here.

My heart beats a little faster in my chest. Even after all this time, she still makes my stomach flutter and my pulse quicken. Although, I think part of it is nerves. She loves pressing our buttons and one of them being the outfits she chooses to wear to these events.

I stand from the desk and just as I'm walking out of the office, I bump into Jax. "She's here."

"Joy," he says sarcastically. "At least she has a ring on her finger now."

"At least." I pump my eyebrows at him.

"Knox and Emmett said to take pictures."

"I bet they did."

"Let's get our girl."

We're walking down the steps just as they get into the door. Her eyes look up to find me and she gives me a quick smirk and my heart flutters with happiness. "What have you done?" I ask, trying not to laugh.

"Do you like?" She throws up one foot and her opposite hand into the air.

"That's not really the correct question. I always like." I step towards her, so we're less than a foot apart. My hand cups her cheek. "I like when you're bundled head to toe, or when you're wearing nothing. The question is not do I like, rather do I approve?"

"Wrong." Her brows peak on her forehead.

"I don't get a say in what you wear?"

Her head falls to the side and her eyes catch mine. "No," she says, her voice filled with defiance.

"No?" I move closer to her and she takes a step back.

"I'll be upstairs," Lizzy chuckles. "Not even two minutes. Fucking record."

"We're not fucking," Everlee calls out.

"Not yet." Lizzy throws her hand in the air and doesn't even bother looking back.

Everlee's eyes land on mine. "We're not." Her dilated pupils reveal her heightened state of excitement and betray her lie.

"No. We aren't," I whisper. But goddamn, my cock wants to.

Jax walks behind her. "You don't think we see how short your dress is?" His hand glides up the back of her leg, lifting the edge.

I close what little distance is left between us and she takes another step back, wedging herself between Jax and me. "You flipped your leg up, and we saw your underwear."

"A small gift for you." Her eyes dance with humor as she looks at Jax over her shoulder.

"Underwear?" He chuckles.

"You always complain I never wear them." Her head tilts to the side, her eyes flickering between Jax and me, mimicking the gaze of a caged cat, anticipating the next move.

Jax leans forward. "Anyone could walk by and let their hand wonder. How easy it would be for them to," his words stop and Everlee's back straightens razor sharp as her eyes roll into the back of her head. I glance over my shoulder to make sure there's no one in the hall.

"She's so wet." He leans forward, and his arm moves and she lets out a moan, grabbing onto my shoulders.

"Not fair," she swallows hard.

"You wear a skirt that barely covers your ass. You all but invited my fingers inside of your pussy. Just one quick swipe to move your panties out of the way and there it is."

She doesn't speak, but just stares at me as Jax's fingers slowly fuck her.

"You feel so good," Jax says, pressing his lips to her neck and sucking.

She lets out a whimper and her eyes flash over my shoulder, causing me to look. There's no one there, just the lights flashing from the main floor.

"Are you scared someone's going to see us?"

She looks up at me, teeth nibbling on her bottom lip, and she shakes her head softly.

"You're nervous they won't?"

Her eyes flash wide with excitement, but she doesn't answer.

"Do you want me to make you come right here in the hall?" Jax asks, before biting her neck again.

Her knees buckle, giving the only answer she needs to.

"Oh, love." I press my lips to hers and let my tongue pulse in.

"Cal," Jax calls. Pulling away from the kiss, I look at him and he twirls his finger. Oh, that dirty devil.

I spin her around and wrap my arms around her chest at the same time Jax falls to his knees.

"What are you doing?" she pants out, staring at him.

"Showing you how accessible your pussy is." His fingers glide up her leg and he swipes her panties out of the way and licks.

Her head presses back into my shoulder as she lets out a pant.

"Your skirt is so short, he doesn't even have to hold it up."

Jax's head is nodding up and down as he continues to press his tongue into her pussy. I would have never considered myself a voyeur before, but I love watching the guys bring Ev to orgasm. It gets me off almost as much as doing it myself.

"This isn't fair. No one's going to lick my pussy in the middle of the dance floor."

"He's licking it right now in the hallway."

"Because I'm letting him. If some stranger tried to do that to me, I'd knee th-..." a moan escapes as her hands latch onto the sides of his head.

"You're getting close."

"Fuck you."

"I plan on it." My lips press onto the side of her neck and I gently suck, causing goosebumps to spread down her arms.

If I slipped my fingers into the top of her dress, I know her nipples would be hard.

"You're going to fuck me in the hallway?"

"Do you want me to?"

Her head turns to look at me, at the same time another moan falls from her lips. She doesn't answer immediately because I know she loves the thrill and risk of being caught.

"I can bend you over right here and fuck you while you choke on Jax's cock."

"Cal..."

I press my lips against her ear and whisper, "Did you do that thing we talked about last week?"

She looks at me, her eyes searching my face, and she nods without speaking.

"Good girl." My lips press to her neck. "We're going to put a baby in you this Christmas." Her head falls back and I reach around, grabbing her jaw and press my lips to hers, swallowing her moans.

I'd seen the text on her phone, reminding her to set up an appointment with her OBGYN the week after Thanksgiving. I thought something was wrong, so I brought it up to her in private. She assured me it had nothing to do with the accident and it was just time to get her IUD replaced. I may have casually suggested that she *not*, and her eyes lit up. We haven't told the others because I think she wants to surprise them at Christmas.

Grabbing Jax's attention, I tilt my head to the closet just past his left shoulder, and he nods. He presses his hip against the keypad, waiting for the door to buzz and the light to turn green, before he twists the handle and pulls us in. I close the door and make sure I hear the lock click before I undo my pants.

Everlee's eyes are fixed on me, pulsing with anticipation, as she utters my name.

"I'm going to fuck you, while I watch you suck Jax's cock."

"Watch my hair," she warns Jax.

"I'll be watching your mouth around my cock, love."

With a gentle tug, I raise the hem of her dress over her hips and slide her panties down to her knees. I'd like to rip them off, but she'll need them tonight to catch the come dripping out of her.

After exposing her pussy, I press on her back, causing her to bend over. "Look at her. She's glistening for me." She lets out an appreciative moan when I press two fingers and curl them inside of her. My cock twitches, ready to feel her clamped around it, so I wrap my hand around the girth and line it up at her entrance. There's already a bead of pre-cum on the tip, so I slowly press it to her needy little cunt and watch it disappear. My stomach tightens and a tingle races up my spine.

Fuck.

Emmett and Knox have been talking non-stop about putting a baby in her and I think it's starting to rub off on me. The idea of watching my come meld with hers does things to me.

Focus, Callum.

A sigh escapes as I watch her pussy swallow my shaft. When I pull it out, it's shimmering with her arousal.

"Jax. Pull out your cock and feed it to her. I want us to fuck her at the same time and then fill her with our come."

"Fuck, Callum," she says before she blows out a puff of air.

Jax pulls his pants down just to his thighs and takes a step toward Everlee, holding his cock in his hand and lining it up with her lips.

He presses in slowly, pushing it as far as it will go until she makes a slight gagging noise. Her left hand stays on her knee, holding her body up, while her right hand wraps around his base.

"That's it, Everlee. Suck it like a good girl."

She clinches her pussy around me, and I let out a chuckle. Thrusting my hips, I punch inside of her, sending her onto Jax's shaft. They both let out a groan, and Jax's eyes snap up to look at me.

"Brother," he says through set teeth.

"Brother," I return with a smile.

The bells on the small ornaments in Everlee's hair jingle with each thrust. "It feels like fucking Christmas in here with her bells ringing," I say, reaching around to find her clit.

"I'm about to come down her chimney," Jax says.

Everlee lets out some sort of mangled sound, between a laugh, a moan, and choking on his cock.

Her pussy feels so good. So warm and wet. As my orgasm builds, my balls start to tighten. "Jax."

"Yea," he says, immediately knowing what his name means.

My finger works her clit faster until she presses back on my cock, wanting more. More friction, more length, more fucking. A few more thrusts and she's moaning and bucking as her pussy clenches and tightens around me.

"Oh fuck. Yes, baby girl. Come for daddy. Fuck. I love when you come around my cock." Grabbing both sides of her hips, I punch deep into her. She's crying out around Jax, as her hand begins to twist. She cups his balls and squeezes, causing him to raise on his tiptoes, taking her mouth with him.

"Fuck Ev."

She sucks his cock in, cheeks hollowing out around him.

Watching Jax fuck her mouth sends my stomach tightening and a tingle to shoot up my spine.

"Jax," I pant out again, unable to hold off my orgasm any longer. The tingle shoots down my spine to my balls. They tighten as I explode inside of her. The immediate thought of my come loading her up, causes my head to swim and a groan to lurch itself from my chest.

"Ohhh," Jax cries out, pressing deeper into her mouth.

She's swallowing him down and I swear it makes me fucking dizzy with desire.

After her doctor's appointment last week, I did some research. It could take up to three months before her fertility is back to one hundred percent, but as soon as the guys find out... they're going to be unstoppable.

EVERLEE - ROCKIN' AROUND THE DANCE FLOOR

When I get up to our booth fifteen minutes later, Lizzy is staring at me with a huge shit-eating grin on her face.

"You're such a ho ho ho."

"Stop."

"What? Did Santa Claus not come to town?"

"Lizzy," I warn.

"You didn't jingle their bells?"

"Are you done?" I ask, sliding in, ignoring the wetness that's still between my legs as I lift Emmett's drink to my lips. It's a sugar cookie martini with a sprinkle rim and little mini candy cane shaped sugar cookies he made.

"Did they show you their North Pole?"

"Fuck Lizzy. Thank goodness I'm leaving in a few days. I don't know if I could handle all of your sexual innuendos for the next week."

"Oooh one more, one more. Then I'm done… for now."

I roll my eyes, staring at her and waiting.

"Did they call you Vixen?" She throws her head back, laughing. "Because the reindeer.... Prancer, Dancer... Vixen! Nailed it!" She screams, thrusting her fist into the air.

"How many drinks have you had?"

"I'm not drunk. I'm just horny and need my candy cane licked by Mr. Claus tonight."

"I thought he wasn't getting home until tomorrow."

"He was initially, but decided not to participate in the after-dinner festivities. He's taking a late flight tonight, and this will be his last big trip for the rest of the year. I plan on being the little nutcracker tonight. If you know what I mean," she says, pumping her eyebrows.

"I can't with you."

"You *can* with me and you love it." She lays her head on my shoulder. "So. Tell me about France. What are you all doing? Big plans?"

"I don't know. Sophie has been planning most of it with Callum or Jax."

"Very hush-hush."

"Not really. We're staying with Sophie and her family for the first few days. We'll do some of the touristy things, visit some museums, and some other stuff, but they don't really talk about it. Maybe rent a small house somewhere? At least that's what I'm thinking. Still not sure."

"But not hush-hush?"

"I mean no, not really."

She smiles, "None the less, it's super romantic and a little house?" She laughs as she speaks, "Do you know the definition of little? Watch the men rent out some enormous mansion. I don't think anything about your men is little..." her brows peak on her forehead.

That's true.

A heat races through my body, no doubt causing my cheeks to flush a deep cranberry red. Lizzy miraculously doesn't call me out. "Knox fussed at me a few days ago because he wants this trip to be a surprise for me. He's been very excited about it, so I'm trying not to pry into anything anymore."

"Knoxxy baby. Such a softy." She looks around, then leans in. "Do you want to go dance, or will your men make you stay up here the entire evening?"

I cut my eyes at her.

She holds up her hands. "Fine. Dancing it is."

EVERLEE - DRESS SHOPPING

WHEN WE WALK INTO La Belle's just after ten in the morning, Andre is standing at the front door waiting for us with a tray of champagne in his hand. He hurriedly sets it down and holds out his arms, "My beautifuls! How are we doing this morning?"

"Andre!" Lizzy shouts, nearly colliding into him as she gives him a hug.

"Full of spunk, as always!"

"There's no other kind of Lizzy," I say, walking over to give him a hug.

"And you wouldn't have it any other way!" Lizzy slaps the air.

"True."

Andre lifts the two glasses of champagne and offers them to each of us. "I have the dresses set aside for you to look at."

Lizzy claps excitedly. "I think you're going to love them!"

"I'm sure I will."

"Show us the way, Andre!" Lizzy laughs out loud. "It rhymes! Way. Andre. I'm a poet and didn't know it!" she cheers, following Andre to the back of the store where the private rooms are.

"You're something," I mumble under my breath and Lizzy turns to look at me and sticks out her tongue.

"Has Everlee shared her news yet?"

"Lizzy..." I warn.

She looks over her shoulder and gives me a quick wink that tells me she's ignoring my warning and trudging forward.

Andre stops and scurries over to me, hands clasped under his chin. "Telllll me." His eyes are nearly popping out of his head.

My stomach tightens and my cheeks hurt from smiling.

"Is it one of those delicious men that were in here with you a few months ago?"

Lizzy lets out a mangled chuckle.

"More than one? I mean, I had my suspicions." His eyes grow wide when I don't answer and then he stumbles backwards dramatically with the back of his hand pressed against his forehead. "All of them? Girl. Color me green with envy. When is your date?"

"I haven't said a single word."

"Honey," he grabs my upper arm. "You don't need to speak with your mouth when your eyes and face are telling the entire story." He removes his hand off my arm and places it on his hip, jutting it out to the side, full of sass. "So... date?"

"No date yet."

"Well, we must find wedding dresses for you then!"

"Yes!!" Lizzy cheers, clapping her hands.

"No," I laugh, cheeks flushing. "We're here for Lizzy today, not me."

"Please. We have the entire afternoon. You're leaving me tomorrow for ten days. Give this to me."

"Not the entire afternoon, and don't we need to look at your bridesmaid's dresses?"

"Yes." She bats her hand in the air. "But that will take two seconds!"

Andre flits around the room, removing all the dresses off the hangers clearing space. "Tell me, darling. What are your desires for a dress?"

Laughing, I shrug my shoulders. "I don't know. I haven't thought about it."

"Lies!" Lizzy shouts.

I stare at her incredulously. Is she serious right now?

"Tell me, darling. Just a few things." He claps his hands with a huge smile on his face.

"Fine."

"Yes!" Lizzy shouts, thrusting her fists into the air.

"Long, some bead work, maybe some lace around the top up here," I say, brushing my hand around my chest. "Classic, with a hint of sexy. Not super puffy."

Andre cuts his eyes at Lizzy. "She hasn't thought about it. Right?" He turns back to look at me. "You try on the two dresses Lizzy has picked out. Let us know which one you love and Lizzy and I are going to run and find some dresses for you."

"You don't want to see the dresses on me?"

"No girl. I trust you."

"Seriously?"

"Boo boo. you and me are like one mind. I already know which one you're going to pick because it's the same one I have picked."

"Do I even need to try these on?"

"Duh. I have to prove to myself and everyone else that we're one mind."

I laugh, shaking my head.

They both flutter out of the room like two little fairies. I have no idea how this morning has turned from a day for Lizzy into a day for me.

Twenty minutes later, I've tried on both dresses and decided the off the shoulder satin maxi dress with the high split was my favorite. The other option was a simple strapless a-line dress. It was pretty, but there's something about the off the shoulder one that just speaks to me.

"Oh Everlee!" Lizzy calls just as I'm finishing putting my clothes back on.

Equal parts nervous and excited, I peek around the curtain and see Andre and her putting several dresses on the hooks around the room. "Liz…"

She looks over her shoulder at me, eyes wide, a smile spreading across her face. "Which one did you like?"

"The simple a-line," I lie.

"Bullshit, hooker!"

"No. I like the simplicity of it."

"Well, sucks for you then. I'm going with the other and you're going to love it."

"Fine. I was just testing you."

"I know." She flips her foot in the air. "Now stop playing around. I found us these dresses."

"Us?"

"You know what I mean! Now, let's go."

Leaving the safety of the dressing room behind, I walk over to Lizzy. I can't believe I'm trying on wedding dresses, but something tells me this was her plan all along and she only used the excuse of picking out her bridesmaid dress to get me here.

"We picked six dresses. There are two that I think you're going to love."

"I'm glad I don't need to look for my own dress." I chuckle.

"You can, but you'll be wasting your time. I got you, girl. The other four you'll like, but not love, but I felt like I had to give you options, so it's not too easy for you."

"Well, if that's the only reason."

"It is. Try these on, and then you can go walk around and then come back and tell me I'm right."

I can't argue with Lizzy when she's like this because when I have to tell her she's right later, it will only make the news that much more difficult. "Fine."

"Look at these four first."

She walks me around the room from left to right. The dresses are beautiful, nice bead work, lace tops, but there's just something missing. Something I can't put my finger on.

She waits for me in front of the last two and smiles. "Now these." She thrusts her arms out, waving them.

Standing between the two, I go back and forth. They are gorgeous. "Stop staring and go try them on. I grabbed your size in each," Lizzy urges, grabbing a dress off the hook and nearly shoving me into a dressing room.

"I think you had this planned the entire time, didn't you?" I pull my shirt over my head, fairly certain if I didn't, she'd be in here doing it for me.

"What? I don't know what you're talking about." The sound of her voice gives away her movements as she quietly roams around the room, surely plotting something.

Shimming out of my clothes, I slip on the first dress. When I zip it up, then turn to look at myself in the mirror, my stomach dances with butterflies and my hands slowly rub down the dress as the world stops turning.

I'm in a wedding dress.

I'm looking for wedding dresses... for my wedding.

"Ev... you good?" Lizzy asks, like she can sense my mood change.

The words feel like a lump in my throat, forcing me to cough before speaking in a voice that betrays my nerves. "I'm good."

The curtain quickly jerks and she pokes her head in before fully climbing into the dressing room. "What's wro- holy shitballs. You're gorgeous. Oh my goddess! This is it. This is the dress. Turn," she commands, grabbing my arms to spin me.

I watch her through the mirror. Her gaze travels up and down my body, analyzing the fit of the dress, until our eyes finally meet. There, on her rim, is a tear.

"Liz," I laugh as my throat tightens. "Stop."

"You stop." She grabs my shoulders and spins me back around. "Let's go out here, so you can see yourself in all the mirrors."

I nod, since a ball has lodged itself in my throat... again.

As soon as we step from behind the curtain, Andre's hands shoot to his mouth. "Girl. I swear to the goddess you could turn me straight. Do you need a fifth man in your harem? Because damn."

A mangled chuckle escapes from my lips and I'm embarrassed by the sound I just made.

"You didn't say no, so there's a chance!" He laughs, shuffling over to me, lifting my arms and sticking his fingers in between the dress and my body, checking the fit. "This dress fits you like a dream. Do you love or do you love?"

"I really like it. It's beautiful," I say, spinning around and looking at the dress in the mirrors.

Lizzy walks over and grabs my hands and starts dancing with me.

"What are you doing?" I laugh.

"Seeing how you move around the dance floor with it on." She twirls me then stops, "I'm not dipping you because we'd both end up on our ass."

I have no words, and she is shoving me into the changing room. "Hand me this one through the curtain and I will give you the second one to try. I think you're going to love love love this one."

Just as I hand her the dress, my phone rings.

A video call from Jax.

Feeling a little frisky, I answer in nothing but my panties. I opted for them today since the guys weren't around.

"Hey babe."

He stares at the phone and doesn't speak for a minute. "What the flying fuck, Everlee?" His brow is pinched and his jaw is tight. "I thought you were going with Lizzy to help her pick out a dress or something."

"I was, and somehow it turned into me trying on wedding dresses. You just caught me in between."

The lines on his face soften, and his eyes twinkle. "What are you wearing?"

I angle the camera down to show nothing but my underwear.

"Ev," he growls.

"Stop." I blush. "What's up?"

"My cock. That's what's up."

"Har har."

He angles the phone down to the seam of his pants.

"Jax."

"Tell that boy to hang up. He's creeping in on my visitation," Lizzy yells through the curtain.

"Well, that's an effective way to kill the mood," Jax retorts.

"I can hear you!" Lizzy shouts.

Reaching through the curtain, I feel Lizzy's warm, soft face under my palm and push her away.

"I'll let you go since you're busy." Jax smiles.

"I have a minute for you. What's up?"

"Nothing. We can talk about it tonight."

"Jax."

"Everlee," he retorts, jaw set.

He tosses me a wink when I scrunch my nose at him. "Fine."

"I love you."

"I love you, too," I huff before ending the call.

A moment later, the second dress is being handed through the curtain. Slipping it off the hanger, I stare at it. It's beautiful. It hangs straight down with a slit up the leg and extraordinary bead work hand stitched through. The dress itself is strapless but there is a lace overlay that goes up around the neck and down the arms, with four silk buttons on the back. Lizzy will have to help me with those because I can't reach them.

This dress is almost exactly what I pictured in my mind when I started flipping through bridal magazines and looking at them online. It really is a little scary how well Lizzy knows me. I haven't told her what I was looking for and here she is, nearly picking out the perfect dress.

Pulling it up, I back up to the curtain and call her over to help. Her little fingers sneak through and she buttons it, then swoops the curtain to the side.

"Fuck me sideways and call me Santa."

"I thought Tony did last night." The words slip out before I notice Andre's gaze on me.

He bats his hand like it's nothing.

"Turn. Turn right now," Lizzy says, ignoring me and barely containing her excitement. She's nearly jumping out of her skin.

When I turn, a tear rolls out of her eye and her hands go to her mouth. I haven't even had a chance to look at it yet, but I catch Andre's face and his mouth is gaping open. Lizzy pulls me into the middle of the room, and I appear in all the mirrors. My heart stops beating for a second as images from all sides of me appear. Goosebumps dance across my skin as I stare silently from mirror to mirror.

No one talks.

No one moves.

After an unknown amount of time, I give a slight twirl and watch the fabric swoosh at my feet.

Lizzy and Andre still haven't said a word as they continue to stare at me.

I catch her eyes and they are pleading with me to say something. Anything.

Scrunching my nose, my hands fiddle near my waist. Her eyes get big and her feet start dancing.

"This is it?"

"Are you asking me?" She nearly shouts.

"No?"

Her head tilts to the side.

"This is it. Is that silly? I haven't looked at dresses and this is only the second one I've tried on."

"When you know, you know," Andre chimes in, sauntering over. "And girl. This dress was made for you."

"Yea?"

"Fucking hell to the yes. I think angels just sang," Lizzy chants. "Damn girl. You've got me jealous over here."

"Stop. Your dress is beautiful."

"I'm not looking for compliments, Ev. I mean this with all the sincerity I can muster. This dress. You." Her hands clamp together under her chin. "You're beautiful. You will need to wear a bag over this through the entire ceremony, because when the guys see you... they're going to stop the ceremony, whisk you away and put a baby in you."

"Lizzy."

"I'm not fucking kidding. Ev. They're going to lose their damn minds."

I look at Andre. My heart is racing and my skin feels clammy. Am I really about to do this? This is ludicrous, isn't it? "Ok... I'll take it."

"Thank Goddess, because I was trying to figure out a way to not let you say no to this dress. Stunning."

"What do we do?"

He glances at Lizzy, then looks at me. "I'll take it and have our seamstress look over it. Make sure that all is in order with the beadwork, then you can pick it up in a few days."

"I'll be out of the country. I can get it when I get back... a few days before the New Year."

"Ok. That's perfect."

Looking at the dress one last time before I walk back in the changing room, a warm wave washes over me. I can't believe I'm buying a wedding dress today.

By the time I slip out of my dress and change back into my clothes, Lizzy and Andre are at the front talking about her wedding. I gently lay the gown on the counter and he takes it, putting it on the hanger behind him.

"Sorry, I could have done that, but Lizzy took the hanger."

"Sure. Blame me."

"You literally took the hanger."

"Tomato tomato."

"You can pay for it when you pick it up after the inspection."

"Ok." I didn't even look at the price tag for this dress, but I know right now that it doesn't matter. This is the dress. This is my dress and I would pay whatever I needed for the guys to see it on me. Lizzy was right, though. They're going to lose their minds when they see me.

Now all we need is a date.

EVERLEE - MERRY BUNCH OF ASSHOLES

WHEN I GET HOME three hours later, the lights are off in most of the house, and Emmett and Jax are sitting on the couch in the living room watching a movie.

They slide apart and pat the space between them. With every step I take towards them, a warmth spreads over my skin. Part of me wants to tell them I found a wedding dress, but the other part doesn't want to say anything because I don't want them to feel pressured into finding a wedding date. When I told my family a few weeks ago, Jax was quick to say we weren't waiting until the end of next year after Beckett and Lizzy's wedding, but he never offered a date or has talked about it since then.

"What have you boys been doing?" I wiggle my butt into the small space they created.

"Waiting for you." Jax's voice lingers in the air, his fingers gently tucking a strand of hair behind my ear before his lips meet my neck.

"So what have you really been doing?"

Emmett puts his hand on my thigh and squeezes. "Waiting for you." He kisses the other side of my neck and my nipples press against my bra.

Trying to ignore the tightness in my stomach and my pulsing pussy, I ask, "What are you watching?"

Emmett lifts my legs and places them on his lap, twisting me so I have to lean on Jax. "Some action movie series. We just finished the first one and the second in series just started a few minutes ago."

Jax loops his arm around my chest and pulls me to him. These men are very touchy-feely right now, which always ends up with sex.

Which I don't mind.

Just thinking about the two of them together makes me hot and watching them together makes me even hotter.

"Where are Knox and Callum?"

"They both went into the office to check on a few things in prep for our vacation."

"Oh."

"So they'll be gone for a couple more hours."

Butterflies dance in my stomach. The way Jax said it... the tone in his voice... there was something laced in the words... in the meaning.

I don't say anything, letting out a soft hum, and sink into the couch to watch the movie. Aside from the fight scenes, the room is quiet.

Five minutes.

Ten minutes.

Fifteen minutes pass.

"Are they going to be home for dinner?" I ask, throat tightening.

Damn it. These men and their pheromones.

"They will not," Jax answers. His arm shifts down from around my shoulders to my stomach.

My eyes flick to Emmett, who looks from Jax's hand to my eyes, back to the movie. I can't ignore the smile that plays on his lips.

Fucking hell.

I'd love for once not to have a needy little cunt that wants their cocks all the time...who could play hard to get for longer than sixty-nine seconds, but no.

"So what do we want to do for dinner?" I ask, trying to sound as normal as possible.

A chuckle tumbles from Jax's chest, catching Emmett's gaze. "I know what I want to eat, but I'm not sure about either of you."

"I'm fine eating what you want," Emmett says, his gaze slowly moving from Jax's hand back to the movie.

A gasp slips through my lips, but nothing else is said.

If I had a knife, I feel like I'd be able to cut the sexual tension in this room.

A few more minutes pass, and Jax's hand slowly rubs on my stomach over my shirt as he continues to watch the screen. Just when I think he's more interested in the movie, his hand slips under my shirt and lands on my stomach. Emmett's eyes briefly flicker toward Jax's hand before returning to the latest action sequence.

Another few minutes pass and Jax's finger circles on my stomach and around my belly button before rubbing over my scar. Since the accident, I've noticed the men like to rub their fingers over the thin white line or plant kisses on it. I don't know if it's more for them, or their way of showing me they love all of me. Whichever it is, I find it sweet.

At first, I was ashamed of it. It marred my skin, but the guys... the attention they give to it... it's made me feel at ease with it.

Emmett's hand slowly rubs up and down my leg, never going below my knee, but inching higher and higher up my thigh. My eyes lock on him, waiting for him to look at me so I can figure out the game they are playing, but he continues to watch the movie. With their roaming hands, I feel like they're teasing me, but it's so hard to tell. Well, two, rather three, can play this game. With my eyes focused on the movie, I act like I'm shifting in my seat, laying my head on Jax's lap, while making sure to rub my leg over Emmett's cock.

I can feel his eyes on me... and Jax's, but I don't look away from the movie. Now they can see how it feels. Freaking innuendos about eating me out and rubbing on me. Merry bunch of assholes!

Their hands continue to rub on my stomach and up and down my leg, so I shift again in my seat, rubbing my leg against Emmett's cock and sweeping my arm to curl under my head, making sure to brush it against Jax's as well. I'm please to feel that both of them are getting harder.

Jax's hand rubs further up my stomach so his fingertips barely brush against the bottom of my bra, so I wiggle again. When he lets out a sigh, I can't help but smile with satisfaction.

Brushing my body along their hard shafts, I slide off the couch. "I'm going to get some popcorn. Do you want some?"

The guys look from one another back at me, but don't speak.

"No? Well, so you know, you're not getting any of mine."

"You think so?" Jax retorts.

"I know so."

"Not very Christmasy of you."

"I'm a Scrooge." With that, I turn and walk out of the room, trying to ignore their bulging cocks. I'm nearly drooling by the time I get in the kitchen. The tile floor feels like ice on my feet. Hell, even the air moving past my body while I'm walking feels cool across my flaming hot skin.

My feet pat pat pat across the tile floor as I make my way to the pantry and look for the popcorn, finding it near the top shelf. Standing on my tiptoes, I try to reach it, but can barely touch the bottom of the box.

"Do you need some help?" A voice booms from behind me, robbing me of my breath.

Jax.

I don't turn around, because I'm fairly certain whatever I would find would make me drool.

"Yes," I say, still reaching up.

Expecting to see his arm above mine, I'm surprised when he grabs me around my legs and lifts me with ease. I let out a little squeal and grab the box of popcorn. "You know, if you put things at a normal level, then you wouldn't have to help me get them down."

"But where's the fun in that?" he asks, still holding me up and not moving.

Turning around, I look down at him. "Are you going to let me down?"

"No."

"No? You're just going to hold me up here like this for the rest of the night?"

"No."

"Did you forget all of your words?"

He looks up at me, but doesn't speak.

"Jax."

"Everlee."

"It's going to be hard for me to make popcorn when I'm up here."

"That's a shame," he answers apathetically.

"You seem heartbroken."

"Devastated."

Letting out a loud huff, I toss the popcorn box onto the counter and cross my arms. Jax lets out a chuckle.

"What was that?" Emmett asks, walking in quickly, then coming to a stop when he sees me in Jax's arms. "Well, well, well… what do we have here?"

"Emmett," I pout.

"Don't think he's going to help you, love."

"Yea. Totally not going to do that," Emmett agrees.

"That's bullshit."

The grip Jax has around me loosens, and I think I've hurt his feelings for a microsecond, before he lets me slide all the way down his body and his hands glide under my shirt and lift it over my head, but leave it around my wrists.

"Jax," I pant out.

"I'll help you now," Emmett offers.

Before I can thank him, he unclips my bra in the front and slides the cups off each breast.

"I thought you were helping me."

He laughs, placing two of his fingers under my chin and lifting. "I am." His lips find mine and he presses his tongue in. He steps closer to me, pressing his chest against mine, pinning me between him and Jax.

Jax's hands slide down the insides of my arms, down to my chest, where he cups a breast in each hand. Emmett slides from my mouth to my neck, down to my breast. He sucks my right one in his mouth, his tongue swirling over my nipple while Jax's hand slides down my stomach and slips under the waistband of my pants and down to my clit.

"Oh," Jax's chest vibrates. "Someone is very wet."

Emmett pulls off my breast and grabs Jax's arm, pulling it from my pants. "Let me taste." He sucks Jax's fingers into his mouth, his tongue swirling around them as his eyes lock on mine.

Fucking fuck sticks.

Emmett sucks Jax's fingers into his mouth like he's sucking his cock and I'm so turned on right now.

"I think you've only made her wetter." I can hear the smile in Jax's voice and feel his deliciously hard cock pressed against my back.

"Let's see." Emmett lowers to his knees and pulls my pants and underwear with him. His finger rubs up the middle of my pussy and I can feel how wet I am. "Oh. She's drenched." He presses his tongue against my center and licks up one time, brushing against my clit.

A puff of air escapes and my hands fall down to find his head.

He looks at me as his hand reaches up to pull Jax's pants down. He slides his hand up between my legs and pulls Jax's cock between mine, so it's right under my pussy. "My two favorite things," he hums, smiling.

Emmett presses his tongue to the tip of Jax's cock, and my stomach tightens as a moan escapes. He's not even touching me and yet... I feel it. He sucks just his head into his mouth and I'm going to orgasm where I stand. Wave after wave of electric sensations pulse over my skin, while my lower stomach clenches and tightens at the sight of him. He pulls off Jax, then licks my pussy.

"It's so fucking hot how wet you get watching me suck him." He presses his tongue inside of me, then sucks on my clit while Jax's cock rests under his chin.

"Fuck me," I grab on his head, need consuming me like a wildfire.

He pulls away just as I feel my climax coming quickly and rubs his hand along Jax's cock. He slowly bends it up, pressing the head of it to my entrance. "I'm going to make you come with his dick inside of you."

A whimper escapes as I watch him and then feel him press Jax's hard shaft inside of me. The familiar stretch is there and Jax inches in slowly, filling me. I rotate my hips backward so I can take more of him, while his arms clamp around my chest and his hands grip onto my breasts.

"Jax." He drags it out, the friction making me ache for more before he presses it back in again.

"I can see her arousal sliding down your cock," Emmett groans out, eyes focused on the place where Jax enters me.

My hand glides through Emmett's hair as Jax fucks me with slow precision. The feelings, my emotions, are so heightened as my head falls back against Jax's chest, cherishing every second of how good this feels. We're always so fast with our fucks, it's nice to take our time to appreciate the micro feelings of everything. The stretch of my pussy, the grip on my breasts, the warm breath of Emmett's mouth on me.

Emmett's mouth on me?

My eyes shoot open and when I look down, I find Emmett leaning forward as he runs his tongue along the exposed part of Jax's shaft, then up to my clit. A guttural groan echoes from deep within my chest as my hands grip in his hair.

"Now I can taste you both at the same time." He rocks back on his hind legs and looks at us with a twinkle in his eye.

"Oh fuck me," I cry out, just as I watch Emmett's tongue slide along Jax's cock, then over my clit.

"I plan to," Jax says, grabbing my hair tightly and jerking my head to the side, exposing my neck and biting me.

Ever since my strange request at Halloween after my dream, he's bitten me a few times and fuck if it doesn't nearly make me come instantly. He bites, then sucks against my skin, causing it to tent. My other hand curls around the back of his neck, holding him against me.

I feel like I'm going to explode. Like I'm going to burst into a flame right here in the middle of the kitchen. An electric energy is humming through my skin, buzzing from my toes, up my legs, through my core, to my head and arms. I'm torn between wanting to watch Emmett-

Ohhh. My vision pulses and my legs buckle for a second. The very idea of him licking my come off Jax's cock each time he pulls it out is driving me wild. Feral. I can't take it.

"Fuck!" I pant out.

Emmett licks up to my clit, then sucks it in his mouth while Jax continues to fuck me, moving a little faster now.

"I'm going to come."

"You already are," Emmett says, dragging his tongue along Jax's shaft. "You're like fucking icing on a cake dripping down his cock."

My stomach tightens and I grip harder around Jax's neck, searching for something to hold on to.

"I got you, love." He abandons my neck and wraps both of his large tattooed arms around my chest and lifts, thrusting his cock into me. He moves faster and faster, while Emmett continues to lick, holding his tongue there so it brushes along my clit.

"Fuck. Fuck. Fuck."

My orgasm shoots through me like lightning whipping through the sky. My legs buckle, but Jax is already there, holding me up. Even though he stops moving, letting me pulse around his cock, Emmett is still licking and pressing his tongue over my clit, pushing it to the very max. The muscles in my toes and legs seize as it becomes too much, but he doesn't stop.

He's lost control.

"Come inside her, Jax. God, fucking fill her with your come."

My heart skips a beat for a second because they don't know I don't have an IUD in, but the chances of me getting pregnant this soon after taking it out are next to nil.

Emmett's eyes dart around the room frantically for a second, like he's looking for something.

"Not here, though. The table. Lay her down," he shouts, running over to it without waiting for an answer from us.

He wants to watch Jax fuck me. He wants to see the come inside of me. It's his thing and fuck if it isn't hot.

Jax pulls out and by the time we're over at the table, Emmett has pushed all the settings to one side.

"Poor table." I laugh, thinking back to all the times I've been on it. Most recently, the clusterfuck surprise that was Thanksgiving.

Emmett is rushing back into the room a second later with the blanket from the living room. "Lay on this." Jax grabs my thighs and rolls me up on my side, then back over onto the blanket.

My hands cup around my breasts, as my head tilts to the side, watching both of my men, cocks erect, staring at me like I'm their dessert.

Jax grabs my ankles, pulling me to the edge of the table. He lifts my legs up and rests them on his chest as he lines up his head at my entrance.

Jax presses into me without waiting, causing my back to slide up the table, and I cry out, pressing my head back.

"Yes!" He fills me, his length pressing in deep and his size stretching me tight. He wasn't able to get this far earlier, but now with me on my back and my legs in the air...

Heaven.

A moment later, Emmett is walking up behind Jax and wrapping his hands around him from behind, gripping around his pecks and then sliding down his abs while his mouth leaves hungry kisses along his neck.

Jax's head swings up to the ceiling in an appreciative groan, and my stomach tightens again. I wasn't prepared to come so soon, but watching them is my drug. Hell, my kryptonite.

Emmett's eyes lock on mine, while his hands continue down Jax.

He knows.

He knows what this does to me.

My fingers clamp down on my nipples as my head languidly bobbles from side to side.

Jax lets out a moan when Emmett takes a step towards him and rocks his hips against Jax's ass. Jax's hands press down on my hips like he's trying to feel his cock moving inside of me and only releases when Emmett lowers towards the ground, planting kisses along his sides.

My eyes meet Jax's and they watch me, just before they grow large in surprise. "Fuck me!" he blurts, freezing before he bends over.

Emmett is there with his tongue playing with his ass and tingles race through my body as my pussy pulsates around Jax. A moment later, Emmett is standing back up and Jax starts fucking me again, then slows. Emmett's eyes focus on me while his teeth scrape over his bottom lip and his arm angles in such a way-

He's fingering Jax's asshole while he fucks me.

Jax moves a little faster, his breaths coming quicker and quicker.

"Ev," he pants. "E..." he drags the letter out.

He bends over, hands pressed to the table on either side of me. He takes my lips in a fevered kiss before he lets out a groan, exploding so hard inside of me I can feel it.

"Fuck. Shit. Shit. Fuck." His words become drawn-out, mirroring the deceleration of his thrusts.

Emmett nibbles on the top of his shoulder and walks away.

"This isn't over Ev. You two. My room."

No, this isn't over. I'm finally going to show them what I bought for us to play with before Halloween.

JAX - MAKE ME PEG FOR IT

By the time I get to Emmett's room, he's walking out of the bathroom, looking and smelling clean. This man.

We participated in No Shave November and he has turned it into No Shave December too. He's like a sexy fucking lumberjack, and I can't get enough.

"Where's Ev?" Emmett asks, only mildly concerned. He knows she can't be far behind.

"She had to get something from her room. She said she's tired of waiting to find a time to use it. Whatever it is."

Emmett's eyes flare with excitement and my pulse races. He and I have talked a few times about what we think it is. It's been toying with us since Halloween and not a day has gone by that we don't wonder. We thought about going into her room and snooping, but we don't... because that's wrong. But damn.

Emmett and I fall onto the bed, legs tangled at our ankles, when the door pushes open, revealing the hallway.

"Ev?" I call out.

She bursts into the room, legs spread apart, and hands splayed to the side in the air like she has jazz hands. "Ta-da!"

"Fuck me," Emmett and I both say in unison.

My eyes rake up her body from toes to head. She's wearing black, thigh-high stockings attached by two clips to a black pair of most definitely cheeky underwear. Her separate top comprises black strips of fabric hugging her body, crossing over her nipples, leaving the bottom curve of her breasts exposed while other black strips form a v, angling down to her underwear.

And there... there, at the center of it all, is a purple silicone cock with ridges.

"Sorry it's taken so long to show you, but..."

Without speaking, Emmett leaps off the bed and grabs her in his arms. "You want to peg us?"

"Only if you peg for it." Her eyes twinkle, then her face falls. "Ok, sorry that was super corny, but I couldn't help it. It just fell out of my mouth."

Emmett murmurs something before his fingers curve around the back of her neck, under her hair, pressing his lips to hers. A long, hard, passionate, bruising kiss. She whimpers out as her knees buckle, causing her dildo to rub along his cock and the sight of that makes my blood pump a little faster.

"I fucking love you so much," he says when he pulls away from their kiss. He rests his forehead on hers and stares at her for a second like there's so much more he wants to say, but doesn't.

"I love you too. I thought...I could play with you and Jax." Her eyes quickly flick to me.

I smile, looking between her and E, and my stomach tightens.

After we got back from the snow-covered chalet, Emmett took me from behind. He was so slow and patient with me as he talked me through each phase. His cock is enormous and while I got used to it, the more he pumped inside of me... I didn't like the vulnerability of it all and I couldn't get out of my head.

Emmett said my reaction was perfectly normal, and some men don't enjoy being the bottom. I must be one of those men. Emmett said he likes either, but prefers the bottom, especially when his cock is buried in Ev. He said the senses are overpowering.

"I'm so down." Emmett smiles and looks at me.

Needing to join the conversation and get my hands on Ev, I stalk over to her and Emmett. Her eyes flash like they do when I'm being rough with her, the mixture of fear and lust. "You want to put *that* in my ass?"

"If you don't want to..." her fingers are fidgeting. "I know... last week..."

"Emmett's cock is like five times the size of that and I would... love for you to fuck me. But so you know," I turn to Emmett. "I'll be fucking you while she does it."

"Are you sure?" she asks, eyes glimmering with excitement.

"I can't guarantee I'll do it after today, but I'll try." My hands scoop her cheeks and I stare at her, lost in her eyes- in her. "I'll try anything for you, love."

She gives an excited hop step as we walk over to the bed. "E... will you help... teach me?"

"Yes, love." He wraps his hands around her neck and presses his lips to hers. She moans into the kiss as it deepens, her tongue dancing with his just before she sucks on his bottom lip. A tingle clenches my stomach as I want to kiss them to. In some ways, it's like the floodgates of want have opened, and I can't get enough of either of them. For once in my life, I'm letting my walls down and I want to experience everything I was so scared of before. There is so much out there I want to try with these two and we have started, but I feel like we're just at the tip. I can't help but chuckle on the inside because a 'that's what she said' joke plays in my mind. While they kiss, I grab the lube from the bedside table and sit on the edge of the bed to wait for them.

"I'm so glad we stock this at Allure now so we can get the employee discount," I quip when they break from their kiss and look at me.

Laughing, Emmett snatches the tube out of my hand, then shoves me onto the bed. Shock pulses through my body at the thought of him trying to dominate me. I am Jax McCall. I don't get dominated. My eyes fall on Everlee with her strap-on. Well, not all the time. Nerves prickle under my skin at the thought of her dominating me. Will she like it? Will I? This power shift will be interesting.

"Roll over, love." Emmett pats me on the ass.

There must be a look in my eyes because Emmett asks again if I'm ok with this and I nod. He knows I wasn't a huge fan of taking him, but we tried it. I wanted to at least experience it one time. Honestly, I have way more respect for Ev now. She's like a fucking superhero, with the way she takes our cocks.

"Words, love," Everlee reminds, using my own words against me.

I cut my eyes at her and she laughs, jumping on my back, causing me to jerk when the dildo jabs me in the ass. "Oh fuck. Sorry. I'm not used to having an extension on me."

Her expression is of embarrassment and I can't help but chuckle, rolling over just a little so she can wrap her body around me. Her lips are right there, and I don't hesitate to take them, to show her I'm fine and to show her she's mine. I try to kiss any question, any doubt away. I want her to experience this and enjoy it.

When Emmett took me, it was just the two of us. We asked Everlee to be with us, but she gave us our space. Part of me wondered if it was because she didn't want to see me getting fucked, because that would ruin all of her ideas about me, but that was just my insecurities creeping in- the evil voice that has pressed these thoughts and feelings down for so long. She stayed with me that night and we talked about it in depth and she explained her reason for not wanting to be in there and it had nothing to do with the way she saw me, but simply it was a big step in my journey and she knew I would feel vulnerable and didn't need an audience.

A minute later, she stands up and I roll over, pressing my forearms on the bed while Emmett talks to Ev, giving her some pointers.

Everlee rubs her hands up and down my back to soothe me, because Emmett pointed out that I'm tense. I try to relax, but it's difficult; however, as I listen to him coach her, walking her through each step, I feel more at ease. Something about the idea of her inside of me causes a tickle to move across my skin. I focus on my ass muscles and force them to relax, dropping my head so I can watch them under my arm.

I love her. I love her with everything inside of me. I love Emmett too. It's so weird to me I can love them both so fully at the same time.

She presses her finger at my entrance, causing me to jerk for a second before I settle back down. Her fingers are small compared to Emmett's. Everything about her is small compared to Emmett, except for her personality.

A moment later, I feel lips, two pairs of lips on my lower back, planting kisses up my spine and around to my side. Goosebumps erupt under my skin like a wildfire with dry brush.

"Do you like that?" Emmett asks in his low, fuck me voice.

He's still trying to relax me.

Everlee's hand scoops around to the front and runs along my hard shaft. "He's hard."

I let out an appreciative hum.

Everlee gives a few more strokes before Emmett continues walking her through how to prep me. After several minutes, she has two fingers pulsing in and I feel like I'm about to come. Emmett's hand wraps around my shaft and I nearly fucking explode. I have both of them servicing me.

Everlee's breasts brush across my back and the dildo hanging between her legs jostles between my ass. Her lips are pressed against my ear and she whispers, "Are you ready?"

"Yes," I nod.

"Good, because I'm going to fuck your ass until you come."

Butterflies erupt in a flurry inside of my stomach.

I make the mistake of looking at Emmett. His hand is on his cock, rubbing it up and down slowly and suddenly I don't want to fuck his ass, I want him to fuck my mouth. I want to be fucked by my loves. Give over control. This feeling that sweeps through me is new and... exciting.

"E..." His eyes pulse wide for a second like I snapped him out of a trance. "I want you to fuck my mouth instead? Is that ok?"

Is that ok? I'm asking? Not telling? Fuck me. What is going on?

A smile curls on his lips. Does he see it? The submission. This will not be an everyday thing because I like to dominate too much, but tonight. For him. For Ev. I will submit for them. I would worship them on my knees tonight, if they asked.

Emmett climbs on to the bed and stands on his knees in front of me.

"Fuck me," Ev cries from behind us in that low sultry moan that she does too often when she's around us. I love it too, knowing that we can be us and she finds it so hot.

She throws the lube back on the bed after she adds more to my ass and I presume her dildo. She lines it up at my backside and I try not to clench, but she must see I'm tense because her hands run up and down my back for a minute at the same time Emmett strokes his cock right in front of me. The bead of pre-cum is glistening on the tip of his head and I fight the urge to lean forward and lick it off until he inches it closer to me.

"You want my cock?"

I nod.

"Oh no, love. You need to use your words for us while we fuck you."

"Yes. I want your cock. I want your cock in my mouth. I want to suck you in so hard that you hit the back of my throat until you are coming down it. I want to play with your balls while our girl fucks me in the ass. I want it all E."

His eyes pulse wide.

So much for being the submissive tonight. No wonder Ev has such a hard time with it. It's too fun knowing what words can do to someone.

"Ready?"

She waits for my go then slowly presses in, just the tip before she pulls out. She grabs some more lube, coats the dildo again before pushing in a little further, pausing at my ring of muscle. I can feel it tight around her, so I try to relax again.

"Such a good boy. On your hands and knees for us," Emmett says, pressing the head of his cock to my lips. "Lick my cock."

"You trying to dom me?" I ask, looking up at him with humor in my eyes.

"No trying. We are and we will." His words are soft and low.

A low moan rumbles out of my chest as Everlee pushes in a little further, hitting that magical spot that Emmett did. My cock jumps in excitement.

Emmett adjusts his knees on the bed, inching closer to me. "Now, I'm going to feed you my cock."

I open wide as he presses it in further. Never would I have thought I would enjoy sucking his cock so much, but the rush it gives me. I suck him in hard until he's at the back of my throat, his piercings running along my tongue. Fuck, he's so hot. Everlee's so hot, the way she's working my ass.

With one hand on my lower back, she maintains a steady push and pull rhythm. Her hands glide across my hips, her confident grip igniting a surge of excitement within me. She presses all the way in, her hips pressing at my backside, and pauses, "How are you? How does it feel?"

I hum out around Emmett's cock and hold my thumb in the air. If I had ten thumbs, I would hold them all up because that is how amazing it feels.

"Good. Because this... this is..." Her words fall off as she moves again, faster, more confident. "I want to fuck you. I want to fuck you until you're coming in your hand. Grab yourself."

Her words come out quick and heady.

My free hand grabs my cock and it is so hot and hard right now and as soon as my hand touches it, my stomach clenches again and my hips buck. Fuck me. I'm going to blow my load.

She moves faster and faster, and this is so different from what I felt with Emmett. His cock is huge, but this one is smaller. Perhaps I can work up to his cock, because this feels amazing right now.

I need more.

I want more.

Emmett presses his cock in and I use that to push me back a little, so I meet Everlee's thrusts. God, it feels so good. I press my hands to the bed and off my cock, because I don't want this to end. I want to come because of them, the pleasure they're giving me.

"Oh," she says when I push back on her again and again as a wild hunger consumes me.

She gets faster, picking up speed, and I feel the dildo hitting inside of me at different angles. She's wild. I'm wild. We're all wild.

Emmett is fucking my mouth while I fuck Everlee.

And that's when I feel it. I buck and nearly blow my load as tingles and sensations rocket inside of me like fireworks on the fourth of July. My skin is humming and the muscles around my spine grip like a vice as a euphoric wave crashes around me.

Emmett pulls out, and I growl out. "Fuck, fuck, fuck." My heart is nearly beating a hole out of my chest.

Everlee pauses, panic laced in her words, "Are you ok? Did I hurt you? I got carried away."

"No. Fucking. No. You hit my prostate and holy shit. It felt... amazing. I thought I was going to explode. Give me more. Give me all of it."

She hesitates for a second and I can feel her eyes watching me, like she's trying to figure out how serious I am. When I see Emmett toss her a wink with a quick nod, I feel her grab my hips and begin thrusting in hard and deep at the same angle, and my world lights up.

"Fuck me." I don't know if it was a request or a prayer, but Everlee pounds into me at the same time Emmett wraps his hands around my head, feeding me his cock.

The intensity of my need has left me in a disheveled state, my come soaking into the bed with every movement. I want to wrap my fingers around my length so bad and just come, but at the same time I don't want this to end.

"I think I'm going to come," Everlee cries out. "The sensations and fuck... the back side of the dildo rubbing on my clit." She lets out a groan of hunger, then chuckles, "But this time I'm not coming until you do, love."

If I didn't have Emmett's cock down my throat right now, I'd cut my eyes so hard at her she'd feel the burn. She knows my one rule. The only rule. I'd only changed it at Halloween to edge her, but now she wants to top me. She wants to make me come first. Her thrusts tell me she's not playing around and I also know I have no hope of lasting longer than her. She's hitting all of those spots inside of me and with Emmett here... and her... fuck.

Need and want, moans and pants, slurps and thwaps fill the room. It is the only sounds.

"Jax... I'm about to come." Emmett gives me a second to pull off him, but I don't want to. I want to taste him. I use my hand to wrap around his base and twist before I slide it down to his balls and palm them. His hands tighten against the back of my head while he shoves his cock in. A second later, I feel his warm, salty come shoot down the back of my throat. I swallow, trying not to gag, but it still gets me a little. I'm not as good as Everlee, but it only gives me something to look forward to improving.

When he pulls out, he leans down and presses his lips to mine. His tongue slides in, claiming me with pure carnal desire.

"Touch yourself Jax. Grab your cock. I want you to come. I need you to come. I need to know you like this as much as I do, because damn..." Everlee moans. "I really fucking love it."

Without waiting, I fist my cock and pump two, three, four times. This wave of pleasure swells up within me like a tsunami building, threatening to demolish everything inside of me once it crashes, but I don't care. All I care about is this feeling. Us. Now. My kiss with Emmett deepens, turning into a wild frenzy, almost like he can sense everything I'm feeling. Needing.

The wave crests and a tingle shoots up my spine and then back down like one of those games at fairs where you use the hammer to hit the light up to the bell. As soon as the feeling crashes back down to my hips, my balls tighten and I fucking come, so hard it's like a fucking fire hose knocking me back, lodging myself onto Everlee as she presses that one magic spot that makes me see stars.

Emmett breaks our kiss as garbled sounds come out of my mouth. All the muscles in my body turn to mush as my arms give out and I face plant into the bed. I don't even hear Everlee behind me panting, or feel her hands splayed across my back for support.

"Holy shit. I've never come like that before," she says, looking at us stunned, having removed herself from my ass.

Emmett and I look at each other and then her. Without hesitation, we both leap from the bed, causing her to yelp as we grab her and throw her in the middle, ripping her underwear and strap on off her.

She is so wet she is glistening like a pond that's been iced over.

"You threw me in your come," she sighs, with a hint of humor in her eye.

Ignoring her, I find a place between her legs and lick, needing to taste her.

She lets out a small whimper, different from her usual one, causing me to pause.

"Are you ok?"

"I think I've rubbed my clit raw."

Glancing down at it now, I can see it's bright red. The entire area is. I plant a gentle kiss on the inside of her thigh. "Yea. It doesn't look happy."

"Damn it."

"Let's go to the Nest bathroom and relax in that bathtub together."

"I'll go run it," Emmett offers, hopping up from the bed.

Grabbing a warm washcloth from my bathroom, I pull her to sitting and wipe the come off her back. "I think I shot my come through the comforter to the mattress."

"Did you like it?" Her voice is small, shy.

I drop the washcloth and turn her around to face me, lifting her chin with my fingers. "I loved it. It was... I don't know if words can describe it. And it's not to say that Emmett was bad when we did it... but that was..." I press my forehead against hers. "I love you... so much."

"I love you too."

"I was scared I hurt you."

"Not at all. Now I feel bad because you're hurting."

"Nothing I didn't do to myself. I had seen some people talk about chafing. Maybe I should have paid more attention." She chuckles, but she's caught off by my kiss. Her... innocence is the wrong word, because she's far from innocent, but whatever it is, she catches me off guard.

EVERLEE - RIDE THE PONY

"Bon jour! Bon jour!" Sophie chimes, throwing her hand in the air when she opens the front door. Her house, as she calls it, is more like a mini mansion. It's a five-story building with light colored brick and large windows spread across each level equally spaced. The second and third levels have black wrought iron around the balcony, which gives it a sort of aged, yet modern look. There are large trees tucked in close to the window, with several others to the left side that seem to partially hide a walkway to the other parts of her house.

I don't know if it's her or the fact I'm in Paris, but I lean in and kiss the side of each of her cheeks.

"Come in, come in." She waves us in and as soon as the door closes, she grabs my hand and looks at the ring. "Wow-wee, stunning." She pats Jax and Callum–the two closest men to her– on the shoulder. "Very nice job."

The interior matches the beauty of the outside of her house. It's a large open foyer with shiny light brown wooden floors and cream-colored walls with a sweeping staircase on the left side of the room that opens to the second level. There are pictures of Sophie and her family lining the walls from eye level to as high as you can see, the higher ones much larger, putting Knox's poster sized pictures in Jax's room to shame.

"Welcome," a voice booms jovially.

Jacques is walking down the hall, rubbing his hands on a small towel, before he drapes it over his shoulder. He's wearing beige colored linen pants that flow as he walks, with a white short sleeved button shirt. He looks like he just stepped off the beaches of Greece with his deep tan and green eyes.

"Welcome!" He gives me a hug. "Congratulations."

"It's so gorgeous Jacques," she grabs my hand and holds it to his face.

"It's exquisite."

"Jacques, show the men to their rooms," she waves as she grabs my hand. "Come. I will show you around." She flits like what I would imagine a fairy does with wings just floating around, so light on her feet.

We walk down the hall, and it opens to an enormous kitchen that makes me drool. I don't cook and really don't love it, but I think if I had this kitchen I would totally learn. In the center is a large, oversized island with a beautiful slab of cream-colored stone. I'm not sure exactly what it is, but it's beautiful. The base cabinets are a nice rich blue that looks like it was mixed with gray and has brushed gold handles. The wall to the far right is one of the largest ranges I have ever seen, with sixteen eyes and four ovens mounted on the wall. To our right are two–TWO–refrigerators.

"Your kitchen," I say when I can lift my jaw off the ground.

"It's too much."

"It's amazing."

"I like to cater and host parties."

"If I had your house, your kitchen, and cooking skills, then I'd be the same."

"Emmett says you can cook."

"I can barely boil water compared to you and Emmett."

She laughs, batting the air, and we continue walking to the floor-to-ceiling glass doors. Standing there, the cool weather prickles on my skin as we look across her patio-brick flooring with large teak tables and a long fire pit that runs along the center. When I look across the garden area, I see Callum looking at me from the third-story window on the opposite side.

Massive.

"I didn't know your house was a mansion."

She laughs. "It's big, too big. But when Jacques saw the kitchen, he placed an offer on it immediately."

"How is everything going with all of your business ventures and shows?"

"Busy. So busy. I have to go to a taping tomorrow morning, but then I'm off for the rest of the time you're all here." She squeals. "I am so glad you are here. You look so happy and the men. My goodness."

"I'm glad we could make it as well. I thought we were going to my parent's house since we weren't able to for Thanksgiving, but then plans sort of got swirly. My parents won a trip, which is mind-boggling to think, because they never win." I chuckle to myself, "But who makes people travel at the holidays? Oh well. They were really excited about it, and they're getting older, so I want them to take these opportunities as they get them."

"Very sweet."

"And then my brother and his fiancée had to work since they saw us at Thanksgiving and then my best friend."

"Yes. Lizzy. She is a meow."

She catches me off guard, then her nose scrunches. "I said the wrong word, didn't I?"

"I think you meant hoot."

"Hoot. Yes. I know it was an animal sound."

We're laughing when the guys walk back in.

"What are you two talking about?"

"Animal sounds." Sophie looks at me and smiles. "We have some fruit, crepes, and scones for breakfast this morning."

"It smells delicious," I say, watching Jacques pull some items out of the middle oven.

"Where are the kiddies at?" Knox asks, playing with his hands.

"They're at Jacques' parent's house for the next couple of days. We wanted to spend time with you all."

"Aww, but I wanted to see them."

"You will. We will spend some time with them on Thursday before you all travel off to your next destination."

My head snaps at the guys, who laugh as Sophie lets out a laudable gasp.

"Oh, no." Sophie claps her hand over her mouth. "I spoiled the beans."

I can't help but smile at her close but inaccurate saying.

Callum pulls me in, pressing his chest to my back, and lowers his head, causing the stubble on his cheek to gently scratch me. "You didn't. She didn't know, but it's ok. We weren't hiding it, but also weren't telling her."

I slowly turn my head to look at him, trying to figure out what kind of bullshit statement that was. *We weren't hiding it, but also weren't telling her.* Motherfucker, that is the definition of hiding it.

He catches my glance with a twinkle in his eye and quickly kisses my forehead before looking at the rest of the group.

"Where are we going, then?"

"We're not telling you."

A bubble bursts in my chest and when I turn to slap Callum's chest, he catches my hand, holding it to him and laughs at me like I'm nothing but a flea slapping a horse. If fleas slap horses. Weirdest thing I ever thought of. Like now, all I can imagine is a flea standing on its back two legs smacking a horse's ass and oddly enough it's shouting ride the pony.

Seriously, what the fuck is wrong with me?

Callum looks at me, studying my face and I just shake my head, too embarrassed to relay that train of thought.

"You aren't telling me. So you're hiding it from me?" I try to jerk my hands from his grip, but he doesn't let me budge.

"That part's a surprise."

"I see."

"Well, shall we?" Sophie fans her arm to the food on the island.

CALLUM - RAINBOW AFTER THE STORM

It's been a long time since we've been in Paris. We came to visit Sophie and Jacques when they had their first child and Emmett has come a few times to visit some friends he made when he was at school here, but all of us together... it's been a while and Everlee has never been.

Knox and Everlee are leading the group and, of course, Knox brought his camera, which is looped around his neck, to take pictures. Fortunately, we convinced him to leave his Hawaiian print shirt, shin socks, and bucket hat at the house. He's like someone plucked a tourist out of a book and just dropped him in the middle of Paris.

He points off in the distance and Ev is running ahead with a smile spread across her face, before she quickly poses for a picture, throwing her hip out and tossing her hand in the air. I have no idea how many pictures he's taken, but it has to be a ton.

"Sorry about earlier... if I ruined the surprise," Sophie says, falling into step with me.

"No. You didn't. How was your taping this morning?"

"Good. Quick. Easy peasy!" She laughs, then looks ahead at Knox and Everlee, looping her arm around mine. "She seems happy. You all do."

I glance down at Sophie, then watch Ev and Knox run over to a statue and take another picture. "We are. We are very happy. She completes us in a way that we didn't know we needed. How are the kids? Jacques?"

"Great. They're all three in school now. Simon just started this year, so that's been an adjustment, but very exciting. Jacques is fantastic, as always. Things really couldn't be more perfect. It's amazing how things work out the way they are supposed to... you know?"

"It is. If only we know things are going to work out when we're going through all the heartache at the time." That wasn't a dig at her or even about our relationship with her, just a general statement. It's so easy to get caught up in the now, but I have seen it time and time again where things are better in the future than you thought they could have been.

"The rainbow after the storm," her words fall off. She nods to Emmett and Jax a moment later. "This is new."

"Yes. A couple of months now."

"Jax seems happy. Relaxed."

"He is. This is... the most at peace I've ever seen him. Like his... soul. Or just the thing inside of him. You know? He's finally letting down his walls and letting himself love and be loved."

"That is fantastic." She pulls her arm from mine. "I'm really happy that you all found one another. Everlee is great, and she complements you all so well."

"She really is. Her family too. I can't wait until you can meet Beckett and his fiancée, Will. And her parents... they have really surprised me through all of this."

"Yes. From what Everlee has told me, she was scared they wouldn't accept you all. But I suppose it helped when her mom showed up at the beach."

I cut my eyes to stare at her, and she laughs. "That week was probably the most stressed the guys or me have ever been. We were terrified of her mom finding out and then losing her. Knox was going over the top, setting Donna's chair up every morning and just being himself. Beckett was there to help level the emotions coursing between all of us. And we ran... a lot."

"Well, it all worked out in the end."

"It did."

"I'm so happy you all came to visit me in the great Paris this week." She spins in a circle with her arms in the air.

"Ev has been talking about all the things she wants to do while we're here, with the Eiffel tower being top of her list."

Sophie gives me a knowing glance with a smirk. "Yes. I believe she will love the Eiffel Tower very much, but that is for tomorrow! Today we have much to do over these next two days."

"Very much."

"You call me and say we need to keep her busy doing many things. So this is what I do. I plan. I keep her busy. You cannot complain now, dear Callum."

"No. I suppose I can't. So tell me. What are the plans?"

"I thought you would never ask." She laughs. "Today, we have the Louvre and the Catacombs. We finish the evening with a nice private dinner cruise on the Seine. Tomorrow," she pumps her eyebrows. "We take a trip to Versailles for most of the day, then come back to the house and get ready for a memorable and spectacular... dinner at the Eiffel tower."

"Thank you for helping plan... all of this. I know it's been a lot."

"My dear Callum. I would do anything for you five. You make me happy seeing you all together."

EVERLEE - SIGHTSEEING IN FRANCE

I'M IN PARIS. THE city of love... with my men, and at Christmas none the less. It's surreal to think that I'm actually here, in a place that I've always yearned to visit and that has been on my bucket list.

Yesterday, we went to the Louvre, which was amazing, then toured some catacombs which was a little weird, but still interesting. Today, we're headed to Versailles... as soon as we can pry ourselves away from this soft, luxurious bed.

Callum is sitting with his back pressed against the headboard with his tattooed chest exposed, glasses on, reading the newspaper. Well, looking at pictures because I'm not sure if he knows how to read French, but I could be wrong.

Rolling over, I toss my leg and arm across him and perch my chin on his chest.

He lays his paper down slowly and looks at me with his glasses on, and my stomach clenches. Total daddy dom, silver fox thing going on right now. "Good morning, love."

"Morning," I chirp back, smiling ear to ear.

"Why are you so happy?"

"Because I'm in the bed of one of the men I adore, in a beautiful mansion in the city of love. What could be more perfect than that? Well, let me stop you before you even answer. Being in a bed with all of you would be better, but second to that... what could be better?"

He chuckles and brushes the hair away from my face. "I guess nothing." He stares at me with those sultry eyes and I feel the room start to change.

"Callum," I whisper as my throat starts to close.

"Everlee," he says back playfully, taking his glasses and setting them on the paper on the nightstand.

"What are you doing?" My heart beats in my chest a little harder.

"Nothing. What are you doing?" He shifts my body so I'm laying on top of him. His shirt, the one I'm wearing, rides up, exposing my ass to the sheets and my pussy to his stomach. I didn't wear panties last night because I've grown accustomed to the free feeling. I would have slept without a shirt, but it's a new place and I didn't know what would happen.

His cock is hardening, causing his head to push at my entrance and it's everything I can do not to shift my body and sink on it. I want to, but feel like I should try to pretend to resist for more than a second. "Are you excited about Versailles today?"

He chuckles at my poor attempt to change the topic and the mood.

"So excited." His hands slide down my hips, over my ass and then up my back, dancing across my skin like ice skaters on ice.

"Me too." I swallow the ball in my throat as I try to ignore the moisture pooling between my legs.

"What's your favorite part?"

His fingers slide back down and dance on my ass cheeks this time, getting awfully close to my crack. As my instincts take over, I can't help but clench, causing a slight rocking sensation against his cock. The bead of his arousal feels cool against my hot pussy.

"I don't know. I haven't been. What's yours?"

"The roses. I *love* roses."

I feel like roses is supposed to mean my pussy because of all the rose vibrators Lizzy got me.

"Yea. Those are nice."

"I love the smell of them." His fingers knead into my hips and ass. "I love the feel of them." His hips start to rotate a little, rocking his cock against my pussy.

I let out a moan and drop my forehead to his chest.

"You're an ass. You know that?"

He laughs. "If I was an ass, I would tease you until you're about to come and then leave you. I don't plan on leaving you. I plan on pressing my dick inside of you and have you ride it until you come all over me. Then I plan on loading you full of my come. Something about the fact that your IUD isn't in anymore makes me so fucking hard all the time."

"Do you have a breeding kink, too?"

"I don't know." He pushes me down and thrusts his hips up at the same time, sending his cock sliding into me, but only just a fraction of his length.

He sighs, closing his eyes. "Ride me, Everlee. Fuck me." His words come out as a command, but sound like a plea.

"Yes, sir."

His eyes flash open as he watches me press my hands on his chest and push off him, sinking onto his cock further and further until I'm seated completely on him.

"Shirt." He nods, then clasps his hands and tucks them under the back of his head.

I pull it off and toss it to the floor with a bit of flair, letting my hand dangle in the air for a minute.

"You're a fucking dream."

"Your dream."

"My dream." He licks his bottom lip, then sucks it into his mouth. "Now ride me until you come all over me."

I smile, then rock my hips back and forth.

"Yes," he sighs out, holding onto the s.

"Do you want me to touch myself?"

His eyes pulse wide with excitement, but he doesn't say anything.

My hands rove over my stomach, up my chest and around my breasts while I continue to rock on him. After I pinch each nipple, I slide them down to my clit just above my pussy that's stretched tight around his cock. My finger circles as I start to move faster and faster on his length until I abandoned my clit, press my hands on his chest and pop my ass up and down. I can't move fast enough or get the right angle, which is frustrating. He must sense this because in a flash he sits up and drives his cock into me, going so deep I feel an ache in my stomach.

The room fills with grunts and thwaps as our skin comes into contact over and over again.

"You feel so fucking good." He grabs around my shoulders and pulls down, trying to drive himself further into me. It must not be enough, because he pushes me back, pulls out, and flips me over onto my stomach, then pulls my ass up. He's in me less than a second later with his hands gripped around my hips and he unleashes, causing me to cry out.

"Look up," he commands.

When I do, I see the mirror on the other side of the room.

Goddamn, he's a fucking vision. All alpha, fucking his lady hard.

"Watch yourself until I'm done with you." His eyes hold mine in the mirror.

My lips part and my breasts flop back and forth wildly. Not the best image, but that's what they're doing. Thank God they're on the smaller side. If they were much bigger, I'd be getting fucking whiplash right now. A concussion would likely ruin this vacation. So, yay for small miracles.

His hand slides down and finds my clit. It was already primed before so three circles and I'm screaming out his name. A few more thrusts and he's burying himself deep inside of my pussy as he comes. I love to watch his face when he releases. It's like this haze brushes over his eyes, like nothing matters as he rides the waves of ecstasy.

He leans down and kisses my spine, which is also a highly sensitive and ticklish area, causing me to buck under him. He bites at my back, then pulls out.

"Let's go clean you up," he says, rolling off the bed and walking into the bathroom.

Several hours later, we're getting off the train at Versailles. It's beautiful here today, but a little chilly. Knox has insisted I take his jacket as another layer of warmth because 'he's been trained for this' and he also doesn't think it's that cold.

Bullshit.

That's all I have to say about the matter.

I pluck my phone out of my pocket and dial Lizzy. It's the fourth time I've called her today, and she hasn't picked up. The first two times I didn't leave a voicemail, because why? She never checks them anyway and I usually have to repeat myself. But the third time I did and the little bitch-ass still hasn't called back or texted. I even waited and call her until it was a decent hour back in the States.

I gave her a key to the house to run by a few times to get our mail while we're gone and just make sure everything's ok. If she has decided to park her happy ass there... I don't really care, but I know she's going to do some crazy shit. She's the female version of Knox, only maybe a little more... just more.

"What's wrong?" Emmett asks, walking over and throwing his arm around my neck.

"Nothing. I've called Lizzy, and she hasn't picked up."

"I'm sure everything is fine."

"Me too. I just don't feel like getting shit from her when she asks why I didn't call her when I was sightseeing. We've always talked about doing Paris together and I'm here without her." I grab Emmett's arm. "Don't get me wrong. I'm not saying I'm not happy I'm here, because I am. I just... I don't know. I don't want her to be mad."

"I don't think she'll be mad."

"She never doesn't pick up. Do you know how many times she's answered my call while in the bathroom? Too many to count."

He laughs. "I'm sure all will be good. When you talk to her, everything will get sorted out." He kisses the side of my head.

"Picture time!" Knox chimes, skipping to us with the camera already pressed to his eye.

I have all their gifts wrapped at the house, but I may need to figure out how to get him photography classes or something. It would be a two-fold gift. He gets the classes, and I get to watch Jax shit a brick when he realizes that only means better quality inappropriate pictures.

EVERLEE - PRIVATE EVENT

Today has been absolutely amazing... Versailles was stunning and Knox and I got a ton of pictures. It's been pretty much the two of us running around looking like silly tourists, enjoying everything this city has to offer, and taking a bazillion pictures. The guys have been there too, but they've been... off. Part of me wonders if it's weird for them being back here with Sophie and Jacques and me, but that's my insecurity. I've pushed most of it away and know the guys are happy to be here with me, but it's still there. It may always be there. Even though I know they would never cheat... I just... I shake my head, trying to clear my thoughts.

They are here with me.

They love me.

We're engaged to be married.

I glance at the time on my phone and do the math before I call Lizzy. I've called her half a dozen times, and she's only texted to tell me she'll call me later, but still hasn't.

Voicemail.

Again.

"Hey. I'm beginning to think you're ignoring me. I want to talk to you and show you Sophie's beautiful house. More like a mansion. It's huge and beautiful. We hit Versailles today and Knox and I took a ton of pictures out in the garden. He tried to convince me to... you know... in the garden, but it was too busy." I laugh. "I mean, I don't mind a little audience, but I didn't want to get kicked out. Anyway... we're going to dinner tonight at one of Sophie's and Emmett's friends at the Eiffel tower. Can you believe it? It's a very nice restaurant, so I'm very excited for that. We did a dinner tour last night on the Seine, which was beautiful." I hesitate. "I just want to talk to you... everything has been great here... but the guys... they seem off." Stepping towards the window, I take in the view of the gardens, where I notice the men at the bar in the kitchen talking animatedly with Jacques. "I'm sure it's nothing. But it's probably weird for them... right?" I let out a sigh. "I really wish you would pick up the damn-"

The automated voice on the other end of the line beeps and tells me I've been blabbing on for far too long. Not in so many words, but I press the button to send the message as is. I thought about re-recording it, but I don't want to. I have to finish getting my makeup done because we need to leave soon.

As soon as I set my phone down on the makeup table, a quiet knock interrupts the silence. I quickly glance out of the window and hear the laughter of the guys standing in the kitchen.

"Coming," I call out, as I flutter across the room in my robe.

Sophie.

She's standing there in a nice maroon colored satin gown that hangs off her shoulders with her hair twisted up in a stunning updo that looks like it took both hours and minutes to do. Effortless beauty.

"Oh deary. You're not ready." She walks into my room, bringing with her the scent of rose petals and vanilla.

"We still have another hour."

Her nose scrunches.

"We do. Don't we?"

"The restaurant just called, and it seems I may have given you all the wrong time."

"Sophie!" My heart pounds in my chest. "I'm nowhere close to being ready. I just finished drying my hair, but I need to curl it and put it up and I need to do my makeup. My dress will take just a second to put on."

"Yes. I'm sorry about this." She says something in French, but I don't understand her.

"How are you dressed?" I sigh, rushing back over to the makeup table to sit down. My brain is moving a million miles a minute, trying to figure out if I should do my makeup or my hair first. I had this really cute idea to curl my hair and put it up, but now it's going to take too much time.

She bats the air and puts her hands on my shoulders. "How can I help? Do you want me to do your hair?"

I look at her through the mirror, and she is calm, poised, and smiling.

"How about this? I will tell the boys to go on ahead while we finish getting you ready. Emmett is eager to see his friend, so they can get the table and all of that before we get there. That way, we can buy you some time."

"Do you think that will work?"

"Of course!"

I take a deep breath. "Ok."

She walks over to the window and waves her hand, like she's shooing a fly away.

"I'm terribly sorry for this."

"It's ok. It's been a while since I've gotten dressed up for the guys that wasn't in something..." I glance up at her and pause, wondering if it's awkward for her to hear about me with her exes.

"Meant to be taken off minutes after they saw you?" She smiles as she takes pieces of my hair and curls them.

"Yes. Sorry. I didn't know if it was weird for you... to talk about them."

"Not at all. Those men are my friends. My very best friends and so are you now. I'm truly so happy for you all to be together. They were an important piece of my life because they helped me to understand what is important to me. Jacques is everything I could ever want or need. Much like you are for these men. They are so happy. The happiest I have ever seen them. And they are at peace-peace within themselves. It's magical to witness."

She must see the tear that is sitting on the rim of my eyelid.

"None of this now. We are happy. Happy is us."

Forty minutes later, we're leaving the house and climbing into a black car with a driver. He isn't Brady and my thoughts wander, wondering what he's doing right now.

"Are you ready for tonight?" Sophie asks.

"Yes. I'm so excited to see the Eiffel tower. I've been wanting to see it for so long now and to think I'll be having dinner in it."

"You'll make lots of memories tonight. Unfortunately, we're getting there a little later in the evening so the sun will be going down. But that's ok. I think it's most beautiful at night anyway, with all the lights. It's truly gorgeous."

"Lizzy and I used to always talk about going to Paris together and riding up to the top of the Eiffel tower. She was a little jealous I was coming this week, and she's stuck visiting Tony's parents for the holidays, but I told her I wouldn't go to the top without her, so hopefully the guys understand."

"I'm sure they will. Plus, this will not be the only time you come out to visit, I hope. I would say you and Lizzy can do a girl's trip, but I don't know if those men can be without you for that long."

I laugh. "They could. Everyone thinks we spend every minute together."

She cuts her eyes at me, causing me to laugh.

"Ok. So I guess technically we do, but it's just by circumstance, not on purpose."

We pull up near the bottom of the Eiffel tower and when I step out of the car, my stomach drops. It's stunning and the pictures simply don't do it justice. People are bustling around, parents are pushing whining children in strollers and tour buses are honking their horns, but none of that bothers me. As if someone put a dome around me, the noises filter out and it's just me and the Eiffel Tower with its large legs anchored firmly to the ground.

"I'm just going to text the guys quickly to let them know we're here and see where the table is. I hate wandering around like a nomad looking for the seats."

I nod, barely listening to her, and just stare straight up. The lights, the lines, the curves. She is gorgeous.

A pang of guilt twists in my stomach when I realize how excited Lizzy would be if she was here with me. I already promised her I wouldn't go to the top, but my gosh. The sky is cloudless, with only a quarter of the moon shining, just bright enough to cast a beautiful glow on the sky.

"Are you ready?" Sophie asks, looping her arm in mine pulling me back to the present.

As we start to head up, a group of people walk off the elevator complaining.

"The first floor is closed for a private event," a woman wearing a cat shirt with binoculars grumbles.

"It's ok. We're going to the second."

The woman twists her face and throws her hand in the air like I just said her house smells like a barn.

"Come on," Sophie nearly pushes me onto the elevator, paying no attention to the woman.

As the doors close, I notice one is lit up, so I press two.

"What are you doing?" Sophie asks.

"She just said it's closed for a private event, plus we're going to dinner on the second floor."

"But don't you want to see what is on the first floor?" She taps the tips of her fingers together mischievously.

I chuckle. "I don't care. Do you?"

"Oui."

"Well, when the guys get mad that we're late, you'll have to take all the blame."

"Deal."

The doors open and there are flowers lining the walkway with an easel set up with a sign that says private event in beautiful golden foil.

"I think we should go," I say, trying to jump back on the elevator before the doors close. "Plus, I'm hungry."

"No, no, no. Let's see what's going on."

"We're going to get in trouble."

"No." She waves her hand in the air and her nonchalance coupled with her accent makes me believe her.

We turn the corner and see a vast group of people standing there, and I freeze.

Oh shit!

My heart drops to my stomach.

EVERLEE - SURPRISES

"Surprise!" they all shout in unison, staring at me.

"What?" I feel lightheaded and woozy and a second later, there is an arm wrapped around my waist. "What's going on?"

"Hooker, did you think I was going to let you come to Paris by yourself? Well, without me. That's what I really meant because you're never alone."

"Lizzy?"

Trying to process what's going on, I look around the floor and see my men, Lizzy, Tony, Beckett, Will, my parents, Betty, and Gerald standing there.

"What's going on? What?" I swear I haven't had any, well, much, alcohol. There was that one mimosa at lunch today.

"Men." Lizzy thumbs over her shoulder and then waves them over.

They all walk over wearing black pants, white button-down tops, with black vests and bowties, with sharp black jackets. If I wasn't having a heart attack, I think I could appreciate how delicious they're looking right now.

Callum drops to his knee in front of me and takes my hand.

"We know we haven't been engaged very long, but we don't care. We want to marry you here. Tonight. We brought your friends and family in and thought this would be the most romantic place to do it and if you want to do it somewhere else, we can, but we didn't want to wait another second."

"A surprise wedding? I don't have a dress. I don't have anything."

"We would marry you in a paper bag with nothing, but Lizzy has your dress."

"My dress?" Things slowly click into place. "Sunday. That's why you were so desperate to go to La Belle's and get me to try on wedding dresses. You knew?"

"Knew?" she laughs.

"Lizzy told us about how much you love the Eiffel Tower and that, coupled with the fact we weren't going to wait until after Lizzy and Beckett's weddings, this made sense," Callum chimes.

"So Lizzy?"

She holds up her hands. "Woah, woah, woah. It wasn't my idea before you even think or say that. The guys came up with it on their own. I just simply mentioned the tower."

"I don't know how Lizzy was able to pull it off with getting them to close it for our ceremony," Jax says.

She chuckles. "Well, I felt like I had your good fortune. I just asked, what would Ev's harem do?"

Jax and I both shake our head. "I don't have rings."

"Here!" my mother calls out, walking over with her hand deep in her pocket looking for something. "Here. We had these made for you." She hands me four black rings with a silver stripe running through the center. "We melted down your grandfather's ring and put a piece in each band." She points to the silver along the center.

"No. That was supposed to be Beckett's. I can't take the ring."

"Classic. Don't try to sound like the woah-is-me sister, now." His voice goes up an octave or two. "Oh, I can't take grandfather's ring, even though it's already been cut apart, melted and inset into four separate rings for my guys."

"Beckett!"

"Fine! Four *gorgeous* rings."

"Beckett!" She slaps his arm. "That's not what I'm talking about."

"What do you want from me, woman? You're going to leave me with a bruise there tomorrow!" He grabs our mother's hand and holds them and his tone softens, "All that to say that it was my idea."

Tears begin to well in my eyes.

"I thought it would be nice to have a piece of our family in the rings for your men," he leans in. "And our grandpappy had some of the fattest fingers known to man, so it only made sense we use his."

A mangled chuckle vibrates from my chest just as Beckett takes me into his arms.

"I'm not one for the mush, but you need to stop crying before your mascara runs. It's why I never wear it. I'm too emotional," Beckett teases.

I laugh again, feeling the weight of the moment easing.

He pushes away and his gaze immediately lands on me. "You're beautiful, Ev, and we're so glad we can be here to share this moment with you. Plus, when your guys mentioned a free trip to Paris, how could we say no?"

"How did you get off from work?"

"We talked to our housemates and told them what was going on and they were very excited for you, so they are working extra shifts for us."

"Wow. You've got a great team."

"Not too great. The fuckers are making bank on the deal. We have to work double the days for them that they're working for us through the next year and we have to do scut duty for the next month."

"Oh, damn."

"It's worth it, though." Will says walking over. "Is what he means to say, so that we can share this moment with you?"

I give him a hug then push him away, grabbing his shoulders, "Thank you so much for coming."

"I wouldn't miss it for the world."

"You're like the sweet, kind brother I never had."

"Your brother is standing right here," Beckett points to himself.

"I know. I said, sweet and kind. You aren't those things. I wouldn't be able to tell Will he is the pain in the ass brother I never had because I have you. See?"

"And to think I flew halfway around the world to surprise you!"

"For free," I remind.

"Still! That was a long flight and you know how sensitive my skin is," he says, patting his cheeks.

"Oh my God. I can't with you right now."

Dad walks over and grabs Beckett's shoulder, pulling him away, before he comes back over. "Hey sweetie," Dad says, pulling me in for a hug.

"Hey dad. I can't believe you and mom tricked me. I was so stumped on what contest you all entered for and who would make you travel at Christmas," I laugh. "I was really excited for you, but equally confused."

"That was my idea," Mom chimes, holding her hand up with a beaming smile. "I said to myself, self... what would Everlee believe? And wouldn't you sure know it? Boom! A cruise popped into my mind. Us ol' fogeys love going on cruises and then the plan was hatched."

I repeat, "And the plan was hatched." I look around at everyone, reality setting in more and more, even though it still doesn't feel real. "How long have you all been here?"

"Lizzy got in very early Monday to avoid crossing paths with you and we came in on Sunday," Mom says. "We did some sightseeing that day and some on Monday, and then have been working diligently the last two days for this. Lizzy is keeping us all on a very tight leash."

"It's really beautiful up here," I say, looking around at the lights in the distance. Just off to the right is a large picture on an easel of the five of us at the Christmas tree farm bundled up. Knox had made us get a picture with his fancy new camera and tripod.

"Are you ready? I know I am. Your mother has been a nervous Nelly since all these plans started a few weeks ago."

"Weeks ago?"

"Yes. Pretty much as soon as Sophie invited you over, plans were rapidly set into motion."

I look over at Sophie. "That's why you invited us?"

"No. I genuinely wanted to see you, but then your men called the next day and told me their hope and plan, so I said Oui! Let's make it happen."

"I didn't realize the Sophie we were talking with on group chat was *the* Sophie Lorenz. I swear to Pete for someone who doesn't enjoy cooking you know some pretty famous chefs," Mom says.

I flinch at her accusation of not liking to cook, glancing at Sophie, who laughs.

"It's ok. Not everyone has to enjoy cooking."

When I look around again, I see my guys huddled off to the side. Jax catches my attention and nods his head, calling me over with the wordless gesture.

"Excuse me."

"Sure, it's not like you're about to spend the rest of your life with him. We only get you for a little while longer," Beckett whines.

"Beckett. Will you just stop!" Mom slaps him on the arm again.

"Woman! I don't like being spanked, that's Ev's thing."

"Beckett!" I shout, looking over my shoulder at him.

"Kidding, of course." He winks at me.

I mouth at him, "You ass."

He throws his head back, laughing.

I look at my guys, who are all looking down at me with a steel brow. "What?"

"We just wanted to check in with you to make sure you're ok with this. We know we sprang it on you, but... we just love you and didn't want to wait and thought this..." Callum searches for the words.

"Would be magical," Knox finishes, tossing his hands in the air.

"Shut the fuck up," Jax says, hooking his arm around Knox's neck with a smile.

Knox's eyes grow large. "I'm counting this as a hug because there is definitely a warm embrace happening right now. Best. Day. Ever."

"See. You keep running your mouth and you ruin it every damn time." Jax pushes him away.

"I'm never washing my neck again."

My cheeks are hurting from smiling so much.

Once Knox quietens down and is standing still, all the guys look at me, waiting for an answer.

A heat races through my body to my cheeks, and I smile. "Yes. I would love to marry you all tonight."

"So you're ok that you didn't plan it."

"You're asking if it's ok that I didn't spend months and months planning every single detail? This..." I hold my arms out and spin around. "Here. On the Eiffel tower with everyone I'm closest to... this is *magical*." I wink at Knox.

"See." He sticks out his tongue and bumps Jax with his elbow and Jax just cuts his eyes down at him.

"I'm so ready to marry you. I've been ready for a long time."

"So we're doing this," Emmett says as more of a statement than a question.

"Well, I hope so. If not, this is going to be a really awkward dinner." I smile at him, grabbing his hands.

He pulls me into his arms and kisses the top of my forehead. "Let's do this."

A hand slips around my waist, and a cheek presses to mine. "Got room for a sixth?"

Lizzy.

"Just kidding, of course. I have my man." She waves at Tony, who is listening to Betty. I would say they were having a conversation, but the several times I have glanced over that way, she has been talking non-stop with her hands moving as fast as her lips. "But seriously, let's go. We need to get you ready." She grabs my arm and starts pulling me across the floor. "We'll be back!"

"Becks!" she snaps, raising her eyebrows and pointing her fingers all around.

Clearly he knows what she means, because he nods and mumbles something and starts walking somewhere. I don't see where because I'm being pulled into the elevator.

When the doors close, my eyes settle on Lizzy.

She's zoned out, staring at the buttons in the elevator, no doubt running through her list of things to get done.

"Thank you," I say so softly that it's barely audible.

She doesn't move and I don't think she heard me, but then she jumps and stares at me before pulling me into a hug. "I love you big. And you never have to thank me. You are my sister from another mister. My ride or die."

The doors open and we're at the restaurant on the second floor. "What are we doing here?"

"The guys rented it out for tonight. This is where dinner and the reception will be, but for now... this is where we are going to transform you."

Just inside the door is a vertical accordion blind–a makeshift changing room.

"Let's go, love. Chop chop."

Hanging there is my dress. The one I picked out before we left. I had no idea I'd be wearing it a few days later, but it's just as beautiful as it was then.

"Do you know how awkward it was traveling on the plane with that thing? Everyone was congratulating me on my wedding and I had to tell them it wasn't for me and I was surprising my best friend–which didn't clear it up because they thought I was leaving my fiancée for you. Which I totally would, but I can't wear enough strap-ons to take care of you. I mean... I looked, but they don't make a four in one yet... but if they did... those men would have to fight for your hand."

"I can't with you."

"You can." She grabs my hands and pulls me in for a hug. "I love you and I'm so happy for you... even though you're having your wedding before mine. But honestly, I couldn't say no to your men."

She unzips the back of my dress and it falls off me, puddling at my feet. I reach up for my wedding dress and start to slip it on. It feels different this time than it did at the store. Maybe this time it feels heavier because I'm putting it on with a purpose, not just to appease my wild best friend.

When I pull it up, it isn't even clasped, as I run my hands down it. Tears form in my eyes.

I'm getting married today.

CALLUM - SEVENTEEN MINUTES

EVERLEE JUST DISAPPEARED INTO the elevator with Lizzy. My heart is pounding a hole in my chest and I feel like I'm about to sweat through my suit, even though it is cold out tonight.

I look at the men trying to get a sense of their feelings and they seem just as nervous and excited as me. Knox is quiet, not even bothering Jax, which is a sign he's in his head and Jax and Emmett are helping Beckett with switching on the candles and making a path to our makeshift altar.

Lizzy was very clear with instructions. She has the whole thing planned down to the second. Everlee arrives. Everlee meets and greets. Everlee talks to us. Everlee gets whisked away into the elevator. We finish setting up in seventeen minutes.

Why seventeen minutes... I have no idea, but that's what she said, and she's been pretty intense with all the plans... so...

Seventeen minutes.

We grab the mini bouquets of flowers and position them around the candles and makeshift aisle. They are beautiful whites and lavenders–not purples as Lizzy made *very* clear, with sprigs of baby's breath and eucalyptus greenery. She did an amazing job.

Because of the short notice, she went to a florist and just asked for the flowers she wanted and she, Betty, Donna, Will, and Beckett worked on putting them together all day. They didn't have to do a lot, but apparently Ev's bouquet took some time, even though I haven't seen it. Lizzy was adamant about keeping some things hidden.

The dress and the bouquet.

Emmett gave her our credit card again, which I don't mind, but damn. We've had the credit card company call as three times thinking that it's been stolen. I wish I could say it was, but no… all the charges are legit. But at the end of the day, it doesn't matter. Lizzy knows what Everlee would want for her wedding better than anyone, so if Lizzy thinks Everlee wants it, then we want it.

Donna and Dave are finishing with the flowers when Donna shouts Beckett's name, swatting after him, saying something about a dick on the ground. Looking at the candles and the way they loop at the end where we'll stand makes it look like a cock and balls. I feel like Ev would have appreciated the humor, but Beckett fixes the other end.

A hand claps on my back and I glance over my shoulder. Jax.

"Hey brother," he says, coming to stand beside me and looks out at the lights of the buildings in the distance.

In the last thirty minutes, the sun has set and darkness now blankets the scenery in front of us with specks of lights popping up all around.

"Hey."

"Are you ready?"

I glance over at him. "I am. Are you?"

"More than ready. Cal… this is it. I feel complete with her. Like everything in my life has led up to this moment. I know that sounds silly, but..." he sighs, stuffing his hands in his pockets.

"Save it for the vows." I chuckle. "But yes... I feel the same."

"It's not weird?"

Another hand claps on my back. "Are you guys talking about the rash on my stomach? I think it's weird too, but I was hoping you hadn't noticed."

We both turn to look at Knox, whose brows are peaked on his face.

"Shut-"

Knox claps his hand over Jax's mouth. "Not today, brother. Well, at least not in the next... nineteen minutes. I don't know why Lizzy made us set timers. Anyway, I get a pass for any stupid shit I want to say. This is our wedding day." His eyes perk up again and he tilts his chin down like he's waiting for Jax to give his approval before he removes his hand.

"If you ever put your hand on my mouth again..."

"What? You'll lick it?"

Jax's eyes narrow to thin slits.

"That was a test. A perfectly teed up moment for you to say your four favorite words. You passed."

"Knox," Jax warns. "I will give you a twenty-minute pass, but I swear, don't make me regret it."

Knox beams. "An extra minute? You sly devil. It's times like these that bump you up to the spot reserved for my second most favoritist person in the whole wide world."

"Favoritist isn't a word."

"For the next twenty minutes, it is." He pumps his eyebrows up and down and Jax just lets out a low growl, glancing at his watch.

"Eighteen minutes."

"Eighteen minutes for what? I thought we only had seventeen from when Liz got into the elevator," Emmett asks, walking up.

"Eighteen," he glances at his watch, then corrects, "seventeen minutes for Knox to annoy the shit out of me, likely."

"I just simply requested a pass on his four favorite words."

"Ahh." Emmett nods in understanding. "So, are we ready? She should be down any minute. Lizzy did an amazing job with everything. Plus, I got a little taste of what she'll be like on her wedding day, since I know she's treating this like her own in terms of quality and perfection."

"Pardon me," Sophie interrupts.

We all turn to look at her, and she is all smiles. It's weird in some ways to be here with her at this moment. She sort of started all of this and we ended things because we couldn't give her a wedding or kids. Although I'd like to think if we stayed together long enough, something would have happened, but it wouldn't have been right. She wasn't meant to have all of us. It's funny to think how a drop in the ocean can cause a wave hundreds of miles away. She was the drop and Everlee is the wave that consumed us all.

She continues, "The violinists are here. Where would you like them?"

We all look at one another, terrified of telling her the wrong thing because Lizzy didn't mention a location, although I'm certain there is one.

Beckett runs over, "Hi. I will take you to your spot." He glances at his watch. "Three minutes."

Sophie laughs. "Lizzy is very funny and very scary. Very particular about times."

"She just wants this to be perfect for Ev."

"It looks beautiful. I'm so excited and happy for you all."

"Thank you."

Jacques walks up a moment later, slipping his hand on her lower back. "This looks amazing."

"It was all Sophie and Lizzy," I say.

"Lizzy," Sophie corrects. "She is a force to be reckoned with."

The elevator dings and we all look towards it.

Lizzy hops off and starts clapping her hands. "Places, everyone. Places." She points at Dave and sends him up the elevator.

My stomach clenches.

This is it.

Jax pats me on my back and smiles.

Betty walks over and takes her spot in the large circle we created with the candles. When she heard what we were doing, she came to us and asked if she could be the one to officiate the union. She even went online and got ordained, even though this is more of a civil union. She seemed really happy and excited, so we agreed. But I won't lie... I'm a little nervous about what she's going to say.

Lizzy and Sophie decided the best way for us to stand was facing the audience, so we didn't close everyone off since there are five of us. Jax and I are to the right, where the grooms typically stand, and Emmett and Knox to the left. Betty will stand at the center with Lizzy and Sophie standing in between us and her. Lizzy will stand just behind Emmett, slightly offset to the right and Sophie will stand behind me, slightly offset to the left.

My hands clench and unclench at my sides as I sway from side to side, finding the right spot to stand. I notice the others are doing it as well. Nerves seemed to have gripped us all.

A hush falls on the crowd as they take their spots, and the violins begin to play. Modern takes of pop songs filter through the air with a classical flare. It's nice and not the traditional wedding songs everyone hears. Although, I guess nothing about us is traditional.

The elevator number lights up and my lungs freeze and my heart stops beating. Everything over the last few months and days, all the planning, has led to this one moment. To our Everlee, here on the Eiffel tower in Paris.

"Ring check," Lizzy commands. It had to be for Sophie since Lizzy has our four rings.

Sophie presents Everlee's wedding ring, then tucks it back in her pocket. She had met with Laurent the day before we got here and picked it up. It was a custom piece he designed to perfectly match her engagement ring. We had chatted with him several times and had a video call to make sure we approved before Sophie picked it up.

The doors open and the only movement and sound comes from the photographer and videographer who are clicking pictures and moving around the floor. They must have come up with the violinist, because I hadn't seen them before.

Everlee walks into view with her father beside her and I'm stunned by her pure radiance. My body feels like it's being weighed down by lead bricks and my lungs forget how to breathe.

Her dress, her hair, her smile.

I hear the guys around me say what I'm feeling... thinking. One word.

"Wow."

She holds her oversized bouquet in front of her hips. It looks like a much larger version of the ones Lizzy created, but with lilies, orchids, and roses, in addition to all the other flowers in the mini bouquets. Tendrils of eucalyptus hang down, swinging softly, before coming to a stop.

Her eyes lock onto mine and she smiles, and that's all it takes to breathe life back into my chest. A flurry of snapshots filter through my mind- a montage of moments that led to today. The first night she walked into the club, her crumbled on the floor of my shower after she just got herself off with the intercom on, the appreciation and excitement she had when the guys watched me fuck her the first time, her in the gala's hallway. Egg tosses, and canoe rides, airplane fucks, ice skating, her face when she saw the dolphins strand feeding, her on the pool deck, her naked on the table at Thanksgiving and most recently, her bundled up at the chalet with snow all around us. Each one of these moments only further cementing my love for her.

She is ours for the rest of our lives.

EVERLEE - LOVE IS LOVE

My heart feels like it's in a vise in my chest and the air has been pressed out of my lungs. In just a matter of minutes, this place has transformed, yet again, to a beautiful weddingscape. The candles, the flowers, the violins.

And my men.

Damn, they are a wet dream.

They're standing at the end of the makeshift aisle, two on each side, with Sophie and Lizzy standing just behind them and... Betty? She looks at me and her eyes are already glistening as she fidgets from side to side on the platform. She looks more nervous than I feel, which is weird because there is no place I would rather be than right here with my men and my family.

Lizzy is at the front, subtly bobbing her head to an invisible beat and with the large drop of her head the violinists stop their current song and switch to another. I can't place it, but it sounds familiar. Her eyes lock on my dad and he clears his throat and starts walking us down the aisle.

For half a second, all I can think about is how Lizzy is orchestrating this entire thing with head nods and raised brows on her face. She is magical and truly the best friend that anyone could ever hope to have.

With each slow step I take, I lock eyes with each of my men. Knox is nearly glowing with the largest smile spread across his face, Emmett just looks sexy as fuck with this beard trimmed neat and his eyes twinkling, Jax's gaze sets my soul on fire, and Callum looks... like a dream. His eyes are glistening, like he's letting his walls down for once, allowing himself to be vulnerable. I don't imagine I will see this very long, but I will take what I can get now.

Sophie is smiling- pure radiance. And Lizzy... there are tears streaming down her face as she lightly bounces from foot to foot with a smile so big it lights up the entire room.

When I pass Beckett and Will, they grab each other's hand and smile at me, while Beckett tosses me a quick wink. Mom is in front of them with tissue balled up in her hand with red eyes from crying, while Gerald and Tony give me slight nods of approval.

My dad comes to a stop in front of my guys and we stand there for a moment until Lizzy gives a subtle nod and the violinist stops.

"Men. Her mother and I do not give Everlee to you, because she is not ours to give. She is her own woman, which she has made clear from the moment she came into this world. I've already told you once that she is not someone who needs a man, but a woman that you men need. I walked her down the aisle today, not because of antiquated traditions, but because I wanted to show you all that I will stand by my daughter, both metaphorically and physically, as she ventures into this new chapter of her life. She is a big spirit, with an even bigger heart, and we knew it would take someone, or in this case, somefour, special to sweep her off her feet and that is what you all have done. As you all build your family, her mother and I wish you nothing but happiness-"

"And lots of babies," Mom whisper shouts.

Dad nods. "And that, but I also want you to know there will be hard times. There will be times you can't stand each other and times you may want to just quit, but I'm here to tell you those are the moments you dig in a fight because what's on the other side is something so much greater than you could ever imagine. Now enough of all that. Her mom and I happily support you all in this union and wish you lifelong happiness and passion."

If I wasn't crying before, I'm definitely crying now. Lizzy is biting her lip, trying to hold back the tears, but failing. Her eyes catch mine and she smiles.

Dad releases my arm, grabs my hand and kisses it before he walks to stand by mom, who eagerly pats him on the shoulder and whispers something to him.

Lizzy reaches for my hand across the space between us, and points to my spot between the men and circles her finger in the air, so we stand at an angle facing the crowd.

"Whew. My turn," Betty starts. "I's tell you Mr. Dave... that was some speech. You got me all up in my feels up here."

The crowd laughs.

"Well now, where to begin?" She takes a deep breath. "When Lizzy came to me and told me about this wedding on the Eiffel Tower, well my first thought was Vegas and how were they going to get everyone up there, but then she told me the one in Paris and then I thought to myself again. Wow! How are they going to get everyone up there, with no one else there?"

The crowd chuckles and I feel my pulse slow down. I don't know if I would have ever picked Betty to be the one to lead this union, but I'm so grateful she is. She has that effortless charm and way with crowds that brings a laughter and love and general calmness to the situation.

"Then, I thought, well, I'll be. I want to do something special for Everlee and her men." She pauses for a moment to collect her thoughts. "A little bit about me. Growing up... I was the daughter of the town's preacher, so as you can imagine, I spent a lot of time in the church and was told what to believe and what not to believe. I was told what God would like and what he wouldn't like and well... as I got older, I didn't believe all of that malarky because see... I believe God would love anyone. Love is love, right?"

The crowd claps and my eyes pulse with a new sting of tears as a knot lodges itself in my throat.

"I had me a wild streak and did some things I wasn't too proud of..." she nods her head, giving me that knowing glance and I know she's talking about snorting coke off her best friend's boyfriend's cock. "But I changed my ways. I found a man," she waves at Gerald, "Who showed me the true meaning of love and acceptance. He loved me with all my faults and all my quirks. And there are just a few."

The crowd laughs again and I take in a deep, calming breath.

"And that's the reason I'm standing before you today. I met this little firecracker at the beginning of this year, and do you ever get that feeling when you meet someone that they're just going to change your life? Like an instant connection and you may not know how or why, but you just know that person is going to have a profound effect on your future? Well, that's Everlee. She crawled into my car wearing her costume for that party at Vixen and something just reached down from the heavens, into my car and into my soul and said she's a special one Betty, and darn tootin' if she wasn't." She wipes her hands nervously on her dress. "Sorry. I just... when I get nervous or excited, those funny words come out."

"It's ok Betty. You're doing great," I offer, smiling at her.

She nods, tears filling her eyes, then continues.

"Anyway... where was I? Yes, Everlee. She climbed into my car and she looked... well, miserable."

The crowd laughs.

"Not in a bad way... she just had sad eyes. It was Valentine's Day and here she was going to this club. I'm digressing." She lets out a hefty sigh, and Lizzy reaches back and grabs her hand.

"When I saw Everlee beating her own drum without fear, it gave me the courage to do the same. Not four men, of course." Gerald laughs. "But to start my own business. I'd been letting fear of the unknown hold me back for so long and when I saw Everlee pushing forward without fear, I knew I could do it too. The only time you fail are the times you don't even try. Right?" She pauses for another moment. "I know that was a very long-winded way of saying that I am just so grateful to be here with you all, and I felt it in my soul that I needed to be the one to officiate this union. So thank you Callum, Jax, Emmett, and Knox for giving me this opportunity."

They nod.

"Now. Where were we? Yes. We are here today to celebrate these beautiful people. This union is about true love and acceptance, about showing the commitment these individuals have towards one another and their intention to be together for the rest of their life. Today, we will all witness the handfasting of these five as a symbol of their commitment to one another. I know this was sort of sprung on you Everlee, but the men have prepared some words they would like to share with you and, at the end, you may also say something."

"No pressure." I laugh.

Knox steps forward first and grabs my hands, staring in my eyes for a moment as he noticeably swallows down the ball that's in his throat. "Everlee." He blows out a long, steady breath. "You... you are amazing. I've spent the last two weeks trying to come up with something, some words to quantify how much I love you, how much you mean to me and I have struggled. There are no words in the English language that can quantify the depths of my love for you. Growing up, I... had a hard life, and it got even harder when my father went away, but in some ways I'm thankful for that. That heartache led me to these men, led me here to you, and to this moment. I would do it all over again a thousand times. I learned that family isn't just about the people who you are born to, or even blood. True family transcends all of that. Sure, it can be blood, but it can also be those who you would give your blood for. Who you would go to the ends of the earth for. And I would do that for each and every one of you." He turns to the men. "We are here today because of Everlee, but not just Everlee. I love you all just as much. You gave me a home, protection, love, and support when my entire world had been ripped away from me. Jax, you are my brother, not by blood, but in something much deeper forged in a bond that was made on the battlefield."

The tears are steadily streaming down his face, but he doesn't touch them.

"Callum, Emmett. You are my rocks, my guardrails. I measure myself against the men you are to help me become the man I want to be."

Well, damn. I'm crying like a freaking baby now.

"You are ours and we are us. I love you all so deeply that I feel like each of you is engrained into the very fibers of my existence and I would never be anywhere else than right here." He looks at Jax, an evil twinkle in his eye. "So sorry, brother. I will officially be a thorn in your side for the rest of your life." He winks, then leans in and kisses me.

Betty starts to interject, "I, uh. Well, I guess that's ok. I didn't really think about the whole you may now kiss one another part of the union since there are five of you."

I smile through our kiss before he pulls away, then leans in and whispers, "That was a PG kiss for your parents, because I plan on so much more tonight."

A heat flushes my cheeks as I watch him walk back to his spot.

Emmett steps forward, grabbing my hands. "Well then. I was planning on going after Knox and thought I would have it easy. He's never been the one for profound, deep, or meaningful words but that…" he looks over his shoulder, "Well done, brother."

Knox nods and smiles.

"Everlee. Everlee, Everlee, Everlee. My love. When I first saw you at Vixen, I knew you were going to be trouble, and then when you told me I was going to hell after just meeting me, all but solidified the fact I was going to fall for you."

A flashback to that first moment at the bar replays in my mind.

"I watched you that night and ever since, haven't been able to take my eyes off of you when you're in the room. You consume my thoughts when I don't see you and consume my heart all the time. You love fiercely and without question. You are headstrong and loving, nurturing and fearless. I can't see a life for me where you aren't in it. Like these men, my childhood was rough and for a long time I was scared of what kind of man, what kind of father, that would make me. I was scared that I wouldn't be good enough, so I avoided it, pushing those feelings away. But you... you make me believe it isn't solely our past that dictates our future, but the desire to be better than our circumstances that makes us do better. Be better. I've never allowed myself to want kids before you because I let the fear that I wouldn't be good for them dictate my life, but with you, I know I will be great–we will be great. I want to do life with you and that means every part. I love you, Everlee. Men, I wasn't prepared to speak to you, so thanks Knox for that." He laughs.

Knox leans forward and pats him on the shoulder.

"You've always held a special place in my heart. You took me under your wing when my world was shaken and you gave me love and stability. You've helped me grow my dreams into reality and have never once talked me out of an idea, but supported me and helped to see it through. I love you all so much." He leans in and presses his lips to mine in a slow, all-consuming passionate kiss, dipping me backward with his hand splayed across my back. Before he stands me up, he pulls back from the kiss and whispers, "I love you, Trouble. Now and always." Then presses his cheek beside mine, letting his lips brush my ear. "And from this day forward, I'm going to look forward to putting a baby in you."

When he walks away, my head is a little woozy and my skin flushes.

These men and their words.

Emmett walks back to his spot and Jax walks over, so I turn to look at him. His chin tilts down like he's studying me. "Love," he tosses me a wink and all I can think of is that he wanted to call me Squirt, but refrained since that would be hard to explain. Well, not hard, just awkward as fuck. "I'm not one for words, but you… edged your way in when I tried to block you out. I didn't want you to love me and God knows I didn't want to love you, but then I did and I didn't know how to tell you. How to express myself and you were so patient, never asking more than I could give."

Memories of him saying he loved me through songs, replays in my mind and makes my stomach tighten.

"Growing up, much like the others, we didn't get to experience love like most do and Mrs. Mary tried to offer that to us, but it wasn't the same. I was scared to let her in, let anyone in. We shut ourselves off and built a wall around our heart and you came in like a wrecking ball and shattered the wall. You showed us, me, that it's ok to love and be loved." He glances at Emmett. "You've accepted all I have and all I am with love and understanding, and for that, I couldn't be more grateful. We were all broken, and sure we had mended ourselves, putting all the pieces back together, but there were fine lines and cracks and you came in and you were the glue that spread across the cracks and seeped into each one binding us together, making us stronger than before. I can't wait to see how our life continues to unfold and see the adventures we're going to go on. I love you now and always. You are mine." He leans in and whispers, "Squirt."

A chuckle escapes through soft tears. He cups my cheeks in his hands and gently brushes the tears away from my cheeks and plants a soft kiss on my lips, then pulls away to look at me. His eyes are dark and promising. Something about the kiss was unexpected, reserved. Almost like he was holding back. The only thing I can think of is that if he allowed himself any amount of rope to give me the kiss he wanted, it would turn into a deep passionate kiss that wouldn't be parents approved.

He walks back to his spot and crosses his arms in front of his body, then clasps his hands.

Callum steps in front of me and grabs my hands. His piercing blue eyes move slowly across my face, like he's trying to memorize every detail. "Everlee. I don't know what else to say that hasn't already been said. We probably should have all talked about what we were going to say…" he laughs and everyone joins in. "I had rules. They were simple. Don't fall in love. Don't get attached. But you… you captured my attention before you even knew I existed. I watched you the night of the Valentine's party." He looks at the crowd. "Not in a weird, stalker kind of way. But you had this energy that drew me in like the cliché moth to a flame. You've told me from day one that you don't follow the rules and I should have listened. At least I would have been better prepared." He squeezes my hands. "I love you Everlee McKinley with all I am and all that I have. I vow to be by your side through all the good times and the bad. I know Lizzy is your ride or die, but you are mine- ours. I can't wait to do life with you."

His hand grabs my neck as his thumbs brush along the lower part of my jaw.

"I love you." He presses his lips to mine and his tongue pulses in my mouth, claiming me, making me hungry for more as my body reaches out to him, needing to feel him. His kiss lights my body on fire, like a thousand unlit candles waiting for their flame.

A throat clears from the crowd- likely Beckett, bringing me back to the present.

He releases me and stands back in line and I glance across the crowd and see my mother fanning herself before she pumps her eyebrows at me. God help me.

"Everlee, do you have anything you would like to say?" Betty asks.

I swipe my thumb along my lower lip and look around at my guys. "Well. I'm not one for speeches and especially ones that were just sprung on me, so thanks a lot for that. At least I had seventeen minutes." I look at Lizzy and smile. "To think of something while I was getting my dress on." I chuckle and try to swallow the lump in my throat that has been threatening to choke me since this all started. I let out a deep sigh, then look at each of my men for a few seconds as I speak. "I had grown skeptical of the notion that a love as intense and consuming as the ones depicted in movies and books could actually exist. How could it? The love that consumes you is so profound that it resonates within your bones, causing an ache when you're apart, and a tightening sensation in your stomach triggered by the mere thought or recollection of them. It's the kind of love that transcends the physical and makes you eager to share every detail of your day with someone who understands and reciprocates your enthusiasm." I pause, looking at each of them. "But then I met y'all and... that's what I got. It was a little bumpy at first..."

The crowd laughs.

"But you all practically walked in to my family's backyard and I knew then I was never letting you go again. Rules be damned. I was going to make it work. When we first met, you were all about the rules and I wasn't. What I've learned growing up is that rules... rules are habits people put in place, guardrails set to protect you from pain. Sometimes rules need to be broken so that you can grow and find something better, especially if breaking the rules is worth the reason you're breaking them for. And you guys. You are so worth it and more. You have showed me a love that I literally didn't know existed. I know that sounds cliché, but it's true. I didn't know this kind of love existed. With you four men, you have unlocked doors I didn't even know existed because they were so far buried inside of me. You've given me confidence and support and..." a tear trickles from my eye. I shake my head to clear it and take a few deep breaths. "Look... you men are my forever. You say I molded into the family you created, but you molded into mine. The fact Beckett was talking to you about his likely proposal before me is equal parts bullshit, but also amazing."

"I told you first. That should be all that matters," he mumbles.

"My point is, that is amazing you all have that kind of connection. It is one I always wished and dreamed for, but never thought would happen. But you guys... you make the impossible possible. I mean, just look at where we are right now. I love you all with all of my heart and I can't wait to do life with you forever."

I step forward, then back up, then step forward again. "Ok, this is awkward." I just blow them all kisses with my hands and everyone laughs. Knox, of course, catches the kiss and puts it in his pocket.

"Those were beautiful words, thank you all." Betty glances at Lizzy, who must have done something with her eyes because Betty nods. "Right. Times a tickin'. I believe there are rings that need to be passed out."

Sophie hands a ring to Callum. He reaches for my hand and all four men grab pieces of the ring and slip it onto my finger. Lizzy had made me take my engagement ring off and slip it onto the other hand when we were upstairs. "You are ours and we are us."

Lizzy walks around to stand beside me and hands me a ring at a time. I slip them onto each man's finger and look at them. "You are mine and we are us."

I glanced down at the ring and it's simple, but elegant, matching my engagement ring perfectly. It's only been a couple of weeks, but I miss seeing it on my finger. Once we are done here, I will move it back over.

Betty continues, "Beautiful, beautiful. Now for the handfasting."

My parents walk up and hand me a green and red ribbon.

"These ribbons may seem like simple Christmas colors, but they are not. I mean, they are, but that's not the point I'm trying to make. Red symbolizes love, action, adventure, strength, passion, and excitement, while green represents health, loyalty, harmony, prosperity, and safety. These are the colors the men picked out to bind your union. If you will all take one another's hand."

Beckett walks up to stand beside my parents.

"Your parents and brother have asked to bind your hands as a symbol of the interconnectedness and acceptance of you all into their family. Oftentimes, a union is not between two people, in this case five, but their families as well. With your approval, they will start binding your hands."

Tears are streaming down my face at the meaning of this and how involved my parents have been. There is so much love in my body I feel like it is literally going to explode out of my chest.

They each take turns wrapping the ribbon around our hands until we're firmly bound in place.

"While holding hands may seem simple, it symbolizes that you are not alone. You don't have to face battles or endure sadness in solitude. You have a partner by your side, providing a sense of comfort and support. Walking with you, fighting with you. These hands bound by this union are a symbol of your partnership from this day forth, not only with each other, but with Everlee's family. Please join me in celebrating the union of these five."

The guys close in around me and give me a hug while everyone around us claps and cheers.

"We're keeping it PG for your parents, but make no mistake," Callum starts.

"When we get you home, we plan to fuck you hard," Jax continues.

"Until you're dripping with our come," Emmett says.

"And... well, shit... I have nothing else to add. Ta-da?" Knox finishes.

"Idiot." Jax is the first to break from the hug, as we're all laughing.

Lizzy's watch dings, like an alarm has been set. She looks at all of us, eyes wide. "This has been beautiful, but we need to wrap it up. McKinley's, grab the candles and the bouquets. Gerald, the picture. Betty the easel. Jacque the sign." She points to the one that says private event. Then moves back to gently, but quickly, unwrap the ribbon around our hands. "They say to slip it off with the knot intact, but that wasn't with five hands." She chuckles, looking around, making sure that everyone is doing their job.

The violinists and photographer and videographer are already on the elevator going up. She must have talked to them when the guys were talking to me.

"Lizzy?" I ask, concern creeping up my spine.

"Don't worry about it." Her brows furrow.

"Lizzy?" Jax asks.

"Second floor. Let's go!"

Everyone else but us five and Lizzy have gone up to the second floor. We're waiting in front of the elevator when it opens and two guards are standing there with furrowed brows. "What are you all doing?"

Lizzy starts talking quickly like she does when she's trying not to get busted in a lie. "We were looking for the second floor. Silly me pressed the wrong button. Even though this is the second floor, you all call it the first floor. I'm just a dumb American. But we're going to the second floor now... well, technically the third. We're going to the restaurant. We have it rented out for the night." She fans her arms towards me, "Wedding and all."

They push past us and look around and Lizzy pushes us in.

"Lizzy, what's going on?"

She looks up at me with that look that tells me she is very close to getting in some serious trouble.

The doors to the elevator close.

"Well, I knew how magical it would be for you to have a wedding at the Eiffel tower."

"Lizzy..."

"So, I reached out to them and..."

"You got their permission, right?"

"Well, in not so many words."

"Lizzy." The breath leaves my chest.

"Lizzy," Jax says, looking down at her.

"What? I knew we had about a thirty to thirty-five minute window, so I took advantage of it."

"You hijacked the first floor of the Eiffel tower for our wedding?" Knox asks. "Fucking brilliant."

"Lizzy!" I shout.

"What boo?"

"That's why you were so strict on time?" Callum asks.

Well, at least they didn't know.

"Who knew?" I ask.

"Everyone but you five."

My eyes feel like they grow to the size of my head. "Lizzy."

"I didn't want your men to tell me no, and I didn't want you to be worried the entire time. I wanted you to enjoy your wedding."

Emmett wraps his arm around her neck. "I think I love you."

"Well, you're already taken and so am I, but who knows? Maybe you'll want to add a sixth and a seventh."

We all laugh as we tumble out of the elevator. Our picture has been set up on the easel again with candles and flowers tucked around the base. The efficiency of these people in my life is outstanding.

"Welcome," the chef says, with open arms.

KNOX - CALL ME BLITZEN

Tonight has been absolutely amazing. More than my wildest dreams. We had a truly fantastic dinner and Emmett, of course, was in cloud nineteen. He was already on cloud nine from our union, but then with the food. I swear he was dissecting every bite, rolling it over in his mouth, savoring each piece while trying to name all the flavors. At one point, it became this thing between him and Sophie to see who could name the most ingredients. We all tried at first, but realized we were quickly outmatched. Donna, however, held her own for quite a while, even finding some flavors that Sophie and Emmett hadn't even tasted at first.

After dinner, the violinist played for a couple of hours while we all danced. It wasn't the traditional raver that most weddings are, but they played a delightful mixture of pop songs and slow songs. It was nice and beautifully done. Lizzy really went above and beyond tonight.

Sophie walks over to us. "I have a gift for you all."

"You didn't need to do that," Ev says, smiling.

"No, no, no. We have rented you a house for tonight. Close by. The roof has an amazing view of the Eiffel tower. Jacques and I stocked the kitchen and bar with all of your favorite yummy treats and have packed duffels for each of you. We didn't want to go through your things, so Jacques went and picked you up some clothes for tomorrow. If you hate them, you only need to wear them back to our house in the morning."

"Sophie." Everlee wraps her arms around Sophie's neck. "Thank you for everything."

"I've done very little, but I wanted to do this for you all tonight. So, with that said, you need to say your goodbyes, because the restaurant is closing soon and your limo is downstairs waiting for you."

"Shall we?" I ask, holding my arm out.

She grabs my hand and we walk from person to person, thanking them for coming to our wedding and reception. Jax takes this moment to still razz Lizzy for the first-floor debacle. I mean, somehow it all magically worked out, and we didn't get kicked out or have the French police called on us, but my gosh. Note to self, whenever Lizzy is super serious about timing, ask her if what we're doing is sanctioned.

Thirty minutes later, we're all downstairs and climbing into the limo.

Silence fills the air as I'm sure everyone is replaying the events of the night, but also eager to get Everlee out of her dress and consummate the fuck out of our union. Over and over and over again.

She's sitting on a seat by herself across from Jax and Emmett and even from here I can see the vein in her neck pumping quickly and notice her skin has a slight pinkish color to it.

The limo pulls to a stop and everyone looks out of the window to see where we're staying. Callum is closest to the door, and starts to open it, but before he can, the driver walks around. Callum climbs out, followed by me and then Ev while Emmett feeds her dress out of the door. It isn't like those oversized puffy Cinderella dresses, but there's still a lot of fabric and it's really gorgeous.

Callum has the front door of the rental open by the time Jax climbs out of the car. We walk into a large foyer with black and white tiled floors and a marble staircase that curves along the wall to the right. To the left is an office and down the short hall towards the back looks to be the kitchen, dining room, and sitting room.

The door clicks locked and we all stand in the foyer looking at one another, everyone eager to move, but excitement holding us in place.

"Yea, fuck this," I say, stepping towards Everlee. "I'm getting you out of this dress and I'm probably the one with the most patience."

Everyone, including Everlee, laughs.

"What's that supposed to mean?" I retort.

"Only that you have no patience at all. You're the equivalent of a golden retriever puppy, hopping up and down, bouncing from one thing to the next."

"I can be patient." I place a kiss on Ev's neck as my fingers work the buttons on the back of her dress.

Her head falls to the side and when I glance up, all three men have taken a step forward but stop.

"Who's not patient now?"

"Knox," Jax warns.

"I was just asking." I place another kiss on her neck, sliding my tongue down to her collarbone, nibbling on her skin as I go.

She moans again and my fucking cock is going to die of strangulation in my pants if she doesn't stop.

As I unfasten the last button, I let my fingers glide down her neck, over her shoulders, and down her arms, relishing the heat of her skin, and admiring how her dress slides down her body, puddling on the floor. She's standing in front of us in only a black lace thong and high heels, and I can't help but press my lips against her fevered skin.

"You're a dream," Emmett says.

"And ours," Jax adds.

"Forever," Callum finishes.

"Damn it... I'm not going last anymore. I want to be part of your cool little sentence moments."

Everlee laughs and turns to look at me, holding her hand to my cheek. "I love you so much."

"I love you." With a playful flick of my eyebrows, I hoist her over her dress, causing her to squeal out in surprise. "Calling me Blitzen, because I'm making like a reindeer and flying out of here!" With her still in my arms, I race upstairs and hear the men groaning and grumbling with what sounds like buckles and clothes hitting the floor.

Fuck. I don't know where to go. It suddenly dawns on me I should have given more thought to the repercussions before snatching our queen. I'm about to get checkmated.

I shake my head. Why in the hell am I thinking about chess right now?

It's that damn floor. It looks like a big ass chess board.

I test the first door and find a bathroom. For a moment, I thought about taking her in there and locking the door, but I'm pretty sure the guys would knock the door down and Sophie got us this place for the night, so I don't want to do that to her.

The second door opens to a small bedroom with two twin size beds.

"Damn it."

Everlee is still squealing and laughing over my shoulder, smacking at my back. "Put me down."

"As soon as I set you down, I'm sinking my cock in you."

She shifts on my back at the same time I hear noises behind me.

"Knox," Jax warns.

"Oh stop, daddy. Did you want to fuck her in a bathroom or on a twin bed?"

"I'd fuck her standing right here in the hall," he fires back.

"She doesn't like to stand when she orgasms," I remind. "Seriously. Think much." I'm laughing as I open the door at the end of the hall, having passed several others in between hoping this is the main bedroom.

Money!

Without hesitation, I move across the room and swiftly toss her onto the bed. I rip my shirt off as buttons fly across the room, ticking on the floor as they bounce and hit. I'm out of my pants and over her a moment later with the guys behind me.

"Are you going to fuck her through her underwear?" Jax asks.

"Maybe." I look at Everlee and toss her a quick wink before I kiss her. I need my mouth on her before I lose control.

My cock lays across her stomach as her body arches to rub against mine. My hands slide smoothly under her back, sending a shiver down her spine as I unhook her bra. Wasting no time, I toss it aside, and indulge in the feel of her breasts in my mouth.

"Do we have lube?" Emmett asks.

"Oh," Jax says.

The guys disappear into the bathroom. "Not here," Callum shouts.

I hear them walking down the stairs, but don't care. I'm with Ev and that's all that matters to me right now.

Wrapping my fingers around the top of her panties, I take my time sliding them down her legs, planting kisses along the way. By the time I get to her feet, the guys still aren't back in the room, which I don't mind. That's more time with my girl.

Her eyes follow me as I slowly slide up her body, a mixture of curiosity and desire in her gaze. When I get to her breasts, I stop and run my tongue in a circle around her nipple.

"It's a good thing those are attached to me or I would get jealous with how much attention you give them."

My teeth gently clamp down around her nipple until she's blowing out a breath between her teeth, trying not to moan or cry out in pain. It's a fine line between the two.

"No need to be jealous, love." I continue moving up her body until my lips are kissing on her neck right under her jaw and my cock is dancing dangerously close to her hot, wet center.

"I think you like it," I say, running my hand down her stomach and over her clit. She's so wet my finger slides right in.

"I didn't say I didn't like it. I was just stating a fact. You give them a lot of attention."

"It's my favorite thing about you. Well, second to your smile."

"Trying to butter me up?"

"I don't need to. You're already slick enough," I say, pressing two fingers into her.

Her back arches off the bed and her hands clamp around me. "Don't tease me. I want to feel you inside of me. I want your come leaking out of me before the others fuck me."

God damn. I just about came. "Not cool, Everlee," I growl out.

"What? I can't play the game too? You don't want me to tell you how badly," she nearly growls out the word, "I need your big, thick cock in me. Stretching me. How badly I want it to fuck me until I'm coming around it? How I want your come shooting so far and so hard into me I can taste it."

"That's not possible."

"I don't care. I want you to make me drip with your come." She moans and grabs her breasts. "I want to fucking taste it. You make me so hot. I want you to put a baby in me."

I whimper. Fucking whimper.

Before I know what's happening, my body is over hers, cock lined up with my hands pressed to the bed at her head. "I can't wait to put a baby in you."

"Let's practice then. A lot."

My lips crash to hers in an unforgivingly hard kiss. Need consuming me. I can't fucking wait until she gets her IUD removed. It's something we need to talk about because I'm going crazy with the thought. I don't know how much longer I can wait.

"We will." I punch my cock inside of her until she is screaming out my name and digging her nails in my back. That first thrust... tingles shoot up my spine. "When we're trying to put a baby in you, you're going to be on your back for a week as we just fuck you repeatedly, loading you with so much come you can swim in it."

Her bent legs shoot up to my hips so I can inch in a little further. I grab her legs and wrap them in front of me and lift her ass off the bed, notching in even further.

"Oh God. You're so deep," she cries out.

I unleash on her, watching her beautiful breasts bounce up and down.

"Guess what we found?" Emmett asks, walking into the room.

"What?" I ask, not turning around. My focus is only on our girl.

"Sophie hooked us up. Champagne, chocolate-covered strawberries and three containers of lube."

Emmett walks across the room and tosses the lube on the bed and feeds us each a chocolate-covered strawberry. The chocolate chips off of mine and rolls down Ev's pussy and stops under her breasts. "Let me," he offers, climbing onto the bed. He presses his tongue flat and licks up the chocolate and then sucks her nipple into his mouth. "I can't wait to sink my cock into you."

"I want to take you all tonight at the same time."

"You are going to have us all and then some."

"She said she wants us to put a baby in her. So we're practicing." I can't help but smile when I see Emmett's feral reaction. His eyes turn dark as his pupils dilate and his teeth scrape over his bottom lip.

"He may want to put a baby in you more than me, Ev."

She cries out again, as her orgasm inches ever closer. Her pussy is beginning to quiver around my cock. Just one touch... I press my finger to her clit and rub three times like a genie in a lamp and she's crying out as she comes undone. A low guttural groan filters across the room as her hands try to find anything to grab onto, settling on her breasts. Emmett is over her mouth a moment later, and she latches on to him like a newborn baby, looking for its mom's teat.

"Should we start a tally board now?" Jax asks, walking in.

Her pussy clamping around my cock sends me over the edge and my orgasm crashes into me as my balls tighten and I unload inside of her. Fuck me, the thought is making my orgasm even more intense.

"My turn," Emmett says, climbing in between her legs when I pull out.

I give her a kiss and whisper that I'll be back.

"You're going to get more strawberries, aren't you?" she laughs.

"No."

"You lie."

"I was going to bring you some."

Her laughs are quickly replaced by a moan as Emmett presses inside of her. "What was that you were saying?"

"Emmett." She smiles.

EMMETT - I BURN FOR HER...

She feels so good.

"Emmett," she sighs, reaching for my arms, still coming off the orgasm from Knox.

I lean over and slide my hands under her back and scoop her up, so we're sitting chest to chest. She cries out as my cock hits deep inside of her. I've only been able to give her a cervical orgasm once, but I plan to do it again... soon. I don't know if it will be tonight or not, but getting that far inside of her...

My cock twitches at the thought.

"You're so fucking deep."

"I know." My hand slides around her neck and I take her lips, pressing my tongue in while she grinds her hips on me. I rock my hips back and forth and see tears form at the corner of her eyes. "Are you ok?"

She nods, biting on her bottom lip.

Jax climbs on the bed behind her and sits on his knees, pressing his chest behind her. He wraps his hands around to grab her breasts while he bites and sucks on her neck so hard her skin is blanching and tenting.

"You want me hard or easy?" he whispers as his lips brush along her ear.

She cuts her eyes at him. "I want you hard... and rough." Her eyes twinkle.

"I thought he was talking about scrambled eggs and I was so confused," Knox says, walking back in with the entire tray of strawberries.

Jax just cuts his eyes but doesn't say anything, maybe because Everlee catches his attention when she rocks on my cock and lays her hands over his and squeezes them on her breasts.

Callum walks in a second later with two bottles of very expensive champagne.

"Remind me to thank Sophie tomorrow."

"If you can talk tomorrow, then we haven't done our jobs," Callum says, tilting up the bottle just above her mouth.

Some runs down her chest causing her to squeal out, but I hurriedly lick it up, pausing at Jax's fingers.

She presses her head back on Jax's shoulder and begins rolling her hips over and over again driving me crazy. "Your piercings... feel... so good."

"Are you trying to come again so soon?"

"You aren't going to edge me again like you did on Halloween, are you?"

"Not tonight," Jax says, biting her neck with his eyes on me.

They're dark and wanting and I nearly come from his look alone. I want to feel him inside of me so badly, but tonight is all about our queen, so that will have to wait. Unless she asks for it.

I'd do anything she asks.

Anything.

"I want you both inside of me."

Her statement catches me off guard and for a moment, I wonder if I was talking out loud instead of thinking to myself.

"Right now?" Jax asks, his eyes flickering up to mine again.

"Yes." She's still chasing her orgasm and I know she's close.

Do I make her come before we're both inside of her or after?

As if hearing my thoughts, Jax attacks her throat, sucking and biting, while his fingers clamp down on her nipples.

She cries out as her hips rock faster.

"Safe action?" he asks, and I know what he's about to do.

"Four taps on the leg."

"Make her come, E," he commands.

My left hand locks onto her hip as my right circles on her clit at the same time his hand slides up her neck and his fingers tighten around her throat.

"Take his cock like the good girl you are and come all around it."

Her mouth opens and her eyes glaze over as her orgasm is nearing. My finger swirls faster and then I press all the way into her, holding nothing back. Goosebumps erupt across her entire body and tears trickle down her reddening face.

"Now Jax! Oh God damn!" I cry out as her pussy nearly strangles my cock.

His grip falls from her throat and she sucks in a breath and screams out and shakes on my cock. "Holy... fuck... balls! Oh my God."

Tears are streaming down her face.

"So fucking intense. I thought my body was literally going to split in half. Oh my God. Oh my God."

"I'm not jealous," Knox says, laying on his side with his knee up, biting on a strawberry.

"I never realized you loved chocolate covered strawberries so much."

"Me either, but damn, they're good."

We all laugh, even Jax.

Flipping my legs under Everlee, I lean back so she's sitting on me. "Ride me baby." I wink.

"I don't think I can move right now."

Jax presses his hand between her shoulder blades and pushes her over so her nipples brush along my chest. "Good, because you don't need to move for this next part." He grabs my ankles and pulls me to the edge of the bed.

"Damn, show off," Knox says, looking through the tray to pick out his next strawberry.

"Don't eat all of those."

"There's another tray downstairs. On the note, it said this one was mine. So weird."

"Can I have another?" Ev asks popping her head up.

"You can have whatever you want, love."

He feeds her a strawberry and a chocolate chunk falls off and lands on my chest, near my nipple ring. She smiles then bends down and licks my chest, then eats the chocolate before she swirls her tongue around my piercing. Tingles shoot across my body.

"If you want us both inside of you, then you need to stop, baby girl, because I'm about to explode inside of you."

She pops her head off my ring and looks at me with the most adorable, how-dare-you-threaten me look on her face and I melt. I melt for her. I burn for her. I... everything for her.

Jax takes his place between my legs and runs his fingers up from my base and slowly slides one inside of her and rubs around my length. He drags his finger out then adds another splitting my cock inside of her with his index and middle finger, rubbing up and down my shaft.

"Jax," I warn, causing him to laugh.

"She's so wet, plus I'm just trying to prep her," he responds with a smirk.

"I know exactly what you're doing."

He slides his fingers out and presses them into my mouth. "Suck," he commands.

I grab his fingers and suck them like I'm sucking his cock until he has to pry them out of my grip. "Was that good enough for you?"

"Ass," he grumbles.

"Maybe later."

He presses his lips to Ev's shoulder before asking, "Are you ready?"

"More than ready."

He squeezes some lube on his cock then tosses it at Knox, hitting him square in the forehead, causing him to scream out overdramatically, causing us all to jump.

"That was a bit much," Callum sighs.

"You try watching your girl get fucked while dining on some delicious strawberries when out of nowhere..."

"What to my wondering eyes should appear, but..." Jax chimes, then pauses.

"A lube tube... on my forehead."

"I say better on your forehead than in your mouth." Everlee laughs and we all chuckle.

"Gimme." Knox reaches his hand out towards the champagne. "I'm celebrating tonight." He tips the bottle up and wipes the back of his hand across his mouth. "Carry on." He waves his hand at us.

Jax slowly glides his cock in and neither Ev nor I move.

Fuck me, he feels so good.

JAX - JIGGLER THE ASS TICKLER

THE FIRST PUSH IN is always the best, but it's even better when it's on Emmett's cock inside of Ev's pussy. The feel of his rings coupled with the slick tightness that comes with Ev is enough to almost make me be a one pump chump.

Almost.

Everlee's shoulder is there, asking- begging- to be kissed as the muscles flex in her back as she shifts to take Emmett and me. Fuck, I love when we do this. His Jacob's ladder feels amazing as my cock slides over it. I pause for a second, savoring the feel but also allowing Ev to stretch a little more to take us.

Dragging my cock out to the head, I hold it there before slowly pushing back in. I go in easier this time and Ev starts to move a little more.

"Do you like that?"

"Yes, daddy..." Knox answers in a high-pitched voice.

I cut my eyes at him. "If I wasn't buried in her pussy right now..."

"I know... that's why I said it. You love her pussy with Emmett's cock, more than you love punching me."

"It's close. Very close."

"Don't let them hear you say that." He pulls his face.

"Nothing to do with them and everything to do with how much I love punching you."

"Oooh." He waves a strawberry in the air, then bites it aggressively, sending chunks of chocolate pieces all over the bed.

"Try not to get chocolate all in this bed. We have to sleep in here tonight." I must have not been paying enough attention to Ev and Emmett, because Ev pushes back on my cock. "Sorry," I mumble, then place both hands on her hips, giving me better control.

"No need..."

Her last words fall off in a moan as I move inside of her faster and faster. Emmett's cock against mine and the tightness of Ev's pussy is... heaven.

"Harder," she moans out, dropping her head like she's preparing to take over.

"Damn, Squirt. Good news is, we have the rest of our lives together."

She looks over her shoulder and smiles, then pushes back on me in a challenge.

"Fine. I hear you."

Emmett reaches up and wraps his fingers around Ev's neck, pulling her down for a kiss. The one movement shifts his cock inside of her causing my stomach to clench.

He pulls off the kiss for a second and his eyes lock on mine, with his hand still wrapped around her neck. "Fuck us, Jax. Make us come inside of our girl." He gently bites at Ev's ear, with his eyes still locked on mine.

My hips move and thrust as memories of the day replay in my mind- Ev walking down the aisle, Ev's words, then the realization that this is it. We are bonded for the rest of our lives. She is our home, and we are hers.

"Don't forget. She wants to take us all at the same time," Knox says, putting the nearly empty tray of strawberries on the bedside table.

"Well, you've already come inside her."

"There's still more." Knox laughs.

"Cal," I call over my shoulder.

He stands up from the seat he was sitting in and walks over stroking his hard cock.

"You want us all, baby girl?" He asks, letting his hand rub up her leg.

She moans and shifts her back as goosebumps spread across her skin. "I swear each time you all do that, it's only making the hairs on my leg longer and longer. Fucking miracle grow."

I laugh and she yelps.

"You can't laugh with your cock inside of me. It jiggles."

"My cock jiggles?" I ask, smiling.

"Better than jingles." Knox barks out a laugh as a sudden thought hits him. "That's Emmett. Emmett's cock jingles with his piercings. Oh my God. I'm dying. If you were Santa's little helpers, your names would be Jingles and Jiggles."

"Yours would be... Chatty."

"Chatty? That's lame."

"Fine. Chatty McTwinkletoes."

The room erupts in laughter, and even I can't help but chuckle.

"Callum is Daddy Glitterballs."

I shift over so he can start prepping Ev's ass to take his cock.

"I'm not jealous we don't have last names," Emmett says from under Ev.

"At least you have names," Ev pouts.

"Oh, we will come up for a name with you," Knox says, standing in front of her with his cock in his hand. "I even got you a little something from downstairs." He pulls out a small container of chocolate sauce from behind his back.

"Did you just pull that out of your ass?" Emmett asks, tilting his head back into the bed.

"Eww, no. I was just hiding it behind my back." He pops it open and drizzles some on his cock.

Ev lets out an appreciative hum, and she tries to lean forward to taste him, but because of the way we're positioned, she can't.

"Come-"

"We plan on it," we all say in near unison, causing her to laugh.

"Here," she finishes.

Knox steps forward and Ev swirls her tongue around the head of his cock, letting out a low hum as she does, swallowing the chocolate. "Very yummy."

"Ev?" Callum asks.

She looks over her shoulder, eyes twinkling with excitement. "Ready."

He adds some more lube on his cock, then slowly slides it in.

"Got it!" Knox says, feeding his cock to Ev. "Jax is Jiggler the AssTickler." He lets out a raucous laugh, which causes Ev to laugh, choking on his cock. When she tries to back off of him, she sits further on ours, then lets out a yelp as she takes Cal's a little too fast.

"Was that the best time?" I scold Knox.

"Well, hindsight is twenty twenty. It would appear after the fact that was not the best timing, but you have to admit. That's a fantastic name."

"No. No, I don't have to admit that because I'm not in her ass."

Everlee leans forward, the small bit she can move, and grips Knox's ass, pulling him back in. "Give me more McTwinkletoes."

"I can't wait to come down your chimney," Knox says.

"Really?" I sigh.

"Fine. It's not just the stockings that are hung."

"Please stop. We have four cocks in our girl on our wedding night and you are coming up with stupid ass elf names and Christmas sayings."

"When I think about you, I touch my elf."

"Fucking hell, make it stop."

Ev sucks him in deep because his next words are cut off and his hands fly to her head. "Goddamn."

Moans, grunts, and sighs fill the room. Knox grabs some more chocolate syrup and squirts some on his cock. "Some chocolate and cream."

I'm going to murder him. Fucking idiot.

He looks up at me and smiles, then tosses me a wink, like he knows exactly what he's doing.

"That was almost in my eye," Emmett groans.

When I look around Ev, I find a large splat of chocolate sauce on Emmett's forehead and can't help but chuckle.

"I'm glad you find this so funny," E says, looking at me.

He wipes it away, smearing a good portion of it, but no one tells him. Ev presses back on us, taking our cocks at the same time as her hand grabs Knox's balls. She's getting close. When she takes over control and gets more aggressive is usually when she's at the edge. Which means we will be there soon too.

Her moans are coming from deep in her chest and her pussy is quivering.

"Let's go guys. She's close."

"So am I," Emmett says, eyes cutting to me.

Knox pumps harder, sending his cock into Ev's mouth. "Let it Snow, Let it Snow, 'cause here I blow," he sings, saying the last words as his body stiffens and his cock presses into her mouth. "Oh, damn." He raises up on his toes as his eyes roll into the back of his head before he pulls out a moment later. "All I want for Christmas is you," he says, leaning in to plant a soft kiss on her lips.

"All I want for Christmas is for you-"

"I know," he waves his hand in the air, walking out of the room. "To shut the fuck up. Blah blah blah. Your heart could stand to grow three times larger." He disappears around the corner.

"I was going to say for him not to leave because I find his happiness infectious."

Callum chuckles beside me. "Careful, or you will end up on Santa's naughty list."

"It's ok. He can join me," Ev says, tossing a wink over her shoulder.

My hand reaches around and finds her clit. She arches his back and reminds me of a cat sticking their ass up in the air when you rub your hand down their back.

"I'm... com...ing... hard... fuck..." she cries out. Her pussy clamps around our cocks and I assume her ass too, because Cal lets out a grumble before he stills inside of her. When he pulls out, she bursts into a string of words "I... ho... ho... hoooo..." she collapses on Emmett's chest.

"Did you just ho ho ho your orgasm?" I ask, chuckling.

Callum pats her ass. "I'm going to find Knox and wash up."

"I imagine that's what he's doing, too."

"We'll all have to do," Emmett says, pointing to the dry chocolate streaked across his forehead.

"Looks like a reindeer..." she starts, then stops. "Nope. Can't do it." Her head falls back onto his chest.

Two more thrusts, and Emmett and I are coming inside of her. She doesn't move because her muscles are like mush. That last orgasm she had was big.

"How do you feel, love?" I ask, slowly pulling out before helping her off Emmett's cock.

She rolls off him and flops onto the bed.

"Tired... and happy. Just give me a second and I'll get up."

"We'll get the bath ready for you."

CALLUM - LOVE THE UNEXPECTED

Close to an hour later, Everlee, Emmett, and Jax are walking back down. Knox and I were going to help with her aftercare, but the room was a little too small for all of us.

While they were upstairs, Knox and I slipped into a pair of joggers. The other option was a pair of twill pants and a sweater, which I guess we'll wear tomorrow.

Knox grabbed another bottle of champagne, some glasses, and turned the fire place on in the living room. The house combines the warmth of rustic elements with the convenience of modern amenities. The living room has two oversized brown leather couches with a cream-colored shag carpet. Knox grabbed several of the furry plush blankets off the back of the couches and spread them in front of the stone hearth, then grabbed some pillows and propped them up against the couch.

While he was setting that up, I looked in the fridge to see what our options were and found two large bottles of water, a charcuterie board and another tray of strawberries, so I brought those over and set them out.

"This looks nice," Ev says, walking across the room in a silk nighty.

"I get the feeling Sophie didn't think we needed many clothes for tonight," I laugh.

After I had gotten washed up, I dropped the men's joggers upstairs for them.

"I mean..." Emmett says, tossing his hands in the air.

"I think you're fine in your joggers," she pants, staring at all of us, nibbling on her bottom lip.

"Keep doing that, baby girl, and we won't be wearing them much longer."

She laughs. "Give me an hour at least. I'd hate for you all to have to carry me around because I can't walk tomorrow."

"We'd happily do it," Jax says, then stiff arms Knox as he works his way closer to him.

We all find a place on the blankets Knox set out.

"Wow. These blankets are like clouds." Ev runs her hands back and forth along them.

"They are really soft," Emmett says, stretching out his legs and laying on his side next to her.

Knox takes the other side, so I sit beside him, letting Jax sit on the other side of Emmett.

"This is nice," she says. "I..." she looks at her hand. "I can't believe we're married. You..." a tear starts to trickle down her cheek, but she wipes it away. "You all make me so unbelievably happy. Tonight was great and completely unexpected. But great," she repeats. "I don't think I could have planned a wedding more perfect...everything was just... amazing. Thank you so much. Thank you for including my family and for making all of my dreams come true."

"Ev," Knox says, brushing away the single tear that's rolling down her cheek. "You make us happy. You complete us. I know you all laugh at the stupid shit I say sometimes, and that's fine. It's on purpose because I love to see you laugh and smile, because seeing that brings so much joy to my heart and to my life. If having Jax beat the mess out of me makes you laugh, I would walk around every day black and blue. I love you. I've loved you for so long. I meant what I said... you are ours and we are us." He throws his finger up in the air. "And don't think I didn't notice all you fuckers using the very saying you made fun of me for, tonight."

Ev laughs. "Knox. You really do bring so much light and happiness to my life. You all do, but you, Chatty McTwinkletoes... you hold a special place in my heart that no one can touch." She leans over and gives him a soft kiss on his lips.

"Do you want some champagne, love?" I ask, reaching for a glass.

"Yes. Should we all toast?"

I pour everyone a glass and pass them out. "Everlee. Love."

She looks at me, tilting her head to the side.

"I think I speak for everyone when I say the day you walked your red winged little ass into Vixen was the best day in our lives. We love you big, and we will love you always. We can't wait to start a family with you and see where all our adventures take us."

"I'll cheers to that," Jax says, raising his glass, as does everyone else.

We spend the rest of the evening sharing funny stories from our childhood, talking about the funniest gifts we got for Christmas growing up, munching on the charcuterie platter with some of the best cheese and meats I've ever tasted, and sipping on champagne. Well, not sipping. We've casually drank three bottles.

It's three in the morning when I finally take the mostly empty platter into the kitchen, put the empty glasses in the sink, and set the coffee to brew in the morning. Ev passed out an hour ago, with Knox curled into her side. Emmett and Jax are on the other side asleep, tangled in one another, and me... I just spent the last thirty minutes watching them all.

This is it.

Our family.

I never thought I would get to experience this feeling of... completeness. Everyone is so happy and for once in my life... I don't know what's going to happen next. I've always been so careful planning out every detail and putting guardrails in place so things don't change. So unexpected things don't happen. In the past, when those things happened, it was always bad. And who knows... we may have some moments like that in the years to come, but it doesn't matter. I know we will get through them, because the not knowing... the unexpected... for once, makes me excited.

Everything is so perfect.

Small tick sounds tap in between the crackling fire. When I look out of the window, little white flakes are falling against the window. I didn't think it was supposed to snow tonight, but it seems to be a light mixture of ice too.

If it was coming down harder, I would be concerned it was going to stick... but this will probably be gone by the morning.

I hesitate for a moment, wanting to wake up Knox because he loves the snow, but I let him sleep.

"Goodnight, my love." I rub my hand on Ev's head, brushing the hair out of her face.

"Night, daddy," Knox mumbles, curling into Ev.

I'm smiling when I slide down and prop my head on my elbow. With all the nice beds and sheets in this house, we fall asleep on the floor in the living room.

EVERLEE - EIFFEL TOWER IN FRONT OF THE EIFFEL TOWER

THE NEXT MORNING, I wake up to the crackling sound of the still-burning fire and the sight of the men peacefully sleeping. I didn't mean to fall asleep on the floor, but I was so comfortable and sexhausted. When I look outside, there is a thin layer of frost and snow on the bottom of each windowpane and I feel like I'm in one of those smutty romcom snowed in stories. Excitement bubbling through me, I slide out from under the tangle of arms and legs and walk over to the window, to find only a small dusting on the deck. I hadn't noticed last night, but just off in the distance is the Eiffel Tower.

Wanting to go outside and get a better look, but not wanting to freeze, I pour myself a mug of hot coffee and grab a pair of the men's dress shoes. They are three sizes too big for me, but I don't know if walking outside in heels would be the best thing. There's a large comfy looking blanket over the back of one of the office chairs so I wrap it around my shoulders, hold the ends together in front of me like a cape, grab my mug and tiptoe across the floor to open the doors to the deck.

A gust of icy wind smacks me right in the face, causing me to regret this for a second, but the moment passes when I see the white frosted rooftops around me. With the world still asleep, the peacefulness of the hour surrounds everything. I was so hot inside that this feels almost... refreshing. At least for a few minutes it will.

I walk to the far end of the deck, only slipping on ice once. Surrounding the top is a black iron fencing, featuring small decorative spires on every post. Very classical and old looking, but modern at the same time.

The Eiffel Tower.

My mind replays snippets of last night. And to think I was so excited to be eating dinner there and then less than an hour later, I'm getting married there with my family. My cheeks are hurting from smiling so much and a chill nips at my bones, so I take another warming sip of my coffee.

A moment later, arms tighten around me and judging by the tattoos and the way my body hums, I know it's Callum.

"Aren't you cold?" he asks.

When I turn around, he's standing there in nothing but his joggers. "Me? You!"

I take my blanket off and throw it around his shoulders, then step into him. He wraps his blanketed arms around me and we just stand there looking at the surrounding beauty.

I try to ignore his hard cock pressed at my back, knowing it's just his morning greeting, but damn. It won't go down.

"It's beautiful out here," I say, bringing the coffee up to my lips.

"It is."

Something about the tone of his words causes me to look at him. He's staring at me and my heart jumps in my chest.

"Callum."

"Everlee," he growls.

Fuck. When he says my name like that, it makes me moist, and with it being so cold out here, it would likely freeze against my leg.

I swallow the ball in my throat as his right hand travels across my stomach and pulls me towards his chest. "What are you doing?"

"I'm enjoying the scenery. The Eiffel Tower."

His hand continues to rub, inching further down to the edge of my nighty, which does little to cover my ass.

"You are?" I pant out as my body fires up. Any chill that I was getting is quickly disappearing.

"Very much. I'm just trying to figure out a way to work off this small chill I have." His fingers lift the edge of my nighty and a cool wind blows between my legs and I gasp.

"Everything ok?" His finger glides softly over my clit and then presses in between my legs.

"Mmhmm."

"Hold this," he says, handing me the blanket corners and I do as he says.

He slides around and falls to his knees in front of me and licks his tongue over my pussy. The cold air mixed with his hot, wet tongue causes my body to clench. When he presses a cool finger in, I lurch forward, eyes still on the Eiffel tower in the distance.

"You're such a good girl. Do you want to come on my face or around my cock?"

"Do I have to choose?"

He chuckles. "Never."

His tongue expertly slides inside of me. He's working quickly, not teasing, which I can appreciate. The blanket doesn't cover him, so I imagine he's probably freezing. He sucks on my clit while he slides a finger and then two inside of me, searching for that one spot that lights my world up.

"Callum," I pant, moving my hips, urging my orgasm along. He lifts my leg and throws it over his shoulder. Fuck. I want to wrap my hands around his head, but I can't with the blanket.

He starts to hum while he sucks on my clit, at the same time he curls his fingers in that come-hither motion and my orgasm slaps into me. It's the trifecta that nearly brings me to my knees.

As he stands up, the force of his movement causes the blanket to slip from my grasp. He swiftly moves behind me, consumed by an overpowering need.

"We're going to watch the Eiffel tower while I fuck you and then come inside of you. I know your IUD isn't in and the thought of our come inside of you these last few days has been driving me wild."

"Cal-" My words are cut off by the sharp thrust of his cock inside me. I am a little tender from last night, but not so tender that I can't, or won't, enjoy this.

He's rough, but it's not too bad, as his shaft punches inside of me.

"Your pussy is so hot and wet around my cock."

His hands slide up my body, over my breasts and around my neck, but he doesn't squeeze, he just holds it there.

"You're so fucking beautiful."

My legs feel a little weak, so I lean forward, grabbing onto the railing.

"Bend over and take my cock like a good girl." He moves one hand to my hips and the other to my left breast. A moment later, his right foot lifts to the small brick wall the black fencing is standing in and unleashes his thrusts, pounding into me. "God, you feel so good."

"Callum." It's the only word I can get out as he fucks me faster and faster. My breasts are flopping up back and forth in my nighty with the slight jerk that tells me they're bouncing around as far as they can before snapping in the other direction.

"Where's Kn-"

A click of the door tells me we aren't alone and when I turn around, Knox is squatting on the porch with his phone in hand, taking a picture.

"This probably won't make it on the Christmas card. Shit. We probably should have sent those out. Ok New Year's card, but it was worth taking our girl being fucked with the Eiffel Tower in the background. Oh, shit!"

"What?" Callum asks.

"Ev you want to suck my cock, while Callum fucks you?"

Callum unexpectedly laughs. "You want to Eiffel Tower her in front of the Eiffel tower?"

"Am I so easy to read?" he asks, propping up his phone.

"I'd love to, Knoxxy baby."

"That's one of the many reasons I put a ring on it." He finishes setting up his phone, presses a button, then runs over. "Goddamn it's cold out here."

He grabs me by the shoulders and pushes us back a little, no doubt framing us for the picture.

"I'm taking a video, so I can pick out the best picture later."

"Of course you are," Callum smiles, then pushes me over. "Now let me watch you suck his cock, love."

Knox's arms reach out to hold me up while I take his hard length in my mouth.

"It's so warm... like a warm apple pie." He lets out a yelp.

I must have been smiling and not paying attention to what I was doing, and scraped my teeth across him.

"Don't crack jokes with your cock in her mouth."

"Noted."

I suck Knox in until he hits the back of my throat and wrap my hands around his balls, while Callum's hands grip on my hips and he unleashes, claiming me, pressing in deep.

"I'm not going to be able to hold on much longer. Waking up from a sex dream, I could still hear the echoes of moans and whispers, leaving me already primed. I think I heard you all out here and it just set me off. My hand. Fuck." He pants out and takes a deep breath. "Was already around my cock."

"She's already had one orgasm and I'm about to make it two," Callum says, dropping a hand to my clit.

The cock and clit combo is a surefire way to make me come quickly. The pressure with the stimulation. Heaven.

I grab Knox's balls and massage them in my hands, knowing he's close and a moment later, he's crying out my name as he fucks my face, hands clamped into my hair at the root.

His warm saltiness shoots down the back of my throat and I swallow him down, just as the dam unleashes on my own orgasm. My legs buckle under me, overwhelmed by the tingles that travel up and down my body, reaching my arms.

"Knox!" Callum shouts.

"Got her," he says, wrapping his arms around me. "Let it out, baby. Ride the waves because I won't let you fall."

He looks down at me and smiles while I crumble into pieces at his feet.

"Such a good girl."

My pussy is pulsing around his cock and then I feel his release in me at the same time he growls out and his fingers dig into me.

When he comes to a stop, he keeps it inside of me for another second and I feel it pulsing. I stand up and press my back against his chest and let him wrap his arms around me and we just look at the Eiffel tower.

"Hopefully no one saw," I whisper.

"Is that what you really wish?" he whispers back, pressing his lips to my forehead.

"No."

He tosses back his head with a throaty laugh.

CALLUM - GLITZED UP WALK OF SHAME

IT'S JUST AFTER LUNCH when we get to Sophie and Jacques' house. After our morning... festivities... we decided to walk home, while stopping at several shops and stores along the way. The first place we stopped was at a little boutique shop to see if they had any sort of shoes for us to wear. We were all doing a glitzed-up version of the walk of shame because we all had casual clothes on, but really fancy shoes that didn't match the look. Most people didn't pay attention, but a few gave us weird looks.

Sophie had done an amazing job with the details of the clothes and bites and other things for the house, but she forgot the shoes.

The first store didn't have any, but the third one did, even though they were a little on the pricier side. They were some French brand I'd never heard of, but they were very comfortable.

After shopping, we found a cute bistro to have brunch. It was a little cool outside and most all the snow, rather, ice mixture, had melted, and as long as the wind didn't blow, we were fine.

After a few more stores, we were still about a forty-five-minute walk to Sophie's, so we decided to call an Uber. It looked close enough, but it was a long night.

Before we could ring the doorbell, Sophie was throwing it open. "You were supposed to call me!" She waves us in. "Come in, come in. It's freezing outside."

We set our bags down in the foyer and she looks at them, then to our feet.

"Merde," she mumbles to herself. "I forgot your shoes."

"It was great. You didn't have to do all of that last night," Everlee jumps in before Sophie can beat herself up.

"It was really amazing, Sophie." I lean in and give her a hug. "It was perfect."

"Perfect, except you have no shoes."

"It's ok. Ev wanted to do some shopping, so it all worked out."

"Ouf." She bats her hand in the air and walks down the hall. "Your family is here. I tell them I cook them a pleasant lunch today. Did you eat? I see your bag from the café."

"We had a little bite to eat a couple of hours ago, but I can always eat again. It smells delicious in here," Everlee says, following her.

"I'm going to put these bags up in the room," I call after them, but neither of them turns around.

The guys follow me up, and we make quick work of packing our bags. Our car service will be here in a few hours to take us to the little vineyard chateau we booked for the rest of our stay. It's a little place just outside of Bonnieux. Knox found it because of the festival of lights they have every year, but Emmett realized it's the location of one of the wines he's been wanting to try. It's tucked away and quiet, which will be perfect for us because I imagine once Ev gives the guys her Christmas gift, we'll need all the privacy we can get.

We're back downstairs thirty minutes later with all our bags, including Ev's, packed up and ready to go. As we're walking down the hall, echoes of laughter ring through the hallway as they recount their favorite moments from last night. Someone must have brought up Lizzy's hijacking of the Eiffel tower for the wedding, because she's defending herself while laughing. When we get to the edge of the hallway and the living room, I can't help but stare at Everlee. She is glowing, hair twisted in a high bun, no doubt to cool her neck down from laughing so much. I've noticed when she laughs for long periods of time, she gets hot and has to put her hair up. It's cute.

"There they are. Mr. America's," Beckett calls, hopping to stand. Before he's halfway across the room, Knox is running towards him with his arms wide open. Beckett obviously picks up on this energy and mirrors him until they both try to jump in each other's arms at the very end and awkwardly crash into one another with a chest bump.

"I thought you were going to catch me. I caught you last time," Beckett says.

"No. You always catch me. I've never caught you."

"To be fair, the first several times, you just koalaed me because I wasn't prepared. Now I know."

Knox gives him a big hug. "Thank you so much for coming, man. This means so much to Ev."

"Thank you for making an honest woman out of her."

"Beckett!" Donna shouts, stomping over. He flinches as she draws nearer. "I'm not going to hit you. I just came to give these boys a hug."

"You always hit me. That's why I always have bruises on my arm. Cap was concerned about me."

"You're being overdramatic. They are little love pats."

"You call them what you want."

"I will." She hmphs, putting her hands on her hips before walking straight to me. "I trust you all had a good night?"

"Mom!" Beckett and Everlee yell at the same time.

"What? I was simply asking about your evening. What are you two talking about? Y'all are the pervs." She leans in and whispers, "So?"

I laugh, giving her a hug, then lightly push her away. "It was a great night." I smile.

She pumps her fist, then gives the rest of the men a hug.

Everlee scoots over on the couch, patting it invitingly, so I walk over and slide in next to her, feeling the soft cushions beneath me. She brings her feet up and scoots under my arm and lays her head on my collarbone while everyone continues to talk and tell stories. Knox and Emmett are in the kitchen helping Sophie. Well, Emmett is helping Sophie, while Knox is trying and Sophie is being super patient with him. Jax is talking to Will and Beckett about something to do with their firehouses while Betty and Lizzy are in their own little world, with their men watching, while they sing and dance to the Christmas carols that are playing to the radio. The only time they are quiet is when the ones in French play, but they still dance and try to hum along.

Everlee turns her head and looks up at me, "This is great."

"It is." I kiss her forehead.

Never in a million years would I have ever pictured such a full and happy holiday season. From the large Thanksgiving to this Christmas. Friends and family and Everlee. The center of it all. She gave us this, the thing we've all wished for since we were at Mrs. Mary's.

A family.

EVERLEE - MISTLETOE

We've been in the car for almost an hour after taking a quick plane ride. It's getting darker outside and the guys still haven't told me exactly where we're going. I've asked three times and the last time, no one said anything at all.

My face is plastered to the window like a kid at Christmas looking in the sky for Santa's sleigh. Knox is beside me, riding in the middle. It was my spot at first because I like to see where we're going, but as we started driving on two-lane dirt roads and passing by vineyards, we switched so I could try to figure out any clue as to where we're going.

Growing more and more impatient, I peek around to the front and see the GPS says five minutes left. Knox laughs at me and wraps his arms around my stomach, placing his cheek next to mine, looking out of the window.

"Are you ready for Christmas?" he asks.

"I am." I can't wait until I give them the little gift that is packed in my bag in the trunk. We left all our gifts at home except this one, because this couldn't wait a day longer than Christmas. I'm fighting the urge to give it to them early, but I really want to wait. My plan is to keep it hidden until Christmas day and then give it to them at breakfast.

A few minutes later, we're pulling to a stop in front of a large two-story house with a flat front painted in a sort of yellow-gray with chipping paint or stucco. More rustic than run down. The door is an olive green and just above it is a small wrought-iron balcony large enough to maybe hold three people, though I don't know if I would trust it to hold the weight. There are four large windows, two on either side of the door on the main floor, and then one above each of those. The symmetrical house stands tall, with its aged facade suggesting it's been around for centuries.

"It's so cute," I say, pushing the door open.

"It's a private vineyard. The family stays on property and will occasionally rent out their house."

"By occasionally, you mean just for us?" I laugh.

"No," Callum laughs, walking to the trunk of the car and handing off the bags to the men. When I reach to grab mine, he cuts his eyes at me.

"You know... I'm more than capable of carrying my bag."

"I know you are. That doesn't mean that I don't want to do it for you, though."

There's no way I'm winning this battle, so I sigh, throw my hands down by my side and stomp towards the door just as it's being opened. An older man is standing there, just in front of the door with his arm extended, welcoming us inside.

"Good evening. I'm glad you could find it. It can be a little tricky if it's your first time here in the dark. Lots of long roads."

Callum walks in first and sets our bags on the floor. "Your house is lovely. Thank you for opening it up to us."

Will we be sharing this house with him? For some reason, I thought it was just going to be the five of us. This is really going to change the plans I had in mind, if that's the case. It was big, but not big enough. To the left is a large living room with worn, brown leather furniture and several sitting chairs scattered throughout. To our left is a narrow staircase leading to the second floor. They painted the walls a soft yellow color and lined them with hand-carved wooden picture frames. Down the hall looks to be the kitchen, which leads to an outdoor sitting area.

"Of course. My daughter will meet with us tomorrow as well, while we discuss our partnership."

Partnership? Are we here on business?

As if sensing the questions running through my mind, Emmett leans over and whispers, "Just tomorrow. A two-hour meeting to discuss getting their wine for Bo La Vie. After that, no more business, just pleasure." His hand runs down my back and rests just at the top of my ass, where he gives a light pat.

"I look forward to the conversation," Callum says.

"Very well." He hands Callum a set of keys. "Bedrooms are upstairs with towels in the bathroom. There is one up there, and a half bath down here. Leave the lavender on the windowsills. What else? Ah yes. Our house is down the hill about a seven-minute walk from here. We would love to host you all for dinner tomorrow. My daughter is making her mother's, my late wife's, special spaghetti sauce. Once you have tasted this sauce, you will never want another."

"That sounds lovely. Let us know what time and we'll be there."

"We usually try to eat around twenty-hundred hours, maybe twenty-thirty."

Callum nods. "Please let us know what we can bring."

Not me over here still doing math to figure out what time we'll be eating.

"You are our guest." The man bats his hand in the air, laughing at us. He says something in French and Emmett responds in perfect French. The man looks impressed as Emmett walks him to the door, continuing to talk to him, saying who knows what. The man finds it entertaining, whatever it is.

As soon as the door closes, Knox lifts me in his arms by my legs, so my chest and head are above his. "Welcome to our home for the next few days."

"Sorry for the bit of work we have to do while we're here," Callum offers.

"It's fine. I will be surprised if it's only a few hours." I wink.

"What's that supposed to mean?"

"That you have a hard time taking off and relaxing. I'm surprised you've gone this long."

"I-"

I hold my hand up, stopping him. "I'm just giving you a hard time. I know all the work you have to do. It's a lot to run all the businesses you do."

"We do," Knox corrects.

"We do."

He loosens his grip on my legs, letting me slide down his body.

"I know you may think that what we did wasn't official because there were no documents signed. But we have them drawn up when we get home. We are redoing all the contracts and making you equal partner for everything, not just Allure. We are committed to you, even if where we live doesn't see us as a family. The idea of marriage and unions goes back way further than the laws around marriage. Everlee, you are ours and we are yours in every sense of the word. I hope you know that. So from now on, you will be part of every business decision and will have ownership in everything. You are our partner."

That damn knot has reappeared in my throat again. It's like a magic ball, not there one minute, there the next. I swallow hard and try not to let my emotions betray my heart strings being pulled. "I love you all."

"We love you."

Knox darts off down the hall, looking through all the rooms, with his hands behind his back. "Look what I found!" He holds up a mistletoe over his head.

"Yay," Jax deadpans.

I lean in and give him a kiss.

"Your turn, big daddy," he says, moving over to Jax.

"Nope. Nope. Stay away."

"Jaxxy baby."

"Fuck off with that." He grabs the mistletoe and shoves it in his back pocket.

"What was that for?" Knox whines.

"It's so that whenever you're close to me, you'll have to kiss my ass since that's where the mistletoe is."

Knox looks flabbergasted, flitting his gaze between me and the others. "Well, I never!"

I can't help but laugh, and even Jax has a smirk curling on his lips.

Knox yawns. "Well, as much fun as this wasn't," he sticks his tongue out at Jax, "I know this is going to seem really shitty, but I'm tired. We were up so late last night, and it's late now... and..." Jax looks at him and Knox just holds his hand up. "Save it. Add whatever smartass thing you're going to say to tomorrow's list."

Jax laughs. "I was just going to agree with you."

"Oh, thank God. I was going to have sex if you wanted, but I'm so tired. I almost fell asleep in the car three times," I add.

"Is that why your head was pressed against the window?" Knox asks.

"Yes. Well, I was curious to see where we were going, but then it was just so relaxing..."

We grab our bags and head upstairs. Unfortunately, the rooms are small and not designed to sleep five people in a bed. So we decide I will rotate room to room each night while we're here. Tonight is Callum's night.

EVERLEE - WINE TASTINGS

THE MORNING SUN FILTERS through the window, heating my cheek, and wakes me up. Wanting to feel Callum, my hand searches him out, only finding cool sheets. When we had gone to bed last night, he pulled me into his arms and tucked his legs into mine and I'm pretty sure I was asleep before the sheets were even warm.

It's not a gigantic bed, but I still roll over to make sure I'm somehow not missing the bulk of the man that is Callum. Instead of his handsome body, I find a note tented on the edge of the bed with my name scribbled on it in his handwriting.

Good morning darling wife,
I was going to wake you, but you looked so peaceful.
Emmett and I have gone to meet with Pierre and Camille this morning to discuss the wine partnership.
I hope to be back before you wake.
All my love,
C

I lay in bed, replaying the note in my head. Not really the entire thing, just the first line. Good morning darling wife. After I say it a few dozen times, I roll out of bed and realize my phone is dead because I didn't even plug it in last night. I rifle through my suitcase and pull out my charger and the special adapter and plug it in. My gift for the men sits there, staring at me, causing my stomach to tighten. The excitement bubbles under my skin at the thought of their reaction and the possibility that this time next year will look very different.

In some ways, a year feels like a long time and in others it feels like a blink of an eye.

My phone dings ten times in a row, all with messages from Lizzy. A few are pictures of our wedding night, a few others of castles they must have visited yesterday, and a few actual text messages wondering where I am, what it looks like, and some other inappropriate messages not worth sharing.

I shoot her a quick text, thanking her for the pictures, and telling her where I am with the promise of pictures when my phone's not dead.

The room is smaller than I remember from last night, although in those last minutes before I fell into the bed, my eyes were burning and I was getting that weird dizzy feeling that you get when you're overly tired. There's a small bed in the center of the wall with a floral quilted comforter and what looks to be a handmade headboard. There is a small dresser with a mirror and a small ceramic bowl sitting on it next to a vase filled with a fresh bouquet of handpicked flowers. And tucked into the corner of the room is a worn olive-green chair. Quaint.

I chuckle, because every time I feel like I'm in a room with Callum, there is always a chair. My body flushes when I think of him sitting in it, watching me, either by myself or with one or several of the men.

I pad across the creaky hardwood floors and walk into the bathroom. For it being the only bathroom in the house, it is tiny. A single porcelain footed tub stands just off the back wall with a shower curtain that goes from one wall to the other. There is a small toilet- no bidet. And a matching porcelain pedestal sink. On the wall opposite the sink is a small wicker looking shelf with two doors and two hooks on the wall. I imagine they're for towels or robes, but one of them is holding our toiletry bag that is unzipped and hanging open.

Last night when I came in, I was so focused on getting in and out as fast as possible because the bed was calling me like a siren's song. Washing up quickly, I head downstairs to find the house empty, but hear Jax and Knox talking on the back porch. I pour myself a quick cup of coffee, grab a muffin off the platter, and walk outside.

"Wow."

"Good morning, sleepy bones," Knox says, turning to look at me.

"This place." I'm awestruck at the beauty before me. Looking out for as far as the eye can see are rows and rows of grapes on vines. The sky is bright blue with only a few fluffy white clouds spread throughout.

"Yea. We were just talking about how much wine they produce annually and how long they take," Knox says, patting his knee. "Come sit on Santa's lap."

"We were having a nice adult conversation..." Jax groans.

Before I sit on Knox's knee, I lean over and lift Jax's chin and give him a quick kiss on the lips. "Good morning, love."

He winks at me.

"Did you get some good sleep?" Knox checks his watch. "We were about to come and wake you up."

"What time is it?" I just realized that when I looked at my phone, I never looked at the time because all of Lizzy's messages distracted me.

"It's just after ten."

"What? I never sleep that late."

"You've had a busy couple of days, both physically and mentally. Your body needed it," Jax says, running his finger up and down his empty mug.

"Are Emmett and Callum going to be back soon?"

"Yes. They texted just before you got out here and asked if we wanted to go tour the cellars on the property," Jax says while Knox absentmindedly rubs my back.

"Yes!"

"That's what we said. Jax replied, so obviously there was less pizazz and excitement."

"When are they going to be here?"

"In about ten minutes."

"Ten minutes? Give a girl a warning."

"We did. A ten-minute warning." Knox laughs.

I growl at him, only causing him to laugh harder.

"I'll be back. I need to go throw on a bra and some pants."

"Or don't," Knox says, sliding his hand up my leg.

"Knox!" My stomach clenches and if I thought I could fuck him and be ready to go in ten minutes, I would. But I know we can't.

I jump off his lap and they both smack my ass before I walk inside.

Seven minutes later, I'm back downstairs with a long sleeve shirt, some jeans and a puffer vest. I ran a brush through my hair, then threw it up in a messy bun.

"Well, don't you look like you just stepped out of a clothing catalogue?" Knox smiles.

"Shush."

He grabs my arm and pulls me into his chest, pressing his hips against mine. "Do you feel him? I want you to think of him the entire time we're on the tour and walking through those dark cellars, because I'll be thinking of you."

A puff of air escapes from between my lips. "Knox."

"A name you'll be screaming out repeatedly while you ride my cock." He presses his lips to mine, his kiss tasting like hints of coffee.

"Are you two done?" Jax calls from inside the house.

Knox pulls away from the kiss. "Almost." He places a quick peck on my forehead, then walks away.

This man.

When I walk inside, I close the backdoor and meet Jax and Knox at the front. Outside are two four-wheeler looking vehicles with no doors. Pierre is in one and Camille is driving the other. She is beautiful. Long dark hair with that girl next door sort of feel. Emmett is in the cart with her, while Callum is with Pierre.

"Ev. You remember Pierre from last night, and that," Callum turns around to point, "is Camille, his daughter."

I wave my hand and both. "Pleasure to meet you."

"Ev. Over here," Emmett calls, sliding out of the front row and moving to the back. Jax and Knox climb onto the back of Callum's car.

When I slide in, Camille holds her hand out to shake. "Pleasure meeting you. Emmett and Callum have had many wonderful things to say about you."

"Really?"

"Oui. They think very highly of you."

"We paid her to say that," Emmett laughs.

"He is such a joker." She laughs and with a slight jerk of the car, we are taking off following Pierre.

"The grounds here are stunning."

"Yes. Very beautiful. I grew up here and still can even appreciate its beauty. Many get used to it, but I don't think I ever will." Her hands are lazily hanging over the top of the steering wheel as she navigates the dirt road in front of her, staying far enough behind her dad so we aren't eating dirt.

Ten minutes later, the carts are coming to a stop outside of an all-brick structure. When I climb out of the cart, Emmett walks up beside me and loops his arm around my waist.

"How was your morning?" he whispers, leaning over and planting a kiss on my temple.

"It was good. I just got up a few minutes ago," I chuckle.

"What?"

"I was exhausted from the night before."

"Our wedding night?" His nose brushes the top of my ear.

"Yes. Say it again."

His fingers grip my hip, and his voice lowers into a growl. "Our wedding night."

A tingle races up my spine as my thumb rolls my rings over my finger.

"Here we are." She opens the door and we walk onto a small platform, then head down a small path of stairs. "This has been in our family for over three hundred years."

"Wow." I touch the wall and wish for a moment I had the gift of sight. Rather history. These walls under my hands have been here for hundreds of years and I can't help but imagine all the hands that have touched it before me. What were they like? What was it like here?

"You ok?" Emmett asks from behind. The stairwell only allowed for single file, so he guided me in front of him.

"Yea. Just thinking about the history of this place and what it was like three hundred years ago."

He grips his hand on my shoulder but doesn't speak.

When we get downstairs, there are several rows of barrels lined up in rows that run deep, further than the walls upstairs led me to believe. Seems most of this cellar is underground, extending past the building upstairs. I assume it's to help regulate temperature to prevent huge swings during winter and summer months.

"This is amazing," I mumble, more to myself than anyone else.

"We aren't a large vineyard, only producing less than two thousand bottles a year."

"Really? With these barrels?"

"We age our wine longer to get the flavor profile we're looking for, so we cycle the barrels through with a few months in between each. So most of these aren't ready yet."

Pierre grabs a funky-looking metal thing and offers, "Would you like to try some from your barrel?"

"Our barrel?"

"We bought a barrel." Emmett beams.

"Yes. I never turn down a tasting." I'm not a huge wino, but hey... while in France.

"What was the growing season like when the grapes were growing? Sunny, cold, foggy?" Knox asks, and we all look at him.

"It was a warm season," Pierre answers with a quizzical brow and a smile curling on his lips.

He looks at me and shrugs his shoulders. "What? I googled some questions to ask this morning."

My chest swells with love for him. Every day I think I can't love him more, but then he does something so freaking cute that I just want to pinch his cheeks.

He takes the cork out of the barrel and dips the little device into the hole while Camille grabs a small tray of mini wine glasses. I should probably learn what they're doing, but I'd just probably forget.

When the glasses are filled, Camille passes them to each of us, then sets the tray back down. I have no idea what I'm doing, so I'm honed into Pierre. Swirling, looking, sniffing, and tasting when he does.

When the first taste hits my lip, I can appreciate the flavors, but can tell I've shifted into more of a bourbon drinker. Give me a barrel of bourbon and I'd be a happy camper. Speaking of, we should totally do a bourbon tour in Kentucky. There are so many there...

"Ev?" Callum calls my name. His tone had a persistent quality, as if he were trying to catch my attention multiple times.

Snapping out of whatever daydream I was in, I look up and see the rest of the group has sat their empty wine glasses on the tray and walked further into the room. I'd just assumed this was it, but apparently there's more.

I knock back the small shot of wine that's left and try to control my face, preventing it from twisting and contorting. I'm sure it's actually an excellent wine... it's just not for me.

Callum chuckles, taking two steps towards me with his arm outstretched. I set the glass down, then take his hand.

He pulls me into his chest and I peek around his arm to see the others have gone.

"Good morning, love." He brushes the few wild wisps of hair back from my face. "Did you sleep well?"

"I did. You?"

"I did." He kisses my forehead, then grabs my hand and guides me to where the rest of the group is.

There isn't much else down here except a room where the door is closed. Their voices are chatting behind it, but we look at one another, unsure if we should walk in. "Should we knock?"

I shrug, rubbing the chill from my arms.

He raises his hand up, but before his knuckles hit the door, it's opening and an eye appears through the crack.

"Wilkommen," Knox whispers in a high-pitched voice, pushing it open a little more.

We slide in and stand with our backs against the wall. It's a dark room with a single light hanging on a chain. Very forbidden and prohibition-isque.

Pierre finishes talking and from the little bit I gathered, they pick one barrel every couple of years and bring it in here. It's a specialty wine that uses certain grapes, grown at certain temperatures, and something else that we missed. It's an extremely limited batch, which is why it has its own room.

After a few more minutes of talking about wine, we head back upstairs to the carts. Pierre and Camille, take us back to the house and confirm we'll see them tonight for dinner.

The hum of the cart is still in the distance and the door is barely shut when I feel a pair of hands on my hips and a cock pressed to my back.

KNOX - KINKY FUCKERS

This place is gorgeous. When I got up this morning, Jax and I had a delightful conversation about life and nothing, really. It was a rare opportunity to be alone with him, away from everyone else. He asked about the enormous gift tucked behind the tree, but I refuse to tell him what it is. I hate we all decided to leave our gifts at the home, because I don't want to wait a day longer to give Ev hers. I know we agreed to not really do gifts, but it seems like everyone agreed to it then didn't follow through. Which is fine by me.

Christmas day is in two days and I plan on just fucking Ev the entire day, since most things are going to be closed here. I even brought a Santa outfit I put in one of those bags where you can suck all the air out so it would fit in my suitcase.

When we climb out of the carts, Jax and Emmett decide to take a walk around the property. They offer it to the rest of us, but we decline. I have something else I'd rather be doing. I don't know what's gotten into me, but the idea she's ours now, forever... it's like it's flipped a switch and I'm always turned on. Well, I was before, but now I just feel extra turned on. After Christmas, we need to talk about kids. I will give her until then to bask in the sweet glow of our wedding.

Callum nudges my arm, then nods towards Ev. That kinky fucker. He had the same idea I did, although it looks like daddy dom wants to watch.

My hands clamp tightly around Ev, and I press my hips into her and she freezes. Her head turns slowly to look at me.

"Hello there." I smile.

"Hello." She smiles back, then glances at Callum. We both see it, the hunger and fire in his eyes.

"You want to watch him fuck me, or do you want to play too?" she asks, not missing a beat. If I wasn't already married to her, I'd marry the fuck out of her right now. Whisk her away to the closest place that could marry us and do it. Do it so fucking hard.

He shrugs with the ember look in his eyes.

"Daddy wants. Daddy gets." She smiles.

"Knoxxy wins," I add, speaking about myself in the third person. Jax isn't here, so I feel more free to say what I want without fear of reprisal.

She unhooks my hand from her hips and grabs it, leading me upstairs. "Callum's room has a chair in it. Coincidence? I think not."

He chuckles from behind us.

By the time we're in his room, she has discarded her jacket, shirt and bra and has her pants unbuttoned.

"It's been a while," she laughs, jumping and twisting onto the bed.

"A whole thirty hours. How have you been able to manage?"

"Dirty thoughts... and," her lips pinch into a hard line and I see the twinkle in her eyes. "I touch my elf."

"Nailed it!" I high five her, then waste no time yanking her shoes and pants off while Callum takes a seat in the room's corner.

I quickly add my clothes to the pile and climb over top of her, my cock brushing along the inside of her leg. My lips take hers in a soft kiss, but when her hands wrap around my neck, she presses her tongue in, pulsing it in and out while her body softly grinds against mine.

My glance flicks to Callum, who is sitting in the seat with his cock in his hand watching us, drinking us in.

"Taste her pussy," he commands.

I pull off our kiss and slowly work my way down her body, stopping at my favorite two peaks of love. My hands massage and rub while my tongue flicks around her nipple until she's arching her back and moaning out. If she wasn't wet before, I know she'll be wet now.

Continuing down further, I plant kisses on her stomach and then move to each hip bone until she's squirming under my kiss. I love to tease her, but I also love tasting her and pressing my cock inside of her... so there's that.

"You're so wet for me," I say, running my tongue up her center and giving an extra flick over her clit.

Her hands grab onto her breasts as she squeezes them and watches me.

"Turn her this way," Callum says. "I want to see how wet you make her."

She scoots back on the bed while I grab her legs and twist her body so she's facing Callum.

"That's my good girl," he praises her.

If Jax was here, I'd fire back with a thank you daddy in a high-pitched tone, but I feel like it'd be wasted on them, so I hold it back.

I slide off the bed and pull her towards the edge so she's closer to Callum and so I can eat her out without completely blocking the view.

My finger swipes across her entrance and then my tongue. Her back arches and a moan escapes. My favorite sound in the world.

"Spread your legs wider, baby. I want to see it all," Callum instructs, and she obeys. "Such a good girl."

I press my tongue inside of her and swipe up, spearing her and fucking her with it. She tastes like heaven and when her hands clamp onto the side of my head, I know she's getting closer. Almost like she's scared I'll stop the closer she gets. I press my tongue flat against her clit and slide two fingers in.

"Yes," she moans out.

Callum is panting as the soft thwap thwap thwap of his hand hitting his thigh sounds behind me.

Her hips are rocking, seeking more. More friction, more tongue, more fingers. Just more.

"Knox. Fuck me."

"Not yet," Callum says.

"I need a dick inside of me," she pleads.

"I want you to come around his tongue first. I want to see your pussy glisten. I want-"

She cries out and her hands clamp into my hair at the same time her hips buck off the bed, taking my head with it. My hands scoop around to her ass and hold her to my face as I press in deeper, licking and fucking her with my tongue.

"Knox! Knox!"

I fucking love when she cries out my name. The satisfaction that I get when I know it's because of me that her body is reeling and zinging with pleasure. The feel and taste of her come on my tongue.

As she slows down, I release my grip and glide up her body, thrusting forcefully into her, eliciting another cry. Her nails dig into my back as her knees shoot up to my sides, opening herself up to me. I try to suck on her nipples, but I can't stop my hips from thrusting. From claiming her. The need to feel her pussy pulse around my cock is trumping any feelings or desires in my mind. My body wants what it wants and right now, it wants her.

"I can't wait to put a baby in you," I whisper, and she doesn't respond. It wasn't really anything worth responding to, just a statement. It's something I've wanted to do for a while now and I know she wants it too. I just don't know when.

The thought of her waddling through the house only spurs my feelings, pushing my orgasm closer to the edge.

"Come inside her, Knox. Claim her. Press in her deep." Callum spits out commands back to back, his hand sliding up and down his cock and then he stops, plastering both hands onto his thighs, his abs and legs clenching as he fights the urge.

"Are you edging yourself?" I ask in shock.

"I'm going to take her when you're done. So, hurry the fuck up," he growls out.

"Sir, yes, sir."

I grab her legs and push them out to the side and slow my thrusts while I roll my hips more, angling in such a way I know I'm hitting all her favorite spots. "You feel so good like this." I roll my hips in large rolling waves like I'm doing the worm on her.

"I said faster, you shithead."

I toss a wicked smile over my shoulder at him, then pull out, flip her over, and slam into her from behind. From this position, I unleash, pounding into her, sending her straight for the banging headboard. She uses her hand to push against it, face in the pillow.

Moans and grunts fill the air as my balls begin to tighten. My body is on fire and then suddenly I'm coming inside of her. "Yes. Fuck. Yes. Oh." I continue to push through the orgasm, riding it until the very end. When I slow down, her hand drops from the headboard and flops onto the bed.

"Oh, no you don't, baby girl," Callum says, standing from the chair.

She sits up, back against the headboard, looking at him with that defiant grin that gets her in trouble–well, the kind of trouble she likes.

She extends her finger, curling it to her.

"No, baby girl. You get on your knees and crawl to me."

She looks at him, eyes nearly bulging out of her head. Oh, she liked that. For as much as she likes to be in control, she loves to be dominated by him.

She doesn't move.

"Everlee," his voice lowers to a growl, "Get on your knees and crawl over to me and suck my cock into that pretty little mouth of yours before I stick it in your pussy and fuck you until I come."

She swallows hard, her pulse nearly beating out of her neck.

After a moment, she moves to her knees, breast hanging down like bits of mistletoe that I just want to suck in my mouth and kiss. I know you aren't supposed to kiss mistletoe, but mistletoe isn't Everlee's titties. Titties? Fuck, I don't care. Titties is a lot more fun to say than breasts. Breasts is for when I'm serious. Titties is for when I want to play and right now I want to play. Lay on my back underneath them and just suck.

But I won't.

Right now is Callum's time, and I can only watch.

Which I will happily do. Though not as happily as Callum.

Kinky fucker.

She's still crawling, her ass swishing from side to side, with that fuck me look in her eyes and her teeth scraping over her bottom lip.

A whimper escapes as I bite on my knuckles.

Where's my fucking camera when I need it?

"Open wide like a good girl." He lifts his cock and bounces it lightly in his hand like he's weighing something, then guides it to her lips.

She doesn't move. Doesn't suck.

She's being the good submissive.

She has her moments, I smile.

He drags it, bringing with it a little drool down her chin.

He pushes in again, his head tilting towards the ceiling as a steady breath pushes out of his chest. "Suck my cock, like a good girl."

She moves to reach, but he stops her.

"No hands. Just your mouth."

Her eyes are locked onto his and she sucks him in hard as her cheeks hallow out.

Callum lets out a stuttered breath and thrusts his hips faster and faster each time she sucks him in, until he pulls out, grabs her legs and pulls her off the bed before bending her over it and fucking her from behind.

Must be in the wine. I'd say water, but we've only had wine today, which is kind of like water if you think about it. It just had fruit in it… for a while.

His hands grip tightly onto her hips as he unleashes his full length into her, causing her to moan out as his hips slam into her ass.

"Your pussy… feels… so fucking… good."

EVERLEE - IUD OR TREE ORNAMENT?

IT'S CHRISTMAS EVE, AND I'm about to burst out of my skin. My gift is in my bag, literally staring at me, begging me to come out. The last few days have been amazing. After our afternoon fuck session a few days ago, Callum, Knox, and I decided to go walk around the property and found Emmett and Jax on a tennis court. It's seen better days. The net was sagging, the balls no longer had the bright neon green color, and there were cracks in the court. But that didn't stop us from picking up a game with the rackets they had in a storage bin under a little roof. Knox nearly shat himself when he opened it to find a spider as large as his hand.

I don't think I've ever heard him scream so loud.

Callum watched the four of us play first, then subbed in for Jax. We each watched and subbed in and played for hours. By the time we were done, it was getting dark outside, which made the walk back to the house an interesting one, since the tennis courts weren't exactly next to it. Showers were fun, since it was a small bathroom and we each had to wait our turn. The men were gents and let me go first because my hair needed to dry for the dinner at Pierre and Camille's.

The spaghetti sauce was literally the best thing I've ever put in my mouth and I felt bad thinking that because of Emmett, but even he was impressed. By the end of the night, he was in the kitchen with Camille whipping up some sort of dessert, and it ended up being a very enjoyable night. We drank coffee after dinner and just talked like old friends to these people we'd only just met. It was very special and amazing.

Last night, we took the car to the next town over. Camille told us about this little restaurant that serves food and hosts an outdoor movie screen that plays old black and white movies. They were in French without subtitles, but it didn't matter. It was magical.

The restaurant had a pre-selected menu with French onion soup, beet salad, a mini medallion of filet, and chicken with root vegetables. Dessert was hot chocolate and the ingredients for s'mores that we could make at the fire pit they had in the center of the outdoor patio.

I'm going to be honest, the French onion soup tripped me up. I would think they would just call it onion soup, but that sounds nasty compared to French onion soup. It has a certain je ne sais quoi. The food was excellent, and we just enjoyed our time together, silently bundled up on blankets on a field watching old movies. We were close enough to the fire that we got some residual heat, but the blankets Camille told us to pack came in handy.

Tonight, Emmett cooked for us. We wanted to do a special dinner since it was our first Christmas Eve together. He cooked an amazing prime rib with mashed potatoes and sauteed carrots. He couldn't find a few things he wanted at the little market store and didn't have enough time to look around since most shops were closed or were closing soon.

After dinner, we decided to grab some blankets and toss them on the floor in front of the fireplace. It seemed to be something that we were doing often, and I loved it. After a while of sitting between Jax and Emmett, Callum pulled me over to sit with him, tucking me between his legs. Knox scurried off the blanket, flitting up the stairs, saying he found something that we would all love. For a second, I panicked, thinking he found my gift, but I should have known better.

He came downstairs in a Santa costume that looked thick and fluffy with his hands behind his back and a sinister smile on his face. "Merry Christmas. I saw this and thought of you." He tosses Jax a bright green furry onesie.

We all laugh. Well, all except Jax.

"Aren't you fucking hysterical?" he snipes, holding it up and looking at it. "I hope you didn't spend a lot of money on it, because I'm not wearing it."

"Said like an oof," Knox presses, then sits on the chair. He pats his knee. "Now who wants to sit on Santa's lap to tell me what you want for Christmas?"

"Hard pass," Jax mumbles, before tossing the onesie on the couch. "Second thought." He stands up.

"This can't be good," Callum whispers, with a hint of humor in his voice.

Knox's eyes grow wide at the unexpected body sitting on his lap. "Tell me what you want, dear boy. Ho, ho, ho."

"Well Santa, for Christmas... there is this friend I have."

"You said friend. Go on."

"And he's a real pain in my ass."

"Oh. Don't you mean rosy red derriere?"

"Sure."

"Go on."

The sight of Jax sitting on Knox's lap fills me with such happiness that my cheeks hurt from smiling.

"Anyway, my wish, Santa, is that this friend-"

A loud snap cracks across the room and the chair they were sitting in collapses to the floor.

"I'll have to get the little elves to fix this," Knox says without breaking character.

Jax just stares at him without speaking, then stands. "I can't with you."

"Just remember," Knox says, "There's always room for everyone on the nice list. Maybe all you need is a little Christmas cheer and a hug from Santa."

When Knox moves in to hug him, arms open wide, Jax presses his hand to his forehead, stopping him.

"Oh come here," Knox urges, flapping his hands in the air.

"No thanks, Santa."

"I have a wish for Santa," I say, standing up. In a hushed tone, I whisper to Callum, instructing him to retrieve my gift. I can't wait anymore. It's only a few more hours, but it's like torture. He nods and walks out of the room.

Knox's arms stop moving and he turns his head to look at me with Jax still holding on firmly.

"Go on. Tell da- Santa what you want."

He backs away from Jax and sits on the couch.

Jax returns to the floor, where Emmett throws a punch into his arm and says something.

I sit on Knox's lap and begin to whisper, but before I can get any words out, he shouts, "You want me to stick my candy cane where? That will put you on the naughty list."

A moment later, Callum is standing by the doorway, leaning against it with his hands behind his back.

My stomach tightens, and it feels like lead weights are sitting on my chest.

"Well, Santa-" I start, but the nerves are getting the better of me. It's not because I think they won't be happy, because I know they will be over the top excited. I think... I'm just... too excited.

"Go on, my little rum raisin buttercup of holiday cheer."

Jax sighs, then grunts as Emmett elbows him in the side.

I lean in and whisper, "I want you all to put a baby inside of me."

He pulls away slowly and looks at me, eyes wide.

"What did she say? And why is Callum daddy doming us right now against the wall?" Emmett asks.

"I think we can definitely make that happen," Knox says, as he slowly unbuttons his jacket.

"What did she say?" Emmett's voice ticks up an octave with excitement.

"She said-" he starts, but I cut him off.

"She said, she... I, want you to put a baby in me."

Emmett's mouth drops open and Jax looks at me. My heart is pounding out of my chest, so I look over to Callum, who pulls the gift out from behind his back.

"What's that?" Knox says, jumping off the couch and racing across the room to snatch it out of his hands.

"That's my gift to you all for Christmas. Well, one of them. The others are at home."

He unties the ribbon, pulls off the lid of the box, then slams it shut.

"What is it?" Emmett and Jax ask in unison.

"A picture of a tree ornament," Knox says, confused.

Callum looks at me, and I shake my head.

"What?" they ask.

He opens the lid of the box again and pulls out the picture.

Jax sighs. "That's not an ornament you nimrod, that's her IUD."

"Her IUD?" His eyes get big. "Her IUD... is out."

I smile and slowly nod.

"Her IUD is out!" Knox repeats, jumping up and down. "Her IUD is out," he says in a lower tone as realization sets in.

"Are you fucking Groot? Do you know how to say anything else?" Jax asks.

"Out is her IUD," Knox quips.

"Funny," Jax smirks, a smile pulling at his lips.

"I wanted to wait until Christmas morning, but... it's been killing me these last couple of weeks."

"Weeks?" they all ask.

Knox walks over and presses his hand to my stomach. "Is there a little fruitcake in there already because we've been fucking like rabbits? We could probably add a tap to you, to pour out the amount of come that's inside of you."

"That went from sweet to gross in about two seconds," Emmett laughs.

"And you elbow me when I try to keep him from saying dumb shit. This is what happens," Jax retorts.

"So," Knox starts, ignoring everyone else. He drops to his knees, lifts my shirt, and kisses my belly.

"No. I don't think. It could take up to a couple of months for my body to regulate the hormones and such."

"A couple of months?" he whines.

"Not definite."

"We have the rest of our lives with her, Knox," Emmett reminds softly.

"Plus, it gives us more time to practice and try," Jax adds.

"I'm all for practicing," Knox plants kisses along my stomach as his hands grip my ass, holding me to his face. "I think we should practice right now," he whispers, pulling the top of my pants down lower and lower until the top of my pussy is exposed. "You know. If at first you don't succeed, try," he kisses and pulls my pants down further, "Try." My pants are now under my ass. "Try." He kisses my clit. "Again." He runs his tongue up my slick pussy and I let out a moan as my fingers dig into his Santa's hat.

"This is why so many women have daddy issues."

"Why?" He chuckles, tilting his chin up to look at me.

"Because we've been conditioned our entire life to get excited over an older man dressed in a suit, sneaking into our house to give us gifts for being a good girl."

"Oh. So wrong kind of daddy." He laughs.

"Oh, yes. Kinky daddy, not daddy daddy."

"I'll be your kinky daddy... and your baby daddy. I'll be any kind of daddy you need." He lays me on the furry blankets in front of the fireplace. "We should work on that now."

Jax pulls my shirt off and I can't ignore the way the guys are looking at me- Emmett especially. His eyes are dark and hungry and my skin is buzzing like electricity is pulsing through it. Knox jumps up and starts to rip his costume off, but I stop him. "Leave it on. Well, take off your pants." I pump my eyebrows at him.

"Fine, but I have to unbutton the top. It's so hot in here I think I'd melt the north pole."

"How many days are left until Christmas is over?" Jax asks.

"Don't remind me," Knox frowns.

"Jax," I scold, and he snarls at me before he winks.

Something about Knox being pantless wearing only a Santa hat with the jacket open, just looks hot as sin. "I'd like to jingle your balls now." My flirtatious wink is met with an infectious smile from him, just before he skillfully glides over my body.

"I'd like to come in your chimney."

"I'd rather eat fruitcake... than listen to you," Jax snarls, scrunching his nose, then quickly corrects. "Obviously. I definitely want to bury my dick inside of you." When we all stare at Jax, he throws his hands out. "What I was trying to be all Christmasy for Knox."

"Aww boo. Christmas miracles really do exist," Knox coos.

I add. "You keep it up, and you won't be fucking me until you're in that costume. Since Halloween, I've seemed to have grown the same fondness for costumes you all have."

"You wouldn't."

"Oh, baby-" I gasp out as Knox seems to have tired of waiting and has started sucking on my clit. "I... would." In a moment of intense sexual frustration, a growl escapes my lips, echoing in the air. I really wanted to be all Evey dom, but fucking Knox and his tongue.

KNOX - HOME SWEET HOME

When I push the door open to our house, I toss my bags on the ground and take in a deep breath. "Home sweet home."

We left at the crack ass of dawn this morning so we could get back here in the afternoon, to give us a few hours to wash clothes and decompress before we have to go back to work tomorrow. I'm excited about washing up in my shower and sleeping in our bed.

We're definitely staying in the Nest tonight, and likely for the foreseeable future.

It was nice being able to get away and *mostly* unplug for a few days, but I'm glad we're home. After Ev told us she removed her IUD, we pretty much stayed naked in the house for the rest of our stay. We've had so much sex my cock is sore, so I can only imagine what Ev is feeling. Although there has been a lot of pampering.

We all like to fuck, but we also love to pamper, and aftercare is so important.

"It's just after three. I say give everyone an hour to do whatever and then back down here to open the rest of our gifts? Maybe call in a pizza for dinner?" I ask to the group as they filter in through the door.

"Sounds good." Ev gives me a kiss on the cheek and heads upstairs with her suitcase while Callum watches beside me.

They got into a bit of a kerfuffle at the airport because he was trying to carry her bag for her and she stuck her foot down. Which, as you can imagine, didn't go over very well with Cal. He wants to take care of her, but she wants to be Miss Independent. They're both stubborn as shit, so I'll likely carry popcorn around with me for the next several years to watch them go at it with each other. Then I'll watch them make up.

They'll be the new Jax and me.

An hour later, we're back downstairs- well, except Ev. She just called out that she's on her way. Something about finishing up a call with her parents to let them know we got home ok. Callum is sitting on the couch, legs spread apart, arm thrown over the back, casually waiting for Ev to walk down. Jax is sitting on the opposite end with Emmett who is sitting between his legs and I've put my Santa costume back on, since I'll be the one handing out gifts.

When Ev walks into the living room, she looks at Callum, then to Jax, then to me. She seems to still be a little perturbed with him, but I think at this point it's more for fun. She climbs over Emmett's head and sits as close as she can to Jax without being on his lap. Callum glances over at her and chuckles.

"Everlee."

"Callum," she returns with the same low tone.

"Get your ass across this couch and sit next to me."

She gasps like he's ruffled her feathers.

Should have made popcorn.

Damn it!

"No. You aren't going to tell me what to do."

"I wasn't telling you what to do, but suggesting."

"Suggesting?" she scoffs.

Emmett, Jax and I are all looking at one another, uncertain of what to do since mom and dad are fighting.

"Yes," he says cooly in his daddy dom voice. "I was merely suggesting that if you don't come over here and sit beside me, I will come over there and pick you up and hold you on my lap. So I'm giving you the option. Beside me or on me."

Her eyes darken for a second before she remembers that she's still pretending to be mad.

"You will have to pick me up, because I'm not coming over there."

"Shouldn't have said that," Jax whispers.

"He's not serious."

"I'm very serious." Callum stands up and leans over Emmett and hooks his arms around her waist, lifting her with ease off the couch.

"Put me down, you buffoon."

"Name calling?" he asks, with a smile on his face. He pops her ass, causing her to squeal, before he sits down with her on his lap.

When she tries to crawl off, he wraps his arms around her and presses his lips to her ear. "You're in enough trouble as it is. Keep acting out and you won't like it."

"Says who?"

"Me. I know what you like, where you like it, and how fast and hard you like it. I know when you're about to come and trust me... I will handcuff your wrists and ankles to the bed, then edge the fuck out of you until there are tears streaming down your face. Then leave you."

"You wouldn't!" She turns to stare at him.

"I wouldn't want to, but if it's to teach you a lesson."

"All of this because I won't let you carry my bag?"

"Yes."

"Imagine how you'll react when it's something more important... like I don't know... raising a child. You aren't always going to get your way, and you need to accept that."

"Neither are you." He bites at her neck, and she tries to scowl, but this is all foreplay for her. Fuck, for both of them. And maybe me too. I'm trying to think of jiggly fruitcake so my cock doesn't get hard watching them.

"Are we done?" I ask, reaching to grab a gift. I shake it for good measure, until Jax barks at me to stop.

Callum nods his head and Everlee crosses her arms, still defiant.

She's going to be a fun preggers. *Definitely don't see odd ass cravings and late-night runs in my future, he says sarcastically.* Great. Now I'm talking to myself. Pickles and ice cream, peaches and whipped cream. I wonder what her cravings will be. Maybe I should get a book and start reading it just to be prepared.

"Knox?" Jax asks.

"What?"

"Are you going to hand out the gifts, or just go off to lala land? Though some could argue you're always there."

"Some? Meaning you?"

"Boys and girl!" Emmett claps. "We just got married a week ago today and we just got back from our honey-ish moon. And now we're about to hand out gifts. You will not ruin this with your bickering. I'm about to make everyone kiss and make up."

"Ev would like that too much," Callum snipes.

She sucks in a breath and stares at him.

"Tell me you wouldn't." He grabs her chin and presses his lips to hers. She fights, pushing away, but he brings her back in again. She tries to push away, but her arms get weaker by the second until she's moaning into his kiss.

After a moment, he releases her, and she looks him square in the eye. "I wouldn't."

"You lie." He smiles, then kisses the end of her nose. He opens his arms so she can climb off, but she settles further onto his lap, curling her head under his chin.

Foreplay.

The kinky fucker.

For the next ten minutes, I'm handing out all the gifts. Everlee has had to find a spot on the floor because of her gifts, which she is frowning over. "We explicitly agreed no gifts... or very few gifts."

"We did. We put at least three back." I laugh.

She growls out.

"Five... four... three... two... one!" The living room becomes a flurry of wrapping paper, ribbon, and tissue paper.

When it all settles, we look at everyone's gifts. Aside from all the usuals, like clothes, shoes, cologne and so on, there were a couple of gifts that stood out. Ev got a customized set of our dildos and Emmett's even has his piercings. We had them each colored too. Somehow Jax got to change mine to glitter, which, whatever, it's not like I care. But the real present we got her is a set of pearl earrings, bracelet and necklace. When we had gone to an event, she had commented on one of the women's necklaces.

"What is this?" Jax asked, standing beside his picture frame.

"Well, I'm calling a truce. I got a custom sized digital picture frame for you to replace the empty frame over your bed."

His eyes narrow at me, like he doesn't believe me.

"There's a button here on the side." I walk over and find the green circle and the frame clicks on to show several pictures I've taken of our family. Us at the Easter event, the dinner for Emmett, several from the beach and most recently our trip to the Christmas tree farm.

Everyone is staring at it, laughing or awing. After a few minutes, Jax's hand clamps on my shoulder. "Thanks man. This is great."

"I figured this way you don't have to choose a picture to hang above your bed. You can have all of them."

"Thank you." He cuts it off and leans it against the wall.

"I can help you put it up in a little," I offer and he nods.

Jax made Emmett a collage of all the articles that's been written about him, framed nicely with his name etched into a small plaque at the bottom.

I wrapped up the gift Callum had ordered a while ago. It was on back order, then shipping was a nightmare, but it finally came in a couple of weeks ago, but I didn't tell him. Technically he ordered it, but it's more for Ev. It's a wooden paddle with our initials on it. We were going to go with first our names but couldn't make anything with JEEKC, so we went with our last names when we realized it tied to her smutty books she reads. MMFMM. On the other side we got the word *Mine*, etched into the wood, so when we spank her with it, she'll know who she belongs to.

"Is that what came in recently that you were freaking out about and wouldn't let me check in the shipment?" she asks, putting it all together.

"Maybe. Ok, yes. I didn't want you to see it."

Ev got me a camera for my paintball helmet and judging by the twinkle in her eyes and the fact she's nibbling her bottom lip, tells me she wants me to fuck her with it on. Which I will gladly do. She got Emmett a beautiful, top of the line, chef's knife with his name engraved on the handle. Callum got a pen with his name engraved on the side and Jax got a really nice flip knife he can carry in his back pocket.

Silence fills the room as we play with our gifts, tinkering with the electronics and just enjoying the peace and calmness.

EVERLEE - MAKING UP

Fog steams the mirror above the sink when I climb out of the shower. A zing moves through my body when my foot hits the cold tile as I move across the room to grab my pajamas- only they're gone.
I remember bringing them in here and sitting them on the counter...
Right?
The sandman and I were fighting before I got in the shower, and I felt a little loopy. Still so, but not as bad.
After we opened gifts, we all sat in the living room and played quietly with our things, but the time change caught up to us and somehow, we all fell asleep. I don't think anyone expected it, so when the doorbell rang, we all jumped up, completely startled.
It was only the pizza that Emmett ordered when we got home and not Lizzy, thankfully. Not that I didn't want to see her, but I was so tired. I could barely keep my eyes open.
We moved into the kitchen and sat at the table, half-asleep. No one talked and then afterward, we all drudged to our rooms to wash up, before we make our way to the Nest.

"I must have forgotten my clothes," I mumble to myself, swiping my hand along the mirror before leaning in to look at my eyes.

Tired.

Part of me is excited about tomorrow, but the other part is dreading it. Time change is a bitch, but hopefully, the excitement of being back at work will take the edge off.

When I open the door to my room, I almost fall backwards in shock. Callum is sitting on the edge of my bed naked.

Fuck me.

"What are you doing in here?" I ask, using the doorframe to help hold me up.

"I thought I needed to apologize for trying to be nice." He rolls his eyes with a playful smirk.

A chuckle escapes unexpectedly. "You do?"

"Apparently..." he pats his lap, but I don't move. "I can't make you do things."

"Well... not all the time." I wink.

"Right. I can only dominate you in the bedroom." He sighs like someone's had a talk with him and he's here against his will.

"So, are you going to apologize? Don't think I missed the part where you only said you're here to apologize, but haven't *actually* apologized."

He smiles, eyes twinkling in mischief.

"Well, I tried, but you didn't accept it."

"When you patted your leg?"

"Yes. I want you to climb on my cock so I can apologize to you while I'm fucking you. It will be a very quick fuck though, because I'm tired and have been instructed to bring you to the nest so we can all go to sleep."

"What if I don't want you to *apologize*?" It was just a question. I very much wanted him to *apologize*. I want him to *apologize* over and over and over again.

"I think you want me to apologize. I can tell by your nipples."

"They're cold from the air."

"I can tell by the way your knees slightly buckled."

"I'm tired."

"I can tell by the way your lips parted at the thought of your come lining my cock." His hand wraps around his shaft and he strokes himself slowly.

"I... was shocked."

"I can tell by the way you're staring at me, touching my elf right now." He smirks.

"You've been hanging around Knox too long."

"His Christmas spirit may have rubbed off on me." He licks his lips and watches me. Eyes drinking me up. "Technically, we're in the bedroom, so I can make you come over here."

This man. My chest swells. I was tired before, but right now I feel like I just had a shot of espresso. "Are you commanding me to come over?"

"Yes."

My pulse quickens.

I slowly walk over and stand in front of him. His hands grip my ass and he plants a kiss on my stomach. "I'm." He kisses lower. "Sorry." He kisses lower. "That." He kisses the inside of my left hip. "You." He kisses the inside of my right hip. "Are." He hovers over my clit, breathing his warm breath across it. "So." He flattens his tongue along my pussy and swipes up. "Stubborn." He spears his tongue inside of me and lets out a moan.

"That was a bogus..." I moan out as he hits a sweet spot. "Apology."

He continues licking and sucking on my clit. "Was it?" He stops and pushes me away.

"You fucker."

"I know." He smiles, staring at me.

"Do you forgive me?"

"You haven't even apologized! And saying you're sorry that I'm stubborn doesn't count."

"No?"

"No!"

He lifts me up and lines up his cock under me before he presses into me. "Now?"

"Still no."

I slide all the way down his shaft until he's stretching me, though I don't see how that's possible with all the sex we've been having lately.

"Now."

"Still no," I moan out a little slower.

"Hmmm." He rolls his hips into me and my God, the things it does to me. His dick is heaven on a stick. "Now?"

I swallow hard as a heat races across my body. Words will no longer form on my tongue, so I shake my head.

"Hmm." His hips pick up speed, rolling into me like a wave. A delicious wave, fucking the sand as it slides up and down her over and over again. I am the sand and he is the water.

"Callum." My hands wrap around his neck as I bounce, fucking him back. I slide my body closer to him, so my breasts press against his chest and I take him even deeper.

"I'm sorry." He puffs out, taking my lips with his.

I push him away. "I'm sorry, too." Then push him back with all I can muster.

He chuckles, a little surprised, and looks at me. "What are you doing?"

"Showing you how sorry I am."

"Ah, go on."

The sand becomes the wave rolling on top of him, fucking him. His hands grab onto my breasts, but I bat them away and push them over his hand, sliding my hands down his arms. It looks sexy when men do it, but I think it's because they're taller. My breasts are now hovering over his face and I've come off his cock.

"Did that work out for you the way you wanted?" He bites at my nipple with a playful grin.

"Shut up." I push on his chest to sit back up, but he leaves his hands above his head where I left them.

He laughs a deep, throaty laugh. God, this man is beautiful. All of my men are beautiful.

My fingers trace along his tattoo as I sit back on his cock. "You know, you've never told me about all of these."

"Do you want me to tell you now?" His eyes peak with curiosity.

A wave of exhaustion passes over me, causing me to yawn. "Sorry. Not right now, but soon."

"We have all the time in the world, love." He grips my hips, digging the pads of his fingers in, and starts rocking slowly up into me. "But now I'm going to fuck you and then take you into the Nest where the others are most definitely waiting right now so we can all go to bed together."

I nod, watching the lines pulse on his stomach as his muscles clench with each thrust. My fingers move over the ripples as my orgasm edges closer. The lower part of my stomach tightens and goosebumps erupt across my skin, causing my nipples to peak even further, and a wave of tingles starts at my toes and works its way up. I'm rocking faster and faster, then feel Callum's finger pressed on my clit.

"Oh!" I cry out, looking up at the ceiling as my body rides his cock and finger. I was close before, but that just put it on the bullet train. My orgasm crashes into me and my pussy clamps around Callum's cock, causing my muscles to tighten everywhere. He moves his finger from my clit and nearly holds me just off his cock so he can fuck into me.

He must not get enough leverage because he flips me in the blink of an eye, lifts my legs in front of his chest and my ass off the bed, and fucks me.

Fucks me hard. Sending his cock deep inside of me.

"Callum. Callum."

He feels so good and looks every bit the part of daddy dom right now. Eyes set, jaw relaxed, lips parted. He blinks slowly and then his eyes snap to mine. His sign that he's about to come. And he does.

He puffs out a breath through his last thrusts, then drops my legs and lets my ass settle back into the bed. He presses his forearms on either side of my body with his face hovering over mine while his cock still pulses inside of me. "I can't wait to fight with you again, then make up."

"We can skip the fighting and you can just listen to me." I smile.

"Yea?" He shifts his weight to one arm and grabs my chin, swiping his thumb across my bottom lip.

"Yea."

"I don't know if that's going to work for me."

"You better learn."

"You trying to dom me now?"

"Shut up and kiss me."

His eyes flash. "You…"

"Now." I try to keep a stern face, but I can't, cracking a smile at the end before his lips crash to mine.

His kiss is intense. Needy. His tongue pulses in and is hot and wet. Consuming. My arms wrap around his neck and I kiss him back with the same intensity. Like he is my lifeline.

After another minute, he pulls away and looks at me breathlessly. "We keep kissing like that and we won't ever make it to the Nest because I will forgo sleep to fuck you all night."

He makes me smile. Makes the butterflies in my stomach dance. "I love you."

"I love you." He kisses the tip of my nose and pulls out.

Ten minutes later, we're walking into the Nest. The guys are already in bed talking about something when they all sit up or roll over to look at me. Jax and Emmett are on one side together while Knox is facing me, patting the bed beside him.

These men are my everything.

Mine.

My husbands.

A sort of peace flows down my body from head to toe.

When I climb into bed, I give each of the men a kiss, then nuzzle into the magical space between Knox's shoulder and chin and throw my leg over his.

He brushes my hair from the side of my face with the hand that is under my head and whispers, "You smell like sex. Did mommy and daddy make up?"

Jax whispers, "You know it's weird as fuck to call her mommy, right?"

"Shut the fuck up, Jax." Knox bats his hand backwards and chuckles at the same time as Jax lets out a grunt.

Callum climbs into bed and gives me a kiss on the cheek before he lays down, giving me my space with Knox. But I feel him there.

Feel them all there.

KNOX - CANOEING

Being back at work feels amazing. It's been just over a week and it feels like so much time has passed and none at all. When I left, I was dating Ev and now... I look at the ring on my finger. I'm married.

Low was the first to notice, and she lost her mind. She's been bouncing back and forth between Allure and Vixen since Halloween, and while we were gone, she was running the books for both bars.

She was mad that we got married and didn't invite her, but I promised her we were going to have a little party after the new year to celebrate here. It would mostly be for all our coworkers since they've been so supportive.

My phone rings and I look at the caller ID.

Wyatt.

Needing a bit of privacy, I walk upstairs into Ev and my office and shut the door.

"Hello?"

"Knox." His words are soft, almost relieved that I picked up.

"How are you?"

"Doing well. How are you? How was your Christmas?"

"It was... great." I pause for a second, looking around the room like I expect the walls to tell me something, rubbing my hands on my thigh.

"Everything ok?" He chuckles like he's unsure.

"I got married," I say matter-of-factly, blowing out a long breath afterward.

"What?"

"Yep. I got married. Went to France."

"Wow. That's amazing. I didn't know you were with anyone."

"I'm not."

"Wait. What?"

"I'm in a... polyamorous relationship. My wife also married my best friends."

Silence.

"There are five of us in total and we love each other very much. They are all my world."

"So you... with men?" His words are slow with thought etched through each one like he's trying to process as he speaks.

"No. I'm only with Everlee."

"Everlee," he says the name, letting it play on his lips. It sounds weird, and he repeats, "Everlee."

Another long pause.

"Well... I'd love to meet them... all."

"Really?" I'm shocked.

"Yes. I've told you. I want to be part of your life and if they... are part of your life, then I would like to meet them too. I know we were talking about introducing me to your friends before Christmas, but you had to go out of the country." He chuckles awkwardly, "I didn't know it was to get married... but I would still like to meet them."

"Ok. Let's plan for some time next week." My heart is racing as nerves twist knots in my stomach. I hadn't planned on telling him about my relationship status or the fact I was married, but in that moment, it sort of just blurted out of my mouth and there was no chance I was stuffing that back in the box. It's like those mattresses you can order online that come in a box the size of a rolling pin, and then you cut open the package and it's a king-size mattress and they're like oh sure we expect returns in the original packaging. How in the heck is anyone getting a king-size mattress back into a rolling pin box?

It. Ain't. Happening.

But I digress.

"I would love to have you all over to my house for a traditional New Year's Day dinner." He laughs again, nervous tension echoing through the phone. "Well, I like to eat at two, so I guess it's not really a lunch or a dinner. Regardless, I'd still love it if you could all join."

"Let me talk to the others." I look at the calendar on my desk.

Three days.

Three days before my dad meets my family.

"Sounds good. Let me know by Sunday, so I can get enough food at the store. Would one of your five happen to be Emmett Monroe?"

"Yes. Emmett is one of the five."

"Oh."

"Is that ok?"

"Well, yes. Just a bunch of pressure. I hope he likes traditional southern cooking."

"He loves all food."

Silence.

"Well, son. Sorry. Knox. I just wanted to wish you a Merry Christmas and let you know I was thinking about you. I'd hoped it was wonderful and, by the sounds of it, it seems like it was more than wonderful."

"Thanks Wyatt. It was amazing, and I hope you also had a good Christmas."

"It was." His words fall off like he's deep in thought.

"Was it?" Why am I asking this? I'm not supposed to get too involved. Though I guess that ship sailed when I told him I got married and I'm in a relationship with four other people and I'm making plans for a New Year's lunner.

"Yes. It was good. I... I made you something."

"You made me something?" I completely failed at leaving the shock out of my voice and regretted almost immediately it sounded... angry wasn't the right word, but... not happy.

"I did. It's nothing much. I was just sitting on my porch lookin' out at the lake one night and started tinkerin' with some wood."

"You didn't have to get... or make me anything."

"I know. And I'm sorry. I don't have to give it to you. I shouldn't have said anything because it's really nothing. I'm sorry." He mumbles to himself.

"Let me ask the others about Monday and I'll text you."

"Ok, sounds good. Congratulations again and... have a safe New Years, if I don't talk to you before then."

"Thanks, and... you too."

When I disconnect the phone, I flip my phone upside down and press my face into the palms of my hands. What have I done? Fuck. Fuck, fuck, fuck.

"Knox?" Everlee asks, pushing the door open slowly. "Are you ok?"

I look up at her and suddenly tears are filling my eyes and I have no idea why. What is going on?

She closes the door and rushes to my side. "Knox. What? What happened? Talk to me?" She drops to her knees in front of me and grabs my hands, rubbing them between hers like she's trying to start a fire.

"I... I just got off the phone with my dad."

"Oh my God. Did something happen? I can stay here and cover if you need to go."

I chuckle through the tears and wipe them off my cheek with the back of my hand before I lift her to standing and guide her to the desk until she sits on it. Overwhelmed by whatever this is, I lay my head in her lap and her hands immediately start running through my hair, trying to comfort me.

"Do you want to talk about it?" she asks quietly, and I can hear it in her voice. She wants me to open up to her, but she won't push. If I said no, she would drop it and just hold me until I was ready.

But I want to share this with her.

I want to share everything with her.

"I just spoke to my dad... and I told him I got married and about us."

"And he didn't take it well?"

"He invited us all over for New Year's lunner."

"What is lunner?"

"Lunch and dinner. He wants to eat at two."

"That's good, right?"

I sigh.

"That's not good?"

"I don't know. I just told him I married a woman he's never met or heard of and I'm in a relationship with four other men and he all but said ok. That's weird. Right?"

"Is this weird? Us?"

I pop my head up and stare at her, shocked she would even ask such a thing.

She smiles. "This isn't weird to us or to people in our circle. It's just us."

"He said that he wants me in his life and, if this is how I am, then he will deal with it."

"I'm sure that's not what he said."

"Not in so many words."

"He's trying. I know we've talked about him several times. He just wants to make amends, and he's probably thrilled that you are slowing rebuilding a relationship piece by piece. Is it the kind of relationship he probably expected for you? Probably not. But neither did my parents. They still found a way to find love and acceptance. At the end of the day, it's about loving your child and respecting their decisions."

"Like ours?" I rub my hand on her belly and she chuckles.
"I don't think I'm pregnant yet."
"You never know."
"You're right." She kisses my forehead.
"I'm going to be a great dad to all our kids."
"I know you will, Knox." She freezes, staring at me.
"What?"
"I'm not having ten or twenty kids."
"I never said that." She stares at me without speaking, "Ok, I may have said it, but didn't mean it. Six or nine is perfect."

"You're trying to use my love of all these 69 to get me to agree to a bunch of kids?"

"Would I do that?"

She gasps and swats the air at me. "You're unbelievable."

"Unbelievably yours... for all time."

"Lucky me."

"Lucky you." I pull her top to the side, exposing the top of her breast and just bury my face in them.

"Are you motorboating me?"

After a minute, I sit up. "No, I was not motorboating you. I was canoeing you. Like motorboating, but without the motor."

She laughs and cradles my cheeks in her hands for a minute. "I love you so much, Knox, and I can't wait to meet your dad."

EVERLEE - NEW YEAR'S EVE

IT'S NEW YEAR'S EVE and I'm still trying to figure out how we're all going to be together when the clock strikes midnight. Emmett said he can go wherever, but Knox and I are stuck at Allure, and Jax and Callum are stuck at Vixen. I'm trying not to think too much about it because I don't want to stress myself out. Whatever we do, it will work out.

I hope.

Tonight, I'm wearing a silver sequin long sleeve dress that wraps and ties in the front with a low plunging v-neck with a pair of strappy black heels. The guys have already left for the businesses, but Knox gave me a little extra time to get ready since it was his fault my shower was interrupted.

I swear. Since our wedding, these men have been feral. It doesn't matter that my body isn't ready to produce a baby; they are hellbent on making her ready. Standing in front of the mirror, I look at my belly and can't help but wonder what it will look like. What kind of parents will we be? Knox, of course, will be the yes dad and also the one I'll have to fuss at for taking the kid's toys and playing with them. Emmett will be the dad that explains everything, teaching all the time. Callum and Jax... Clearly the more serious ones... What kind of mom will I be?

Does it matter? I shake my head. I'm just going to love our children, but probably not all six to nine of them, even though I'm tempted. That's just a lot of kids.

A car door shuts outside and pulls my attention. Brady must be back from dropping off the guys. I haven't seen him much this holiday season. He took some time off and went on vacation. Apparently, he doesn't have much family, or family at all, really. I'd always seen in movies that those are the people the military recruits. High intelligence, no family attachment.

Giving myself the once over and patting down the few loose strands of hair on my head, I turn for the door.

When I get to Allure, there are streamers and silver spinny things hanging from doorframes. Large silver and black balloons fill the corners of the room with a few clear ones mixed in. There is a ton of glitter just sitting in the bottom of the balloons and the only thing I can think of is if someone pops the balloon how much glitter will spread everywhere and how much of a pain in the ass it's going to be to clean it up.

A moment later, my eyes draw up to one of the sexiest men I've ever seen. Knox walks out of the office adjusting the cufflinks on his black button-down shirt, with his hair slicked back and a smile on his face.

He locks eyes with me and straightens his posture, adjusting his shoulders to perfect the fit of his shirt. When he crosses his arms in front of his chest, the fabric of his shirt pulls tight.

I'm pretty sure my ovaries are trying to push out eggs like a sinking boat would push out people onto a life raft.

He nods his head to the side, signaling for me to come upstairs and I do, my feet moving like he's pulling me with an invisible string. When I get beside him, he looks me up and down, pausing on my exposed chest, making my heart flutter.

"Look. I'm not going to pull a Jax and Callum and tell you what you can and can't wear, but damn. Are you trying to kill me?"

My cheeks hurt from smiling as his gaze travels over my body like heated silk. His hand traces a path down to the delicate tie that secures my dress.

"What happens if I pull this?"

"Knox," I warn, still smiling, but my heart is beating faster in my chest.

He pulls me into the office and closes the door. "Say my name again," he whispers, causing a shiver to race up my spine.

"Knox," I say breathlessly this time, because that's what he does to me when he looks at me the way he is- eyes dark and full of need and desire. He sucks all the air out of the room.

He pulls the tie and I watch the fabric pull through until the knot is undone and my dress is falling open and hanging from my shoulders. Knox brings his fist to his mouth as he stares at me, wearing only my black lace bra.

"No panties," he whimpers. "Fuck me." He bites his knuckles again. "God. I want to bend you over this desk right now and stick my cock in you." He looks from me to the door, to his watch, back to me. "But we have to go adult." His eyes fall. "We need to give the pre-open talk and by we, I mean you, because I can't go out there with this boner." He growls out. "Fuckin' no panties."

"You say that like it's a new thing."

"Damn it." He drops to his knees before I know what's happening and his tongue is licking up my center, then over my clit.

"Knox," I gurgle out in shock and pleasure.

He doesn't answer, but only presses his tongue in further.

"This is so not fair." I press my hands to his head, trying not to make a complete mess out of his hair. "I'm..." Speechless.

He stands with speed, pushes my dress off my shoulders and yanks me to his desk, bending me over. Within seconds, I feel the head of his cock notched at my entrance and slamming into me. My hips jerk into the side of the desk, biting at my skin as a grunt escapes past my lips. He is not gentle. No, he is hungry as he shoves into me with stacattoed thrusts, driving his cock further and further into me.

"Your pussy feels fucking perfect wrapped around my cock. It should never leave."

The paper on the desk grabs my attention, and my eyes immediately lock on the numbers inscribed upon it.

"Knox."

"Say my name."

"Knox." I push back into him, creating some distance between the desk and my hips to cut down on the inevitable bruise I'm going to have from hip to hip.

He bats my hair out of the way and sucks my neck, then gives it a quick kiss.

"Goddamn you feel so good," he mumbles to himself.

His fingers dig into my hips and he unleashes with speed. The friction and the angle he's hitting rubs against my sensitive areas, but it's not enough.

"Clit." I breathe out through thrusts.

It takes a moment for him to realize what I'm saying. His left hand wraps around my waist, hand splayed over my stomach while his right hand finds my clit.

My head falls back for a moment.

"I love you so much, Everlee."

My orgasm builds inside of me like it's the little engine that could. Choo choo, mother fuckers, watch out because this trains a comin'.

When I start to moan out, I catch myself and bite my lip, burying my head in my chest. My pussy is clenching around Knox's cock and a second later, he's puffing through his thrusts as he explodes inside of me.

He pulls out and I stand up, looking at him, his cheeks flush. "Sorry," he shrugs. "I really wanted to wait until the New Year."

"Well, you shouldn't have brought me in here and then untied my dress."

"You should have worn something more difficult for me to climb into and, for goodness sakes, you should have been wearing underwear."

"So you're blaming me for your lack of control?" I laugh, watching him shove his semi-hard cock back into his pants.

"One hundred percent that's what's happening."

"Good to know."

"Are you going to apologize?"

"Fuck off," I say, tossing the tissue in the trash. I tried to squeeze as much of his come out as possible so it's not dripping down my leg all night.

"I'd rather fuck in... you." He grabs my hand, causing the bow I was tying to fall. "It sounded better in my head."

"I'm sure most things do." I pucker my lips and chuckle when his eyes grow wide in feigned indignation. "You'll be alright." I grab his chin and give him a kiss on his lips. "I love you."

"I love you." He turns and walks towards the door, stuffing his shirt back in his pants. "Now finish getting dressed so you can join me out here for our last kick off speech of the year."

By the time I get out of our office, he has everyone lined up below looking up at us. "Team. We're about to say goodbye to this year, and welcome in a new one. I'm sure when you started this year, you didn't know you'd be under new management. I want to commend you all for the work you've all done, but more importantly, since we've taken over. It's hard to go through management change, because you never know how they're going to be, but you all have stuck with us."

A voice in the crowd yells out, "You both rock!"

They all clap and scream.

"You all rock. You've been there for us as we navigated the intricacies of this place and have patiently tolerated all of Ev's eccentric ideas."

"What?" I gasp, slapping his arm.

"Mine were all brilliant. Yours were wild."

"Yea, right." A female voice calls from the audience, but I can't quite make out who.

"Hey! You have to be on this side of the speech giver. It's like the rule or something."

"Team Everlee!" someone else shouts.

"Team Kinky BookNook!"

The crowd claps again, and Knox and I just bask in this happiness for a moment. This is our amazing life. These people are amazing. This place is amazing.

When the crowd quietens down, Knox continues. "Tonight is going to be a busy night. Remember, service first. Give these people an experience they'll remember forever."

Everyone claps before the crowd breaks apart.

"This is it," Knox says, turning to me. "This is our last night of this year… and what a wonderful year it's been." He pulls up my hand, thumbing over the diamond on my ring finger, before he kisses my knuckles.

"It has been a pretty outstanding year."

I hear a loud voice pierce over the music, "Where's my married boo thannnggg?"

"Lizzy," Knox says.

"At least she isn't at Vixen with Jax."

"Could you imagine?"

I haven't seen Lizzy since the day after our wedding and even then it felt like a blur. Heading down the stairs as she walks over, we meet at the bottom. She throws her arms around me and gives me a long hug.

"It's dead in here," she says when she pushes me away.

"We literally just opened."

"I know. I wanted to see you as soon as possible since the guys have been hogging you."

"You mean while we were on our honeymoon?"

"Tomato tomato." She bats the air and pulls me up the stairs towards our office.

We don't usually allow others up here, but since she's helped manage this place a few times this year, I guess it doesn't seem that odd.

"Where are you going?" Knox asks, still fixing the cuff of his shirt.

"Talking to my boo. I haven't seen her in so long." She pouts and pushes the door open into the office.

"I'm going to make some rounds. You two behave."

"Always," I say at the same time she says "Never."

"What?" she asks, laughing.

"How have you been?"

"Smells like sex in here." She looks around like she can see into the past to watch where it happened.

"I see you're good."

"I'd fuck you too if you wore a dress like that around me."

"I *am* wearing this dress around you."

"You know what I mean."

I sigh. "How are you? How was the rest of Paris?"

"It was amazing! We did all the tours and drank lots of wine. Hung out with your family. Your mom is so happy and excited."

I grab her hands and catch her gaze. "Thank you. Thank you for being an amazing friend and for putting all that together."

"It wasn't just me."

"I know, but you're here now, so I want to thank you. It was... it was more than I could have ever dreamed of. I still can't believe the little stunt you pulled on the Eiffel Tower to get us married. We could have been kicked out."

"Ehh. You have your men and let's not forget your mother. I'd hate to see what she would have done had they tried to stop the wedding of her precious baby girl."

"There's no telling."

"Any big plans tomorrow?"

"We're going to Knox's dad's house."

"Say what?"

"Yea. He's pretty nervous about it, so don't give him a hard time. It's hard for him because I think he wants to let his dad in, but other parts are scared of getting hurt again. But his dad is trying. He calls or texts at least every two days, doesn't push. Just a simple hello or how is your day?"

"That's really great for Knox. I hope everything works out. How are the others taking it? Are they sad because their family hasn't reached out to them?"

"No, I don't think so. Emmett was too young to remember or care. It would be more the idea for him and Callum and Jax. I don't know. I think they moved on a while ago. Knox was the one who always held out hope because he was old enough to remember and the situation was a little different."

"Well, I'm happy for him."

Silence fills the air for a minute before Lizzy claps her hands on her lap. "I'm going to go get my sex on now. Tony and I rented out one of the rooms in Infernus and I'm very excited."

I pump my eyebrows. "Will I see you when the ball drops?"

"Of course. It's our tradition. We're always together on New Year's Eve. Now, until forever. You and me, boo." She leans over and gives me a hug.

"Now stop making me all teary-eyed."

"I didn't do anything. You're hormonal right now. I can feel it. I told you... I'm an empath."

"You're *empath*-able."

"Did you just try to call me impossible?"

"It sounded-" Suddenly, Knox's 'it sounded better in my head' words come back to me. "You know what... nevermind."

EVERLEE - NO PHONE IN THE SEX CLUB RULE IS THERE FOR A REASON

Ten... nine... eight.

My eyes hurriedly search the crowd. Callum and Jax still aren't here yet, but Emmett said they were on their way twenty minutes ago.

Seven... six... five.

My heart is pounding in my chest with both the excitement of what's coming in the new year and worry about where my guys are. It's so funny. I've been up at midnight more nights than not since taking over Allure with Knox and not once was it anything special, and tonight is the same, really. Just a few more seconds, but it symbolizes so much more.

The end of one year and the start of a new. Promises that can be made to do better, to be better, because it's a different year. Why can't these same promises be made month after month? It's a new month. Do better. It's a new week. Do better.

Four... three.

My gaze flickers between Knox and Emmett, who also have furrowed brows. I know Emmett was definitely planning on kissing me tonight, but was he also hoping to kiss Jax? Does he have the same nervous butterflies I do?

His lips pinch into a thin flat line and he shakes his head slowly and a sadness creeps in.

Two... one.

The room erupts in loud cheers and excitement as thousands of balloons fall from the ceiling. I hadn't noticed them tucked away in the nets all night, granted, I don't usually look up.

"Surprise," Knox says, turning in a circle, batting balloons. "I've always wanted to be in a balloon drop at New Years, and now I can do it whenever I want."

He wraps his arm around my back and presses his lips to mine, kissing me hard and long with so much emotion that it causes a knot to form in my stomach.

"My turn," Emmett says, grabbing my shoulders.

I turn from Knox and find Emmett there, looking sexy as ever. I nearly leap into his arms, standing on my tiptoes, throwing my hands around his neck. He grabs my hips and kisses me, his tongue pressing in, making me melt on the spot. The world fades out around us as his kiss consumes me. The feel of his tongue dancing in my mouth, pulsing, moving.

"Champagne?" someone offers, but I ignore it, letting myself get lost in his world.

We converted all the staff to servers for the ball drop, each carrying around trays of champagne for all our guests.

"Champagne?" they ask again, tone dropping.

When I pull out of Emmett's kiss, Callum is standing there with two champagne flutes in his hand, with Jax right behind him.

They made it!

Jax steps forward and kisses Emmett and my heart explodes out of my chest at the same time Callum lowers his chin and looks at me with those come-hither fuck me eyes.

"I was scared you both wouldn't make it."

"Love. We would walk through fire to be here with you."

He hands the champagne flutes to Knox, letting him juggle three in his hands, and picks me up. My legs wrap around him, causing my pussy to press up against his stomach.

Well, that's going to leave a mark, because I'm definitely wet. With one hand wrapped around my back, he uses the other to wrap around my neck, holding me there. "Happy New Year, baby."

Before I can say the same to him, he's pulling me towards him and kissing me.

These men and their kisses are going to be the death of me.

"Bro," Knox starts. "She doesn't have any panties on. I know. It came as a shock to me too, but her ass is on the precipice of being displayed for all."

Callum stands me back up, releasing me from our kiss, just as Jax's hand grabs my neck and swings me around. "Now it's your turn," he says, eyes wild.

It's heaven.

My life.

These men.

Last year I didn't have a man to kiss and this year I'm married to four. A year. It's only a fraction of our life, but it's amazing how much can change. Imagine all of those years stacked up and the change that happens.

When Jax stops kissing me, I'm in the middle of my men. They're standing shoulder to shoulder looking at me, eyes on fire. But so much more. Hope. Possibility. Excitement of what's coming next in our life.

"Who let her wear this outfit?" Jax chomps, bringing me back to the present, like a bucket of cold water being dumped on my head.

Defiantly, I answer, "I did. I am my own woman, so you better get used to it, buddy." I pat him on the chest and he just looks between the guys.

"Get used to it?" he retorts back, stepping closer to me as his hand brushes up my leg. "Will you get used to this?"

His hand continues to slide up my dress and brushes over my clit.

"Jokes on you, because Knox already bent me over our desk and fucked me," I lean in and whisper.

His eyes pulse wide and his fingers dig into my ass, but he doesn't speak. He just stares at me, almost daring me to keep talking.

"I could fuck you right here and right now in the middle of this room."

There are balloons all around, and the lights are dim. "Don't threaten me with a good time."

He leans in to press his lips to mine, but a loud dramatic sigh floats in the surrounding air. "Damn it! We missed it! We missed the count down. I told you to take the butt plug out!"

Jax leans back to standing and closes his eyes slowly, then opens them. He had to be repeating wooosaaa in his head.

"Lizzy." I smile as she pushes her way in between Emmett and Jax. Tony stays back a good distance, smiling.

"I missed it, boo boo. Can you forgive me?"

I won't tell her I forgot about her. I mean not like forgot, forgot. But totally wasn't thinking about her as the clock ticked down.

She kisses me on the lips quickly and then pulls away. "Happy New Year!"

Baffled, I stare at her and she just shrugs it off. "Don't pretend like that's our first time kissing on the lips. In all honesty, I didn't mean to. I was aiming for your cheek, then just got flustered and forgot to move my head around." She illustrates what she meant by move her head around, which is exactly what anyone would think, so why she feels the need to show it, is a testament to how fast her brain is working right now.

"Calm down. What's going on?" I say, grabbing her by the shoulders.

"I missed the countdown with you. I never miss it."

"Should have taken out the butt plug," Jax taunts.

"Right? That's what I sai-" She turns and casts an angry scowl. "You're making fun of me."

"No. Never. I wouldn't do that," Jax laughs.

She turns back to me and grabs my hands. "Will you forgive me?"

"Already forgiven. Didn't even have to be a thing."

"Good." She snatches the champagne out of my hand and knocks it back. "Oh shit. That's the good stuff."

"We don't do cheap here," Knox chimes, holding his fingers in the air to call a server over. There are still a few left making passes through the people left in the main area. When the server walks over, Knox grabs the last three off the tray and hands one to me, to Lizzy, and Tony, who has since stepped into the circle the men have made wider.

"Happy New Year." Callum thrusts his glass into the air and we all follow.

Jax continues, "Wishing all of you, including Lizzy, a very happy New Year. And a special wish to you, Tony. May you have the fortitude to endure her for the rest of your life. I won't threaten you with keeping her happy, but unfortunately, she seems to be a package deal with Ev. So hurt her... and you know the rest of the saying."

Tony's face is pulled somewhere between a smile and concern.

"Jax, you big softy!" Lizzy bats across his chest. "Did you just admit you liked me? AND on New Year. January 1st! It's January. Man! What a way to start the year!" Lizzy wipes the tear under her eye. "You just made my year and we are barely five minutes into it."

He sighs and pulls her in for a hug.

With her face buried in his chest, she yells out, "And a hug!!" Her hands pat him wildly on the back. When he pushes her away, the smile drops from her face.

"What's wrong?" I ask.

"Did we fall through some portal? Are we still on Earth? Are we in the Twilight Zone?"

"I'm really regretting saying anything nice about her."

"Nope!" She claps. "We're still here. Obviously."

"How much has she had to drink?" I ask Tony.

"Hardly anything!" Lizzy answers for herself. "I'm just so happy and looking forward to this year. One hundred and sixty days until we get married. I'm rounding, of course, since we just started today."

"Of course." I pull her in for a hug just as my phone rings. "Is that the McKinleys?"

"Yes." I press the answer button and walk to a corner of the room so we aren't smack in the middle of it.

"Happy New Year!!" Lizzy shouts before anyone can get a word out, rocking her body from side to side.

"How much has she had to drink?" Beckett asks before saying anything else.

It looks like he's calling from his firehouse, while mom and dad are at their house.

"Nothing. Well, a glass of champagne."

Beckett throws his head back, laughing hysterically. "I bet Jax is loving all that," he pauses and twists his hands in the air, directing it at Lizzy, "energy."

"Stop. He just made my year, and all but admitted he liked me."

"He said that?" Beckett's eyebrows peak on his forehead.

"Not in so many words, but then he gave me a hug."

"More important question then, how much has *he* had to drink?"

"Stop. We're making progress, him and I. Who knows, by the end of the year we'll probably be best friends. Well, he'll still be second because no one takes over my number one spot." She wraps her arm around my neck and pulls me in for a hug.

"Wow." Beckett smiles.

"Happy New Year, dears," Mom says, leaning into the frame. "I was going to say it earlier, but your brother just jumped right in and didn't let me get a word in."

"Happy New Year."

"Where are those delicious men of yours?"

"Hopefully you got a kiss tonight," Beckett chimes.

"Beck! Be nice. I swear. I'd love it if for just one call, you were nice to your sister without some... some..." she scrunches her nose. "Some comment."

"Sorry sister." He rolls his eyes.

"I can see you through the picture on the screen, Beckett," she scolds.

"We're here," Callum calls and I flip the camera around so she can see them all.

"Happy New Year, men. I hope you had an *enjoyable* honeymoon."

"Mom!" Beckett and I both shout.

"Can't a mom simply ask how the honeymoon was?"

"Donna," Dave pats her shoulder.

"What are you doing?" I ask, flipping the phone around.

"Was that a woman leading around a man on a chain like a dog?"

"What? No." I gasp in horror.

And this is why we don't allow phones back here. Fuck. I glance at the guys and their lips are pinched tight.

"No, mom. Geez. Probably funny shadows. You know, like we used to play growing up?" Beckett chimes in.

"Oh yes. I loved when we would do those." She claps very fast, "and just think we can do that again for all the littles that will be running around here in no time!"

My eyes connect with Beckett's, and I scream a wordless thank you to him. Surest way to get mom off any topic is to somehow bring it back to babies. She is a dog with a bone on that one. I toyed with the idea of telling her we're trying, but I don't want to get her hopes up or be inundated with all things baby planning. Knox has already ordered a book called *Preparing to Become a Mom*. He reads it out loud to the men and me every night. I can already tell he is going to be super hands-on during the pregnancy, so that will be interesting.

"Are you busy tonight, Becks?" I ask.

He looks around the fire station. "Not too much action right now. We had a small house fire a couple of hours ago, but nothing too serious. Now we're just playing darts. Thought about going to bed, but apparently that's not a thing on New Year's. It's bad luck. Cap said in the past every time someone went to bed on New Years, they would get a massive call. So now they don't go to bed."

"That's miserable," Mom says. "I can barely stay up until midnight. It was easier when you kids were here, but now it's just me and dad."

"What's that supposed to mean?" he calls from beside her and inches into the frame.

"Oh nothing. You're just a little... boring."

"Mom," I scold.

"Next year we need to plan to be together like a family. You all can come down here and I will fix you a proper New Year's dinner. Although, from what Knox said, his dad may do that tomorrow."

My eyes flick to Knox, who shrugs his shoulders.

"Oh stop. I'm allowed to talk to your men if they call," she defends.

Knox called to talk to her? No telling what those Chatty Cathy's or Chatty Charles McGurt's were talking about. No doubt babies. I don't know who's more excited.

"Ok. Well, I will let you kids get back to your fun evenings. Beckett don't go to sleep and be safe. I'm about to call Will. Have you talked to him?" Mom asks.

"Yes, I was on the phone with him earlier."

"Ok. Well, I just want to call him really quick too and wish him a Happy New Year. I feel like it's bad luck if I don't wish all my kids a Happy New Year. Extended included."

"Mama McKinley!" Lizzy holds her arms out towards the phone.

Mom laughs. "Oh Lizzy. You are a light. We need to get you on the baby train too!"

Through the camera on the phone, I see Lizzy's eyes get big, but she says nothing.

"Good night loves! You all be safe. Beckett, I will have you some breakfast cooked when you get home."

"Aww so sweet," I tease.

"You're just jealous," he retorts.

"She lives with a world class chef Beckett. I doubt she's jealous of my cooking!"

"Always jealous of your home cooking, mom." I smile.

She tilts her head to the side. "Well, aren't you just the sweetest?"

Beckett's eyebrows jump to his hairline with an accusatory look while he pats this nose. Our symbol that we're being called out for being a kiss ass. I simply pump my eyebrows with a smirk. "Thanks mom. It's a tough job, but someone has to do it. If only Becks could learn."

"Oh my God." He throws his hand up in the air dramatically. "I can't with you." He does something on his phone and a second later, Knox is laughing and holds the phone up to me.

Beckett texted Knox. **Get your girl under control. There are four of you and one of her!**

I look back at the phone and stare at Beckett, who is smiling, then he texts again.

Knox laughs again and holds the phone up. **It was better than what I was going to say since I knew the little shit was going to show you!**

"Well, we better be going. Love you kids and please be safe, Beckett. My heart hurts when you're out all night."

"Good night and Happy New Year. Love you all and do be safe, Becks." I blow him a kiss.

"Love ya, sis!" he says in a super chipper, mocking-like tone.

"Goodnight men! Love you!" Mom shouts through the phone, but I don't dare turn it around, so I hold it down and they all lean their head over the top and say goodbye to my parents and Beckett.

Once I put the phone back in my pocket, we all stare at one another and I feel like they are waiting for me to address the elephant in the room. "Ok. My bad about the whole flipping the phone around. I'm sorry."

"Yea. Probably need to be a lot more careful with that in the future," Callum says. He loops his arm around my waist and pulls me in. His hand brushes my hair behind my shoulder and he leans down and whispers, "If not, I will have to punish you."

Looking up at him with my chin resting on his chest, "That's not the thing to say to get me to behave."

"I know." He smiles.

KNOX - MORNING SURPRISES AND NEW BEST FRIENDS

We got home early this morning just after four and all fell into bed and passed out. Last night, rather this morning, was a great night and the balloon drop. I've always wanted to be in one. I know it's silly, but there's just something about it and it didn't disappoint. But now it's January.

A new year.

It's crazy to think about how far we've come in twelve months. We're married, planning a family, and I co-own a sex club- a sex club that we used to own years ago.

Everlee looks so peaceful sleeping. Her bottom lip is trembling and her eyes are moving back and forth under her eyelids. What is she dreaming about? Is it me? Her mouth parts slightly, like she's panting as her body subtly wiggles.

Is she having a sex dream? Excitement prickles under my skin.

Quickly glancing around, I see everyone is still asleep. Given the hour we went to bed last night, getting up this early seems crazy, but I can't sleep. We're having dinner, rather lunch, with my dad today and he's going to meet my family.

Everlee's tongue sticks out of her mouth for a second. Just the tip.

That's what she said.

Too bad Jax isn't awake to appreciate my joke and give me shit for it.

I'm really beginning to think she's having a sex dream because her breathing is getting more rapid.

A smile curls on my lips.

I suck my fingers into my mouth, then slide them slowly under the covers. She's only wearing Callum's t-shirt, so access won't be an issue. I'll just give her what she's searching for in her dream.

Tenting the sheet that is barely draped along her stomach, I brush my fingers over her clit. Slow, gentle. I don't want to wake her up… yet. Can I make her come this way without waking her?

My finger slides between her legs and she's a little wet, but not as much as she usually is. I press my finger softly between the lips of her pussy and drag my finger up to her clit. She shifts a little and I freeze, but she doesn't wake up. As I put my finger in my mouth, I relish the subtle hints of her flavor, yearning for another taste, yet reminding myself to be patient. I remember when she did this to us once, and it was the hottest fucking thing ever.

I take my time, caressing her clit with a slow, deliberate touch, tracing circles that cause goosebumps on her legs. Gradually, my finger inches down to her slick entrance, entering her just a fraction, using her growing wetness to glide my finger in.

She lets out a low whimper and shifts her body again, spreading her legs a little, so I pause. When she settles, I move my finger again. Fuck, I want to taste her, so I do.

When I suck my fingers into my mouth, it's more to fuel my selfish need than to help get her wetter.

Fuck it.

Sitting up, I pull back the sheets covering her legs and see her pretty pussy there, looking up and smiling at me. Yes. It wants me, my mouth. Gently, I open her legs a little wider, so I can slide between them and pause, staring at her to make sure she's not going to wake up.

Leaning over, careful not to put a lot of weight on her legs, I hover and run my tongue up her center. Fuck me. I love the taste of her. I could live on my knees in front of her for the rest of my life. My tongue passes a few more times, flattening against her clit before I slide it down and press it inside of her, spearing her softly. I twist my tongue around like I'm making out with her pussy, because I just want to drag this out and taste all of her. I want her to orgasm and come on my tongue before she wakes up.

Her hands move across her stomach, raising her shirt a little higher. She feels me here, even if she isn't awake. The thought we're connected on that deep of a level causes my cock to become even harder. I gently blow a warm breath on her pussy and watch the goosebumps shoot up her legs and over her arms in response.

Leaning back down, I keep my eyes fixed on her, eagerly awaiting the moment her eyes flutter open. I want her to find me with my tongue inside her pussy, bringing her to orgasm. I want to see her eyes, heavy with sleep, suddenly widen in complete alertness as her orgasm surges through her body. Moving my tongue faster and faster, I continue until her legs move, sliding back and forth beside me, her heels digging into the bed. She's getting closer, so I pull my tongue out and suck on her clit at the same time I put my fingers into her pussy, slowly pulsing them in and out.

Her head moves, so I pause, lifting mine to rest my chin on the top of her pubic bone. Her eyelids open slowly and her head tilts up as the sleep slowly washes off her.

Smiling, I hold my finger over my lips and pump my eyebrows a few times. She blinks slowly, like she's trying to process what she's seeing and feeling, so I dip back down and suck on her clit, never taking my eyes off hers. It doesn't take long until her hands are rubbing over her stomach, as her legs dig deeper into the bed. The guys shift around us, so I freeze and she does too. Her eyes are watching me, but I can see the haze that still lingers.

I press my fingers in slowly, savoring the sensation, before curling them and feeling the satisfying grip as her body pulses around them. Her abs clench, lifting her off the bed as she watches me, teeth clamped tightly on her bottom lip. I pull my fingers from her pussy and lick and suck, drinking her down.

After another minute or two, I slide off the bed and blow her a kiss.

There's no way I'm going to go back to sleep, so I head to my bedroom and turn the shower on. Fuck, my cock is hard. By the time I rinse the shampoo out of my hair, the glass door of my shower is opening, and she's standing there completely naked.

"What are you doing?" I ask.

"Do you think I could just go to sleep after that?" She sighs, pushing her way into the shower, and closes the door behind her. "It took me that long to get out of the bed without waking them."

I blow out a quick breath and grab the soap.

"What was that for?"

"What was what for?"

"Don't play dumb with me," she says, pushing me against the wall of the shower.

I can't help but let out a small chuckle as I turn around to face her. "I wanted to taste you."

"So you just eat me out, then leave?"

"Well, I thought you could go back to sleep."

She looks down at my body, and I look down at hers. My mouth is salivating, eager to take her nipples between my teeth.

"Well, that is the stupidest fucking thing you've ever said."

"Someone woke up on the wrong side of the bed, which I don't know how that's possible because it should have been the most glorious wake up ever!"

"Was it?"

She pushes her body against mine and my half hard cock is now fully hard and sandwiched in between us.

"What are you doing in here, Ev?"

"Do you want me to leave?" She thumbs over her shoulder and turns to walk out of the shower.

I grab her arm and pull her into mine. "You know that's not what I want."

"What do you want?" Her eyes flick up and catch mine in a daring glance.

Wrapping my arms around her, I spin, pressing her back against the tiles. She lets out a gasp, no doubt from the ice cold feel of the wall. A shiver works its way down her body, leaving a trail of goosebumps and hard nipples which draw me in.

But not yet.

I fight the urge to sink my mouth onto them, so I start at her neck, planting kisses along her soft skin. Working my way over her collarbone. "What I want-"

She moans out as her fingernails dig into my back and her body arches against me.

"Is to stick my-" I reposition my body so my hard length is lined up at her entrance like a snake coiled and ready to attack. "Cock inside of your sweet pussy, and fuck you until you come around it."

"I-"

Before she can get any other words out, I turn her around and press her chest up against the tile wall and notch myself between her legs.

"You'll need to stop me," I warn her, giving her the out.

Silence.

I punch my cock into her with one powerful thrust. Her hands splay out against the tile wall and her lips part in a silent squeal. Hot water drips down my back as I drag my cock out and slam it in again and again. The only sound in the room is the water hitting the floor and the thwap thwap thwap of my hips smacking against her ass.

"The thought of my come shooting inside of you, through you, gets me so hard all. Of. The. Fucking. Time." My stomach clenches at the thought. "I want to press my dick so far up in you, that you feel it in your throat." I pull her away from the wall and bend her over. She searches for the wall, placing her hands on it for balance as I fuck her harder and faster. "Goddamn baby. Your pussy was made for our cocks." A tingle shoots up my spine, then back down to my balls, so I push my dick inside as far as it will go just before I come inside of her. I want her fucking pregnant with my baby so fucking bad. When my cock stops pulsing inside of her, I hold it there for another second before I let her stand up. My hands wrap around from the back and I grab her tits and squeeze them in my hand softly. "Good morning."

"Morning."

"Shh. I wasn't talking to you. I was talking to them." I give a light squeeze.

"Oh. I see."

Wanting to look at them, I twist her around and plant a small kiss on each.

"I feel so used."

"I love you, too," I say, thrusting my hips against hers and sending her back against the wall. The tile feels cool under my hands as I trap her between my arms and my body. "Want to get some breakfast with me for the rest of the house?"

"Yes. I'm starving."

"I have something I can feed you."

She smiles. "I'll take you up on that later."

Twenty minutes later, we're standing in line at the little corner café, picking out some muffins and getting coffees and teas for the house. When we left, I was so hot from the shower that I just slipped on a sweatshirt and some joggers, but damn it if it isn't freaking twenty degrees outside and the wind. The wind is whipping around and makes it feel like ten below zero. Everlee, of course, is bundled head to toe in the teal and gray ski outfit Callum bought her last February.

We get to the door and I pause with my hand on the handle, trying to psych myself up to battle the cold.

"I can go home and get the car if you want?"

Cutting my eyes at her, I puff out a breath and push the door open.

"Let's go. I'm no pansy ass."

"The way you're whining says otherwise."

"Take off your outfit and see how cold it is."

"I know how cold it is, which is *why* I bundled up." She laughs.

A metal trash can lid rattles loudly on the ground, pulling our attention down the alleyway we're passing. The hairs on my neck stand on end and we pause.

Our eyes lock on the desolate alley, anticipation building. Suddenly, a wave of relief washes over me, only to be swiftly overtaken by a wave of sorrow. There's a dog. It looks no older than a year or two, hobbling around garbage cans, no doubt trying to find something to eat. Its hair is long and stringy, covered in a dark oil or mud and when its eyes catch mine, we just stare at each other.

"Knox," Everlee whispers, and I know what she's going to say before she even says it.

"I know." I hand her the drinks in my hand after she readjusts the bag of muffins to hang on her arm.

"Be careful," she calls after me.

"Hey puppy," I say in a soft voice. "Are you looking for some food?"

The dog looks scared, but it doesn't run away, so I stop walking and squat down. I don't think it's going to attack me, but I don't know if it'll come to me either. A second later, a blueberry muffin is being passed over my shoulder.

"Can it have this?"

"I think in moderation it'll be fine. I'm not trying to give it a dozen. But it seems like it's starving."

"Ok." I break off a piece and hold my hand out. The dog just stares at me, so I toss the small bit of muffin and it lands right at its feet. It smells it for a second, then licks the muffin up and looks at me.

"I think the pup liked it."

The dog takes a small tentative step towards us, then stops, so I break off another piece and toss it between us. The dog looks at the muffin on the ground, then at me. After another second, it steps the few feet forward and eats the muffin.

"Good puppy dog. My name is Knox, and this is my wife, Everlee."

Wife.

It's weird saying that. I don't think I've said the words out loud since France.

The dog just stares at me and takes another step forward, almost within arm's reach. Its eyes look tired and scared.

"Here puppy." I let the muffin roll off my fingertips and again, it hesitates, then steps forward to eat it. I reach my hand up to pet it, but it steps back. "It's ok, puppy. I won't hurt you. I just want to make sure you're ok."

"It looks so hungry," Everlee says, putting her hand on my shoulder.

My legs hurt from squatting, so I sit on my butt and cross my legs and a second later, the dog lays down, paws outstretched towards me.

I can't help but chuckle. "Aren't you a friendly puppy?" I toss another piece of the blueberry muffin and it reaches forward and licks it up, then crawls forward a little, closing the distance between us. "I think it wants to be pet, but it's scared."

Another wind whips through the alley and the dog and I both squint, trying to block out the biting cold. "Do you want to come home with us? We can feed you and give you a nice bed. After we clean all the dirt off you, of course."

The dog crawls forward a little more, so I hold my hand out with the muffin on it. The dog smells, looks at me, then slowly licks the food off my hand. Moving slowly, I reach up and pet the dog, rubbing its head and behind its ears. "Good puppy dog. It's cold out here."

"How are we going to get it home?"

"I don't know." I look around at all the trash piled along the alley and see a short rope that has been tossed to the side sticking out underneath a garbage bag. "Go grab that rope and bring it to me." I don't stop rubbing the puppy because it seems to appreciate the affection. "We're going to take good care of you, puppy." I hand it the rest of the muffin and it laps it up quickly. There's no telling the last time it ate.

When Everlee walks back over, I instruct her to create a small loop at the end and tie it into a knot so we can feed the other end through to make it a collar.

"Good puppy. We're going to slip this around your neck so we can bring you home with us and get you cleaned up and fed." The dog doesn't move, almost like it understands every word I'm saying. When I slowly stand up with the other end of the rope in my hand, it just waits.

"Ready?" Ev asks, shifting the drinks in her hand.

"Yes, I think so."

We start walking, and I have to give a small tug, and the dog walks with us. The rest of the way back to the house, I continually talk to it and it walks beside me, not pulling or tugging. It's almost like it feels relieved or happy to be going somewhere with someone.

When we get in the house, the guys are in the kitchen talking.

Ev rounds the corner ahead of me and cheers, "We bought muffins and drinks!"

"What the fuck?" Jax asks as soon as I round the corner.

JAX - THANKS A LOT PHIL

"It's a dog," Knox says, bending down to rub its head.

"No shit. I can see that. What's it doing in our house?"

"It was looking for food and it's freezing outside. And look at it."

Emmett is walking around the dog, which steps closer to Knox, watching Emmett cautiously.

"Her. It's a girl."

"We couldn't leave her outside."

"So you thought you would bring it back here?"

"Obviously that's what we thought since that's what we did," Ev says with a bite in her voice, putting the muffins and drink container on the counter. She pulls out the cup with Ev written on top and cradles it in her hands while she drinks it.

"It's filthy."

"I know, Jax. It's been outside on the streets. I'm surprised she didn't die from hypothermia or something. There are still little ice patches on the ground and sidewalks."

I look at Callum who is standing with his back pressed against the wall watching us, and Emmett who is sitting by the dog petting her.

"I'm going to give her a bath and then bring her back down for some food." Knox turns to look at Emmett. "Can you fix her something?"

"Yea. I'll cook up some ground beef and rice. Maybe toss in some green beans and carrots."

"Are you serious?" I look at him in complete shock. "Cal?"

He laughs, shrugging his shoulders.

Ev walks over with my coffee in hand. I snatch it away from her and she gives me a hug. "She's cute."

"Adorable," I mock.

She gives me a quick kiss on the cheek and when she tries to walk away, I sit my cup down and grab her arm, pulling her back in for a hug. "She doesn't go in my room."

Ev pushes away and stares up at me, her eyes nearly dancing with excitement and joy right out of her eye sockets. "Of course! Of course!" She wraps her arms around me, then raises on her tiptoes and gives me a kiss. "I love you."

"You better. I'm letting you keep a dog."

"You aren't *letting* me do anything." She swipes me on the nose. "We had a conversation and came to an agreement."

"I don't know about that."

Ev drops on her knees in front of the dog and begins rubbing her face and ears and the dog stands there, wagging her tail.

Great.

Emmett's cooking a freaking five course meal for the dog. Knox and Ev are already smitten, Cal is... doing nothing. Just watching us all with a fucking smile on his face.

"I'll go upstairs and bathe her. Wish me luck."

"No."

"Grump," Knox shoots over his shoulder before he disappears with what is likely going to be the second biggest pain in my ass.

"I'm going to run to the store to get some food for her."

"I'll come with you," I offer. I try not to hover, but it still makes me nervous letting her go out on her own, especially since there's an entire house of us that can go with her.

"What time is dinner at Knox's dads?" Callum asks, just as we're opening the back door.

Ev steps back and pokes her head in the house under my arm. "It got changed to four."

I grab the keys off the wall and walk over to the car, opening the door for Ev.

Twenty minutes later, we're walking into Phil's pet store. It seems like a little boutique store, but the other chain pet store was closed.

"Happy New Year, folks! What can I do for you today?" The older man, who I would presume is Phil, says walking around from behind the counter. He's wearing jeans and a red and green flannel shirt and has salt and pepper disheveled hair.

"We just got a dog and need to get some things for her."

"How sweet. How old?"

"Maybe one or two. We aren't sure. We just found her on the side of the road."

"Well, look at you two. Doin' the lord's work."

I try not to roll my eyes. It's not even twelve hours into the new year yet, so I'm trying not to be a complete dick to everyone, but Knox makes it hard.

"You will need some food, bowls, toys, treats. Are you going to crate train?"

"Crate train?" I ask, less than amused.

"Let her sleep in a crate at night."

"Oh no. I'd hate to lock her up after we just got her off the street," Ev says, interlacing her fingers in mine.

Phil nods, not even bothering to look at me, knowing I clearly have no say.

"Let's go look at food and bowls," Phil says, walking down the aisle.

"I'll be here... waiting," I call to no one.

Ev and Phil are chatting several aisles over about the different types of food, so I wander around and end up on the toy aisle. My fingers flick through a few shaped like ducks and pigs, a few balls, and some rope toys. There are way too many options. Apparently, they found some food and have brought it to the front and are now going back for bowls and beds.

Thank God Knox didn't come with her. They would have bought half the store. I grab a few toys, having a hard time deciding if she'll want a duck or an alien-looking thing, so I grab both. She'll probably want some sort of ball, because dogs like those, so I grab a couple of different sizes. One flashes different colors when you squeeze it and has spikes on it. I grab a few more toys with ropes and one that squeaks, and drop them off at the front counter, then walk around to find Ev looking at different types of beds.

So glad we aren't going overboard on a dog we just brought home.

She hands me the bowls and a bag of beef jerky treats and a box of milk bones. "Which bed do you think she'll like?"

"She was sleeping outside, so I'm pretty sure she'll love any bed."

"Not helpful." She sticks her tongue out at me, then turns back to Phil, who is apparently her new best friend.

Sorry, not sorry, Lizzy.

"This one is an extra-large. It's a solid option if she doesn't have a crate and it will give her a space to lie out and relax. It has a nice little pillowed border around the edge that she can put her head on. I know my pups love that. My little humans." He laughs, rubbing his hand absentmindedly along the small bed on the shelf in front of him.

"Let's do this one." She points to the biggest fluffiest one on the bottom that our good friend Phil was recommending. It's one hundred and fifty dollars. Fuckin' aye Phil.

I reach down and grab it, knowing it's pointless to talk her out of it.

"Do we have everything? There may be something left in the store we haven't added to the front counter."

Ev looks at me and pats me on the ass, scooting me along the aisle towards the front.

JAX - THANKS A LOT PHIL   221

"Ok. You have food, bowls, bed, treats, and an excellent selection of toys. Very nice. I'd recommend taking her to the vet when they open tomorrow to get her checked out. Make sure she doesn't have worms or anything. It's so common with street dogs."

"Worms?"

"Yea, they get in their belly. Their heart. So sad."

"Her belly looked a little bigger than the rest of her."

"Yea. I'd definitely have her checked out, then. Watch her poop to see if you find worms moving around in them."

My fingers clamp onto the edge of the counter. That sounds disgusting.

"Probably need a leash and collar for her."

"Oh yea!" Everlee laughs and Phil walks her to the correct aisle and I hear them talking about the different types. Of course, she comes back with a purple leash, a pink collar and a harness because that's better when walking them so you don't hurt their throat.

"Is this it?"

Phil starts ringing up everything and I can't help but watch the price go up, higher and higher and higher. She better be glad I love her so damn much.

"How long have you two been married?"

Ev shakes her head, shocked, then smiles. "Right. Twelve days."

"Twelve? Newlyweds. How exciting."

"Yea, they surprised me in Paris."

"They?"

She glances at me. "My best friend. She blocked out part of the Eiffel Tower for the wedding. We nearly got kicked out after."

"Oh my goodness. Some friend you have there."

"She's the best." Ev claps her hands.

"Totes the best," I mock.

Phil laughs a hearty laugh. "You two are adorable."

Ev grabs my hand, slipping her fingers in between mine and squeezes. I pull my hand out of her grip and wrap it around her, pulling her in. I'd do anything to see that smile on her face. So if that means buying out half of a pet store and adopting a dog, then so be it.

By the time we get home and unload the car, Knox is walking her downstairs with a soaked shirt and messy hair. Happiness, like a radiant flame, glows inside of me, knowing he appears to have had a difficult time with her.

"Perfect timing!" Emmett calls. I've had her food cooling, so it is nice and ready for her.

"Phil said about a cup right now."

"Phil?"

"Our new bestie," I tease, setting the items by the door.

"Did you buy out the entire store?" Callum asks with that same smile on his face, like he knows something I don't.

"Almost. Just be glad I went and not Knox."

Everlee fills a bowl with water and puts it on the gray silicone mat we bought while Knox brings the dog over. She sniffs at it for a minute, then drinks the entire bowl. I hand Emmett the other bowl and he fills it with a cup of food, while Everlee gets some more water, then takes both bowls over to her.

"So I've got some news."

"A name?" I ask.

"I think she's pregnant."

"For fuck's sake," I snap out at the same time Everlee squeals in delight.

The Gods are pushing my 'all things to see that woman smile' statement.

EVERLEE - LUNA AND WYATT

It's almost time for us to leave and visit Knox's dad. I'm excited to go but at the same time I don't want to leave Luna. That's what we all voted on. Jax tried to get us to going with money pit, and thought he could say it with an accent to make us want it, but Luna just seems to fit her. When we said it, she even gave out a bark. Since getting bathed and getting some food in her belly, she seems like a completely different dog. We ended up giving her two and a half cups of food, because we didn't know the last time she ate and we plan to give her some more when we get back. And if she is pregnant, we figure she'll need more food.

    Jax is still keeping his distance from her, but I catch him watching her several times. Almost like he wants to love on her, but can't let himself admit it. Knox is in the living room trying to teach her commands like sit and here. We've had to remind him several times to get ready for his dad's, because he doesn't want to leave her side. Emmett's been there when Knox isn't and Callum just watches. Not sure what he thinks because he hasn't really said much.

"What are we going to do with her when we leave?" Jax asks.

"I don't want to leave her out, but I also don't want to close her in somewhere."

"We should have gotten a gate," Jax says.

"I've ordered one. It should be here tomorrow," Emmett says, rubbing Luna's head, her tail still wagging.

Jax just watches him and sighs, rolling his eyes.

"Who's a good dog?" Knox says, walking over to her. "Do we bring her with us?"

"Would your dad care?" Emmett asks.

"I don't know."

"Do you want to call him?" I suggest.

"Yeah. Yeah. That's a good idea." He grabs his phone out of his pocket and walks out of the room.

"What are we doing with a pregnant dog we just picked up off the street?" Jax asks, blowing out a breath.

"We're giving her a suitable home. Do you want to put her back out on the streets, or worse, a shelter? Put her in those tiny little cages with all the other dogs barking. She's pregnant."

Almost like she can understand what we're saying, she rolls over on her back and kicks her feet in the air, looking at Jax.

"I think she likes you," Emmett says, rubbing her belly.

"She doesn't know me or any of you. She's just happy to be some place warm with a full belly... for the babies she's about to have."

"I've always wanted to see what it's like to watch babies being born," I say, walking over to pet her.

Now that she's been washed and dried, her hair is a long beautiful golden color, like a golden retriever, but who puts one of those out on the road? It would make sense though, because she seems house broken and good with people. Poor thing. Maybe when someone found out she was pregnant, they dumped her? Which makes me want to keep her all the more.

"Ok!" Knox skips back into the room and Luna rolls over, popping to stand, tail wagging. "Wyatt said we can bring her."

"Yay. I call shotgun," Jax deadpans.

Callum jumps behind the wheel while Jax takes the passenger seat and Emmett takes the third row, leaving Luna, Knox, and me in the second row. Before we left, Emmett grabbed her bowls and another two cups of the food he made and put it in a to-go baggy. Jax was giving us shit because we were making her a lunch to go.

Luna sits in the middle seat and circles a few times before she lays down, putting her head on my lap. She looks up at me with those puppy dog eyes and I about melt in my spot. Seriously, how could anyone turn her out? Then something else tears at me. What if they didn't, and she escaped and people are looking for her? My heart aches in my chest. I know I just met her, but I've already grown attached. I've given her a name, damn it.

Secretly, I pull out my phone and start searching for missing dogs, praying that I don't find anything for a missing golden, or golden-looking dog. If she ran away, then we'd have to do the right thing, even if I don't want to.

It's just under an hour to Wyatt's house and the entire trip, I'm searching my phone while Knox stares out of the window quietly. The entire car feels... a little intense. I don't know if it's meeting Wyatt or the pregnant dog that is now licking my wrist.

After looking for forty minutes, I put my phone back in my pocket. I've looked on every site that I know of, trying to find anything for a missing dog. It's baffling how many I found, but none of them look like Luna.

"Your- Wyatt, is in the middle of nowhere," Jax says.

"He said he was in a cabin on a lake and it's quiet. I didn't really ask much about the area."

"I'll say so. We haven't passed a house or a road with a sign in two miles."

Up ahead, there's a house with smoke billowing out of a chimney. We can't see anything yet because of the tree cover, but it's definitely a chimney and a house under that steady stream of smoke.

When I glance back at Knox, his leg is bouncing up and down as his hands rub along his thigh. Luna sits up and turns her body before sniffing and licking Knox's ear.

I reach across the space and squeeze his leg. He stops bouncing it and looks at me, so I mouth, "Are you ok?"

His lips twitch and his eyebrows lift on his forehead.

He's nervous.

I know he's seen his dad one other time since before my accident, but this is different. This is the official meet the parent, only it's five of us and a dog.

Callum turns onto a gravel road and slows down as rocks fly up and tink on the metal under the car. We can see the house now. It's cute. Nice, big front porch that wraps around the back with several rocking chairs on it that look out to the large lake. Tucked on the bank of the lake are several colorful kayaks, oars, and boards.

Wyatt walks out on the front porch and grips the top of the railing with one hand and waves at us with the other.

"Thanks, y'all. For coming with me."

Jax turns around. "There's no place we'd rather be, brother." He nods his head and gives Knox a look that warms my heart.

We stop and climb out of the car. I take Luna's leash and walk her to a small spot of grass by a tree where she handles her business. I bend over and stare at her feces for way longer than is usual to make sure there are no worms. Nothing. Clear.

I'm sure the vet will be able to tell us more tomorrow, but that's a good sign.

Knox and the guys are talking on the front porch and I feel their eyes on me, so I take Luna up to meet them.

"Wyatt. This is Everlee and Luna."

Wyatt's eyes are warm and kind with a weathered look to his skin, but my gosh the resemblance is uncanny. "Pleasure to meet you Everlee, and Luna," he says, rubbing her head. "She seems like a friendly dog. You just found her this morning?"

"Yea. Knox and I were getting breakfast and saw her in an alley, searching for food. Poor thing." My gaze flicks over to Knox, whose hands are clasped together in front of him. His eyes are darting back and forth, and I can tell he's uncomfortable.

"Knox. Can you hold Luna?"

His eyes snap to me like I caught him in a dream, and then he looks down at Luna and nods.

The leash will give his hands something to do and maybe she'll help calm him down a little.

I pass the leash over and she nearly sits right on his feet.

"She seems to like you," Wyatt says. "Do we want to head inside? I don't know how long you all can stay, so dinner is ready." He looks at Emmett. "It's not going to be as good as yours, but I like it."

Emmett laughs. "I'm excited to try it and I'm sure it will be wonderful."

"I used your recipe to make the collard greens. It reminds me of home with the fatback. I'll tell you. I was really shocked to see that in your cookbook. And I don't want you thinking that I bought it because you were coming. I've had it for a while now. Big fan of your work."

"Are you fan-girling, Wyatt?" Knox asks, with a hint of a smile on his lips.

Wyatt chuckles and we all head inside.

The inside matches the rustic outdoor log cabin feel, but with a more modern twist. He has a hand-scraped dining room table with dark spots and knots throughout and stainless-steel appliances. His furniture is a mixture of brown leather, blue, and natural wood.

"Where would you like her?" Knox asks, pointing at Luna.

"You can let her lose. I've closed all the bedroom doors so she can't get into anything."

Knox unhooks the leash and curls it on the table by the door, but Luna doesn't leave his side. Almost like she can sense his discomfort and she's trying to soothe him. Maybe I'm thinking too much about it, but I don't know. She seems like a smart dog.

Wyatt shows us around his house, pointing out the pieces of furniture he made, commenting on the time each took and the mistakes he made and what he learned. He's very talented it seems and my gosh, he looks like Knox, just a little older.

We sit down to eat, and the table falls into an awkward silence. Luna is still beside Knox and I can't help but love her more and more with each passing second. Wyatt looks at each of us and then lands on me. "So, your wedding was nice?"

My gaze nervously shifts between the men, then lands on Knox, who gives a slight nod. "Yes. It was magical. The guys had worked with my best friend and they planned a surprise wedding on the Eiffel Tower."

He leans back in his chair and claps his hands. "My word. That is very special. How were they able to get it rented out?"

I laugh. "They didn't. My best friend put up a sign directing people off the first floor and we had a very tight window. I didn't know that until two security people showed up to see what was going on, but by that time we had already broken down everything and were heading up to the second floor for our dinner."

"That is some story. One you'll always remember." He smiles, his eyes warm. It's easy to see why Knox would have a hard time not letting him in. He seems so genuine.

"How was your Christmas?" I ask.

"It was good. Sat out on the porch and drank some nice spiced peppermint and chocolate tea."

My eyes snap to Knox. That's what he's been drinking this season as well, but he doesn't say anything. I can tell he's thinking the same thing, and taking that piece of information and putting it in his pocket.

Wyatt continues, "Then, after watching the ripples on the water, I got ready and went to my therapist's house. She invited me over, so I got to spend time with them. It was nice." His words fall off as he puts another bite of pork in his mouth.

He fixed a southern dinner with a pork loin, collard greens, stewed potatoes, and black-eyed peas, with some corn bread. It reminded the men and me about home, each commenting that we had this growing up.

Wyatt asks about the guy's history, how they all found each other, and they dote on Mrs. Mary, which I thought was going to be awkward for Wyatt, but he handled it well, listening to all the stories. The men started letting down their guard by the time we finished dinner, and were sharing more and laughing. It felt more natural, which was nice. Luna finally laid down, but at Knox's feet.

Knox and Jax wash the dishes and when I walk into the kitchen, I see them talking quietly, so I let them be. I'd seen a shift since we've been here with Jax. He's been very supportive and protective of Knox, acting like the big brother. It just shows me the depths of their love for one another. Beneath all the joking and jabbing is an unbreakable bond that can't be touched.

I love these men with all of my heart.

When I walk back into the living room, Luna is sitting between Emmett's knees with her mouth hanging open, panting and smiling.

We spend the next several hours talking about Knox's childhood growing up, his time in the service, and Allure. Part of me wonders if he's being so open because he's trying to throw everything at Wyatt, to push him away or test his commitment to really being part of his life. Wyatt has handled everything with acceptance and openness.

He asked about Allure and Vixen and, instead of judging, asked questions and congratulated him- us- on our recent accomplishments.

For dessert, Wyatt fixed a seven-layer chocolate cake with a sort of chocolate sauce in between each layer. It was absolutely delicious and Wyatt nearly fell out of his chair when Emmett commented the same and offered him a kitchen tour of Bo La Vie. Knox doesn't seem surprised, so I have to assume that they talked about it at some point before he offered.

We wrap up the evening and head home just before nine. The car ride is silent as we all wait for Knox to lead a conversation, if that's what he wants. Luna jumped in the back with Emmett and is laid out on the seat with her head on his lap, so I've curled into Knox. He's looking out of the window, lost in thought, while his hand rubs along the skin under my shirt. It's comforting.

As we pull into our driveway, Knox asks, "Dinner went well, right?"

"Yes. Wyatt seems very nice." Callum cuts the car off and turns around.

"You're going to be a stud when you get older." Emmett claps his hand on his shoulder.

"Thanks for coming with me. I really appreciate it."

"There's nowhere else we'd rather be, brother," Jax says.

We sit in silence for a moment and when Knox moves to get out of the car, so do the rest of us.

After showering, Knox pulls me to the side and asks me to sleep in his bed with him tonight. He seems vulnerable, and I just want to wrap my arms around him and hold him. We decided while we showered we would move Luna's bed into his room, since she seemed to feel the strongest bond with him.

"Can I put my cock in you tonight? No sex. I just... I want your pussy to hold it."

I smile. "You can put your cock in me anytime you want." I take my shirt off and toss it to the side of the bed, so

I'm naked for him because I know how much he likes my breasts, and he seems to need comforting right now.

I gently press him backward, so he's laying down and climb on top of him, slipping his boxers off. His hardening cock springs to life and it takes all the control I have not to suck him in my mouth.

Climbing up his body, I straddle him and he tilts his head to the side and stares at me, while his eyes rake over my body and his hands rub the outside of my legs. "I love you, Everlee. Thank you for being there tonight."

"I love you too and there's nowhere else I'd rather be than by your side." I smile. "Well, maybe one other place." I grab his cock in my hand and stroke up it and his eyes roll into the back of his head.

"I don't want to come tonight. I just want to feel you around me. It's just... relaxing."

"I was doing some research on cockwarming and it's a dom sub thing."

"I know." His words are soft.

Is it possible for a heart to grow so big it bursts out of your chest? The amount of vulnerability Knox shows me at times literally makes it feel like that's what is going to happen. I know I say it all the time to the point where it feels like it's too much, but I love this man.

These men.

I feel like if I say it, then it's like a volcano letting off some steam so I don't fully explode with the amount of love I feel for them.

I slide along his cock, making it slick enough for me to ease onto him. This is going to be so fucking hard for me. I raise up and notch his head at my entrance and slowly sink down. His hands grip into my hips as his eyes close, savoring the feel of my pussy hugging his length.

Fully seated on him, I don't move and neither does he.

His teeth scrape over his bottom lip as he just stares at me. After another moment, his hands slide up my body and wrap around my breasts. "You're so beautiful."

My hands glide up his chest, over the ripples of his muscles until I'm leaning over him. I take his lips in a kiss- soft, delicate. The kiss deepens and my body moves, grinding on his cock. He pushes me away. "Everlee," he warns.

"I'm sorry. It's not like I meant to."

He chuckles and I sit up. "Here." He rubs my clit. "Don't move. You ride my cock and I stop."

"Knox."

"Everlee." He smiles. "I want to feel you come around me, and then we'll go to sleep."

"Seems like torture for you."

"If I could just crawl inside of you and have your pussy hold all of me, I would. I can't, so I'll settle for my cock." He laughs. "Thank God Jax isn't here. He would have lost his shit. It sounded better in my head, but as the words were coming out, I was visualizing crawling up there and it just got really weird, really fast." His laugh is soft. I'm sure there's a lot of emotions going on inside of him that he's trying to process. The pull to have a relationship with Wyatt and the fear of getting hurt again. Perhaps he also feels guilty for Wyatt being back in his life when the others don't have their family. If what he needs tonight is just my pussy on his cock, then that is what I'll give him.

His finger works my clit, slowly, as our eyes lock.

"Can I touch my breasts for you?" I ask, letting him lead.

"Please." He smiles. "But don't be too sexy. It's taking everything I have not to fuck you."

My hands grip my breast, squeezing and clamping as his eyes never leave me. His finger presses a little harder and moves a little quicker. His hips buck once and I freeze, staring at him.

"Fuck." His lips pinch into a line. "I thought this was what I wanted before you sat on my dick." He shakes his head. "No. This is what I want. I don't want to come tonight. I just want to feel you come around me and then I want to fall asleep with me inside of you. It... comforts me."

"I'll do whatever you want, babe."

His voice is soft. "Don't let me fuck you tonight. Even if I want to change my mind."

I lean over and kiss his chest, then move up to his neck, then to his lips. "I love you."

"All your moving could constitute a soft fuck."

I smile against his lips, give him a quick kiss, then sit back up. I can't fully understand why he doesn't want to fuck tonight, but that's not for me to decide. He clearly needs something from me, so I will give that to him. Five minutes later, my pussy is pulsing around his cock as my orgasm slowly washes over me. It's not intense, just slow. Like a low rumble, echoing through the woods that sort of just lingers.

His head presses into the bed and his eyes close as he savors the feeling. "I'd ask you to climb off and turn around so I can spoon you, but..." he blows out a cool breath, then bites on his bottom lip. "I want to fuck you so bad."

"No, Knox." I hate saying the words, but I told him I wouldn't let him change his mind earlier. I lay down on his chest and press my lips against his muscled pecs and lay my cheek on them. After a minute or two, he wraps his arms around my back and kisses the top of my head. The steady beat of his heart lulls me to sleep.

EVERLEE - OVARY EXPLOSION

By the time I get downstairs the next morning, Callum, Jax, and Emmett are at the island eating breakfast. Knox has already taken off to the vet with Luna. Apparently, when he called, the vet had a cancellation first thing this morning, so that coupled with the fact we think she's pregnant and been on the streets, the vet wanted to see her.

"Good morning, love," Callum says, opening his arm wide.

I climb onto his lap and wrap my arm around his neck. "Good morning, husband number one."

"Why does he get husband number one? Why not me?" Jax asks, setting his coffee cup down.

"Or me?" Emmett stalks around the counter, closer to me.

"Back off boys. You heard her. I'm number one." Callum uses one arm to squeeze me tighter to his chest and the other to block Emmett.

Emmett looks at Jax, and they pass each other a curious glance.

"Boys. It's too early in the morning for this," Callum says, shifting his legs out from under the bar.

"It's almost ten and we've been up for three hours. Princess here is the only one who just got up."

"I've been up for thirty minutes. I was in the shower."

"Hair's not wet."

"Because I don't wash it every time. I had it wrapped up."

"Likely excuse." Emmett flicks my hair playfully.

The back door bursts open, pulling all of our attention.

Burst may be a little dramatic, but given where I thought I was heading, it definitely startled all of us.

Knox is carrying Luna into the house, then sits her on the floor.

"Knox?" I ask, standing from Callum's lap and walking over to Luna. Kneeling in front of her, I rub behind her ears and she gives me a quick lick on the forehead. "What's going on?"

"So she's definitely pregnant."

"Yay," Jax mumbles from behind.

"Why does your face look like that?"

"Vet said she could go into labor any day."

"Fuck me," Jax groans.

"Oh. Wow."

"Yea. Vet gave me all this paperwork for dog births and her private number so I could call, should there be any complications."

"I'm sure that's why she gave it." I shove him in the shoulder.

"She's sixty something years old and called out my unique ring, so yes. I think it was because of the dog." He shoves me back. "Jelly belly." He laughs. "Don't be jealous."

"So what do we need to do?"

"Find a hotel for the next week," Jax continues.

"Oh stop. You and Luna are going to end up being best friends and we're all going to hate you for it. We know it, you should know it. So let's just stop pretending like you don't like her." Emmett shakes his shoulder and Jax doesn't respond.

"Keep an eye on her. I've got a list from the vet and I'm going to run to the store to get some supplies."

"Yesterday has been the most expensive breakfast ever," Jax quips.

"Do you want to come with me, Jax?" Knox asks.

"I think I'll pass."

The doorbell rings and then a head pokes in. "Yoo-hoo."

"Second thought," Jax adds, walking over to Knox.

"What the?" Lizzy screams when she sees the dog. "When did you get a dog?"

"Careful, you're scaring her," Jax warns, and we all look at him. "What? I'm not heartless. Lizzy is a lot for humans, have to imagine it's worse for dogs."

"Hey Lizzy. Bye Lizzy," Knox says, darting out of the house, followed by Jax.

I thought he was kidding, but apparently, he was serious. Part of me thinks he wanted to go and didn't want to admit it. The other part wonders if he's trying to make sure Knox doesn't go overboard with the supplies.

Lizzy drops to her knees and starts rubbing Luna behind the ears. "Aren't you the cutest wutest thing ever?" She looks up at me. "When did you get her? Where did you get her? I didn't know you were looking for a dog. Why didn't you say anything?"

"Slow your roll. Knox and I went out for breakfast yesterday morning to the little café on the corner and found her in the alley on the way back. She looked hungry and was filthy, so we befriended her and brought her back here. Turns out she's pregnant. Knox just got back from the vet a few minutes before you got here and she'll likely go into labor soon."

"How fun!" She claps her hands together. "So that's where Knox and Jax went?"

"Yes. To get some supplies per the vet's directions."

"What's your name, pretty girl?"

"Luna."

"Luna. Are you a good girl? Yes, you are."

"What are you doing here?" I ask.

Lizzy stands up and Luna walks over to her bed and lays down. Knox must have brought it down from his room this morning. We'll probably need to buy two... or more, so we aren't hauling it back and forth all the time.

"Can't a girl come say hi to her BFF?"

"You can, but the look in your eyes tells me there's a reason behind the visit."

"I wanted to bring you my gift. We haven't had a chance to do our gift exchange, so I thought today would be the perfect day!"

"Yes! Thank you. I've been wanting to get your gift to you so we can take down the decorations."

"Not a good idea. Knox will not be happy. It takes us like a month of bribing him every year. If it was up to him, he'd get a fake tree and leave it up all year round and decorate it with whatever holiday is closest. Hanging hearts, hanging Easter eggs. You name it."

"Oh."

"I'll meet you in the living room," Lizzy says.

"Oh lord."

"Stop." She turns to go back outside, but peeks her head in and shoos me away when I'm still standing there.

"Fine." I walk into the living room and grab the small box under the tree.

She walks in a minute later with something huge and flat in her arms. If I didn't know better, I'd say it's a huge picture frame because it looks to be of similar size to the one that Knox got Jax, which shockingly enough there haven't been any shenanigans with it yet, even though I know Knox has something planned.

"What is that?"

"Your gift." She smiles and props it against the wall.

Callum and Emmett walk into the living room and sit on the couch beside me.

"Can you open my gift first? Obviously, bigger means better."

"I didn't think size mattered," Emmett teases.

"It does, Jacob." She pumps her eyebrows.

I tilt my head to the side and look at her, eyes wide.

"What? I'm fairly certain they know we talk about our men's sticks of love. I just get the benefit of hearing about four instead of one."

Callum looks at me and all I can do is shrug and smile.

"Don't worry studmuffin. It's all good things, all good things." She fans herself.

"Let's just get on with this before I have to swap out my gift for a sock to shove into your mouth."

"Kinky." She tosses her head back laughing, then throws her arms to the side like a game show host, showing which prize I've won.

When I start to unwrap it, I see a thick metal frame and the nerves that fill my stomach… It's a picture. A big fucking picture. But which one, I have no idea.

Anxiety getting the better of me, I rip the paper down and burst out laughing.

"Do you like?" She wraps her arm around my neck.

It's the picture she took of her motorboating me back in the summer. She had it blown up and framed.

"I think this is one of the best pictures of you I've ever taken. Your face."

"Lizzy. What can I say?"

"Thank you. You can say thank you. Do you know how long it took me to get this picture in this frame? It's a fucking five-foot tall frame. That's one big picture."

"I love it. I was wondering whatever happened to this picture."

"I know how all the men have pictures above their bed, so I thought you needed one, too."

"This is great. Thank you. I love it."

I hand her the small box and she gives it a shake. "Sounds small."

"It's definitely not a near life size framed picture of you motorboating me."

"No, I suppose not." She pulls the lid off and then closes it quickly, with tears filling the brim of her eye.

"This is from all of us."

"Stop." She stomps her feet up and down, then opens the lid again. She pulls out a key with cartoon princesses on it and holds it up.

"It's a key to our house. Jax insisted if we were doing this, then he got to pick out the design of the key."

"That rascally rascal!" She holds the key to her chest and hugs it tightly.

"There are still rules. You can't go wild."

"I will! I mean I won't! I won't! You so totally won't regret this!" She stomps her feet up and down again, then sighs. "Well damn. I was going to surprise you with the second part of your gift later, but you freakin' ruined it with your amazing gift! I'll be right back!" She runs outside and we hear the door lock, then unlock. A few minutes later, she's running back into the house with a large tube.

"I had to make sure the key worked, and it wasn't some joke."

"I wouldn't do that to you."

"I know *you* wouldn't, but I could see Jax changing out the keys."

She wasn't wrong. I could see him doing that to be funny.

"Here." She thrusts the tube in my direction.

"What is this?"

"The other part of your gift."

With caution, I pop the lid off and peek inside the tube to find another rolled-up piece of work wrapped in a thin sheet of tissue paper. I gently coax it out of the opening and undo the tape holding it together, and unroll it. My heart stops beating in my chest for a moment.

"Liz." A single tear trickles down my cheek.

"Stop!" she shouts, batting her hand in the air. "This is your actual gift. I mean, they both are, but this is it. I was going to figure out a way to sneak in and swap them."

It's a photo from our wedding night on the Eiffel Tower near the end when we were all holding hands.

"Thank you. I love it."

"I'm not even going to ask about the first, although I clearly remember the night in question," Callum says, walking over and wrapping his arms around me.

"I feel like we should get another frame. I will put the first in my room and this one should go in here above the couch and replace the picture of that random cliff in the ocean. It looks sort of magical- mystical, but this would look better."

Here I am.

Friends and family.

It's a new year. I've got a new job. I'm married to four amazing men and I have a dog.

I don't know what could make this life any better.

Later that night...

When I roll over in bed, the cool sheets under my leg wake me up. I'm used to rubbing up against a warm body. I open my eyes and find someone missing, and quickly realize it's Jax.

Rolling over, I look towards the bathroom to find the door open and the lights off. I wait for a few minutes for him to come back into the room, but when he doesn't, my heart beats a little faster.

I climb out of bed and walk into the hall and see the light on downstairs. When I get to the edge, I hear a low voice talking and confusion settles in my brow. Who could he be talking to this early in the morning? Creeping down the stairs, trying not to make a sound, I pause on the bottom stair and look across the room and my heart nearly jumps out of my chest.

Jax turns his head slowly to look at me, cradling a puppy in his enormous hands against his chest.

"She's having the babies," he whispers.

I'm frozen in my place, staring that this large shirtless tattooed man who is always tough as nails and eyes wild like fire, and he's sitting with his knee bent up cradling a puppy.

I'm pretty sure my ovaries just exploded and decided to release all my eggs. All I can see when I look at him right now is what he would look like holding our baby. That same look of warmth and love in his eyes.

Damn, call me Frosty, because I just melted.

"She has two out right now and working on the third," he says, putting the one in his hands back down. "You may want to get Knox. I know he didn't want to miss this."

Stunned, it takes me a minute to move.

I hurry upstairs and find Knox in bed. I lean over and plant a kiss gently on his forehead and whisper in his ear. "You need to wake up."

He stirs for a second, but doesn't open his eyes.

"Luna's having her babies."

A second passes, then his eyes shoot open and he stares at me. Fully awake, but also confused, like he's waiting for me to repeat myself.

I nod. "She's having them. Jax is down there with her now."

He shoots out of bed, shaking it and tossing the sheets to the side. As I follow him down the hall, he starts rattling off everything we need, repeating the list the vet gave him from memory.

When we get downstairs, Jax is holding another puppy. "We've got three right now."

"How's mama doing?" Knox asks, dropping to his knees by her head and giving her a rub.

"Good. She's tired, but doing everything she needs to be doing."

How does he know what she should be doing?

He must see my expression, because he rolls his eyes at me. "I did some reading today about what to expect," he says, helping the puppy find a nipple.

I shake my head in disbelief. Mr. Grumpy-pants- I don't want a dog–Jax was reading about dog delivery.

"Stop. I don't like not knowing things."

"Just wait until you're pregnant," Knox quips, looking over his shoulder. "We'll have a new daddy in the house."

"Shut the fuck up, Knox."

"Good morning to you too, brother." He grips Jax's knee then stands, rushing to get the bag by the back door. He brings it back over and has strips of colored fabric, a scale, and a booklet. "We need to weigh them and tie these strips around them so we know who is who."

I watch these two in silence for a moment, working together without speaking. They know what each other needs without saying anything and it's mind-blowing. After Knox weighs the first, I tie a red piece of cloth around its neck and place it back down, just as Luna is pushing out the fourth one.

"Do we know how many?"

"Vet wasn't sure. Could be a few, could be ten."

Jax's eyes lock on mine and I see the dread in his eyes and I smile and mouth, "I love you."

This is going to be a long morning. I walk over to the coffee machine and flick it on at the same time Callum and Emmett walk downstairs.

"It's four in the morning." Callum wipes the sleep from his eyes.

"Luna is having her babies."

"No shit?" Emmett says, moderately more awake than Callum as he looks over at Jax. If he had ovaries, they too would be exploding because Jax is holding another one who thinks Jax's nipple is Luna's as its head wobbles uncontrollably.

He sits the pup down against Luna's stomach and leans back against the wall with his forearm propped on his knee. He catches us staring at him and rolls his eyes before flipping us the bird.

"The big mush," Emmett says, grabbing me around the waist from behind. "He's all bark and no bite."

"Well, he does bite sometimes."

Emmett squeezes me tight. "Let's go see what we can do to help."

By the time we get over, Luna is working on puppy number five and we have a red, orange, yellow, and green puppy.

Our rainbow colored puppies.

What's Coming Next?

AHHHH!! This was the second to last book of the series. The last book, (working title) Happy Holidate Ever After, will not be based around a specific holiday but will wrap up loose ends and take place throughout the year. We may get some new holidays mentioned like St. Patty's day and of course, the men will have to defend their title at the Easter get together! Will they keep all the puppies and how many were born? Can anyone else picture Jax being a doggy daddy? Haha.

I don't know about future spinoffs, but there is definitely a Beckett one (MM firehouse forbidden romance and coming out). It's already written, I was just waiting to publish. Still TBD on Lizzy. I don't know if I will ever be able to stop-stop with these characters because I love writing them so much, so expect random pop-up scenes throughout the year :)

About the Author

Hello lovelies! Follow me below for all the updates, behind the scenes and bonus content!

You can always email me at authorsnmoor [at] gmail.com or message me below. I do rely more on facebook, Insta and TT for most of my communication.

Websitewww.snmoor.com
Etsy Shop AuthorSNMoor
Tiktok@authorsnmoor
Instagramsn_moor
FacebookSN Moor Author — Author SN Moor Fan Group
GoodreadsS.N. Moor
Amazon

Made in the USA
Columbia, SC
10 January 2024